ROGUE ENTERPRISES

SPACE ROGUES

BOOK 10

JOHN WILKER

EDITED BY

CHRISTINA SHORT

Rogue Publishing

Cover art by: Greg Bahlman

V 1.1

ISBN: 978-1-951964-16-0

CONTENTS

PART 5

For Abbi.
Gone too soon.
I miss you, my friend.

You're about to embark on another fun adventure!
The crew of the *Ghost* is at it again!

When you're done reading, I hope you'll take a minute to leave a review!

PART 1

CHAPTER ONE

WELL, THAT WAS FUN

"You know, I didn't know what to expect, but that wasn't it," Wil says. He finishes his bottle of grum, wiping his mouth on the back of his hand. "I mean..." He shudders.

Barbara Mress, sitting on the large sofa next to Maxim and Bennie, says, "Galactic Commonwealth justice." She shrugs, holding out a hand for a fresh drink, fingers wiggling. Bennie sighs and scoots off the couch, grumbling about betting and cheating.

Mress continues, "The trial was for the public. Janus' fate was sealed the moment they took his grotesque ass into custody." Bennie comes back with a fresh bottle, taking the empty from the Tygran woman. "Thank you, Sir Knight."

"I still think you cheated." He jumps back up onto the sofa, scorching against the back of the much-too-large-for-his-frame seating.

Mress says, "After the Harrith thing, he was on stolen time. Toss in trying to invade the GC with hybrid Palorian monsters, and well... molecular disintegration was too kind."

Wil, Cynthia on his lap in the overstuffed chair, says, "I can't believe he let the Source merge with him." He shakes his head. "Three eyes...that one tentacle..."

Zephyr and Maxim are in the kitchenette portion of the lounge, preparing lunch. The big man looks over his shoulder. "Plus, those fangs. He had to be pretty desperate to put himself through that." He turns his attention back to the meal. "Lunch in ten." He hands something to Zephyr. "You always under spice this."

"I do not."

Wil eyes Mress. "They destroyed all the...raw materials?" He knows that raw materials means the remaining Source monsters and those Palorian soldiers unlucky enough to not get killed in the fighting. The Hybrids they rescued earlier, as far as he knows, are still living comfortably under the watchful eye of the GC Science Directorate. Living tissue samples, but comfortable.

Mress nods. "And the data archives. Councilor Grythlorian assured me that all materials relating to this nightmare have been destroyed." She sips her drink. "I'm sure she's lying, but at least for now, the entire thing is too toxic to be caught with."

Wil grunts. "She better let it be another sixty years, at least. Then I'll be dead and won't care."

Cynthia looks at him. "Sixty? That's it?"

"If I'm lucky."

Cynthia looks at Bennie. "You have someone?"

The Brailack hacker nods. "Yeah, the autodoc has his entire genome. Shouldn't be hard."

Wil looks at each of them. "Hard to...?"

Mress smiles. "Extend your life."

Cynthia adds, "I need at least a hundred cycles of you."

Wil wiggles his eyebrows. "Yeah, you do."

Cynthia frowns, sighing. She turns to Bennie. "Never mind, I'll just re-bond with someone else."

Bennie bobs his pale green head. "Good idea. I'm already tired of him."

"I'd throw something at you, but I don't want to get grum all over our client," Wil says.

"Appreciate that." Mress laughs. "I really like you all. You're fun."

Wil adds, "Didn't we already do some life extension, human-body-tweaking stuff?" He looks at Bennie.

The Brailack nods. "Sure, but that was a while ago. I bet that the autodoc, plus that bio hacker, has had enough time to really get creative." Wil shudders.

Bennie grins. "Gills?" Wil makes a face.

Zephyr clears her throat. "Meal time."

Once everyone is seated, Wil says, "You know, I think the thing that bugs me the most is they wouldn't let me see him, and I have all this stuff I'd have loved to say to him." He takes a breath. "I mean, he killed the crew that saved me back in the Sol system. Sure, they were pirates and smugglers, but I'd be a dried out little husk in my pod in a wide orbit somewhere near Neptune if not for them. He stripped the only thing I had going for me away with a smirk." Cynthia puts a hand on his shoulder. "I just really wish I'd been able to see him one last time and show him he'd failed. He didn't break me. He didn't win."

Bennie tuts. "I think he got the *didn't win* part when his molecules lost cohesion." He reaches for a plate with pale pink rolls on it.

"This is delicious," Mress says.

Wil beams. "She's been practicing."

Cynthia smiles. "It's an Earth dish." She looks at Wil. "Lassoona?"

"Lasagna," he replies. Turning to Mress, "My mom's recipe."

The Tygran woman inclines her head. "Your mother would be proud." She turns to the Palorian couple opposite her. "My compliments." Zephyr's cheeks shift to a darker shade of blue.

Mress turns to Gabe, who has been standing off to the side of the common area since everyone settled into the lounge. "Tell me, Gabe. When do you plan to announce your intentions on Arcadia?"

As everyone turns to look at their mechanical friend, the droid makes a choking-like sound. "I was not planning any announcement to that effect."

"You running for president?" Wil asks, then turns to the others. "Space President Gabe has a ring to it." He grins. "Probably get us more lucrative projects, too."

Zephyr opens her mouth but stops when Gabe says, "I am not. For the last several spans, interim Governor Mitch and several members of the provisional Governing Council have requested that I put my name on the upcoming ballot to elect Arcadia's first governor." Tilting his head, he adds, "I have declined. Repeatedly."

Bennie burps. "Why? You'd win in a landslide. You'd be the most powerful droid in the GC."

"I do not crave such power or even notoriety."

"Dummy." The Brailack waves one hand while scooping up another bit of lasagna on his fork with the other. "They don't hand out nicknames like 'Gabe the Liberator' to just anyone, you know."

Gabe makes a face but says nothing further.

Wil looks from Bennie to Gabe and back before saying, "Well, I'm glad you're not going into politics. We'd miss you."

Gabe smiles. "I would miss you all." He turns to Bennie, chewing noisily. "Except Bennie."

The team hacker looks up. "Floo oo," he says around a mouthful of food, some of it escaping back onto his plate.

Mress grins. "I'd love to discuss the political situation on Arcadia more if you're interested, Gabe." She stands and grabs her plate, heading for the washing unit.

"So long as your goal is not to entice me to run for office, that would be enjoyable." He moves to the hatch that leads aft to the computer core and engineering space. "I was going to perform a systems-check on the backup atmosphere processing system, if you would like to join me."

The older Tygran executive nods. "Of course." She looks at the others. "If you'll excuse us."

Wil watches the pair head aft, the hatch closing behind them. He turns to the others. "Did any of you know he was getting pressure to run for office?" Head shakes all around, except Bennie.

The hacker finishes chewing and says, "Sure."

Maxim raises a brow. "How?"

"Listening to his comms." Everyone just stares at him until finally he adds, "What? Don't worry, I don't listen to yours."

"I don't believe you for even one millitock," Cynthia says. Bennie shrugs.

SPACE TAXES

"G OOD MORNING," Wil says as Barbara Mress opens the hatch that closes off the stairwell connecting the three main decks of the *Ghost*. The crew and guest berths, along with the small brig, are all situated on the topmost deck of the small warship.

"That smells wonderful." She nods to the cooktop before Wil and the sizzling skillet of bacon he's working with.

"Eggs will be done soon. They're not as good as chicken eggs, but chicken eggs are too tough to export from Earth. Well, that, and you don't know what a chicken is, so..." He shrugs.

"I look forward to visiting your world someday," the Tygran executive says, taking a seat at the dining table. Wil has already put out table settings for everyone.

Wil turns. "Don't go in with high expectations. Humanity is a ways away from GC membership still."

Mress nods. "My understanding is that with your help, a global government has been formed. That's a big step."

Wil deposits plates of eggs and bacon in the center of the triangular table, taking a seat opposite their longtime client and, more or less, friend. "Yeah, they're getting there, but well, it'll be a while still. In my opinion."

Mress nods absently as she takes a bite of bacon. A purr escapes her lips. "So good." Behind her, her tail is swishing back and forth. Wil grins at her. She says, "It might surprise you to learn that the United Earth Government has reached out to the GC."

Wil stops chewing, his eyes locked on the woman opposite him. "What? Really?"

She nods. "Nothing has come of it yet, mind you. But a delegation will be sent out sooner or later to investigate the potential for next steps."

"Holy hell," Wil murmurs. He takes a slow sip of his chlormax. "I didn't think they were that far along. The last time I checked in, they were still squabbling over petty crap." The woman opposite him shrugs.

"Hey, losers," Bennie says, opening the stairwell hatch. Maxim and Zephyr are on his heels. He looks at Wil, then Mress. "Ooh. Bacon." The hacker rushes to his seat, hopping into it. He reaches across the table, standing on his chair. Wil smacks his little green hand, sending it back. Bennie growls and sits down as Wil lifts the bacon plate and offers it to him.

Cynthia opens the hatch and joins the group. She looks at Wil. "I think you got another message from the tax board."

Wil swears, offering her a mug of tea.

Mress raises an eyebrow. "Tax problems?"

Bennie chuckles. "Someone thought Fury was some type of backwater tax haven."

Wil folds his arms across his chest. "It's a dirty shithole. If there were taxes, it'd be nicer."

Mress tilts her head. "That's not how taxes work, exactly."

Wil scowls. "It's fine. They're going to let me make payments."

"Out of your share," Bennie says around a mouthful of eggs. Wil pinches him, the screech sending half-chewed egg into the air.

Between bites, Maxim says, "You really thought that Fury had no taxes?" Wil nods. "So, all this time we've operated from there...?" Wil nods. Maxim whistles.

"Good evening. I'm Klor'Tillen, and this is GNO News Break." The Brailack journalist shifts in his seat. "With the public execution of disgraced Peacekeeper Janus for his crimes against the Commonwealth, a chapter longer than many citizens realize comes to a close." A display comes to life behind him, showing a file photo of then-Peacekeeper Janus.

"For those viewers that may not have known, or forgot, Janus was responsible for conflict that later became known as the 'Harrith Incident.' He and several thousand loyalists fled that sector when their plot was exposed. Many assumed the traitors had fled into the outer territories, never to be seen again." He takes a breath and looks down at his PADD. The inset display behind him updates to show the Farsight Corporation logo. "It's unknown how Janus and his forces came to be connected with Farsight's vile genetic experiments, but it happened. Peacekeeper Command is still investigating that aspect of this strange and tragic story."

Composing himself and smiling, the Brailack says, "The GC has weathered worse. In other news, the Rit Sohj Grand Prix is on schedule despite the ion storm that ravaged the area a span of five rotations ago."

CHAPTER TWO

On the bridge of the *Ghost,* Wil is leaning over his command and flight console. "Is this right?" He looks up and over to Zephyr.

His first officer looks up from her console. "Is what right?"

"We're cleared through to a spaceport." He looks over his shoulder to Cynthia at the communications station behind him. "You call ahead?"

She shakes her head. "Guessing when you're transporting one of the most powerful people on the planet back to her home, you don't sit in queues."

Wil tilts his head. "Fair enough." He adjusts their course. The planet Tyr and her four moons swing into view. Gruet, the largest of four moons, is almost as brightly lit as its parent. The other moons, less habitable than Gruet, are also colonized, but to much less extents. Nonetheless, the planetary system of Tyr Prime is almost as overwhelming as Tarsis.

As the *Ghost* drifts toward the central planet of the Tygran civilization, more and more details become visible: massive cities forming glowing webs across the dark side of the planet.

On the screen, the familiar ghostly green arrows of the auto-navigation system are guiding the ship toward the planet.

Wil looks at the ceiling. "Babs, we'll be entering the atmosphere in a few min—tocks, a few microtocks, if you want to get your stuff down to the hold."

From the ceiling speakers, their guest says, "Acknowledged. Thank you, Captain."

Wil nods, still looking at the ceiling. "Gabe, mind helping our client with her belongings? We'll be planetside shortly."

"Of course, Captain," the ceiling speaker replies in Gabe's voice.

Wil makes a few course adjustments, then asks, "Good to be home?" A moment of silence, then, "Cyn?"

"Oh, me."

He turns and looks over his shoulder. "Who else would I be asking?" He hitches a thumb toward one corner of the bridge. "Green Goblin over there came out of a pouch." He tilts his head toward the two Palorian crew members. "Those two—"

"My pouch was on a planet, you krebnack. A planet you visited. A planet with food that wrecked your insides, if I recall," Bennie says.

Maxim and Zephyr both make faces remembering their adventures on Brai, saving Bennie's sister from Xelurian kidnappers.

Wil waves a hand. "Anyway." He turns his attention back to Cynthia. "You haven't been home in a while."

Cynthia shrugs. "For a reason. Several, actually."

Wil's console beeps, pulling his attention back to it. The planet has grown to fill the entire primary display.

The bridge hatch opens and Barbara Mress walks in, followed by Gabe. Wil glances over his shoulder. "Come for the show?"

The elder Tygran woman nods. "Why not? Gabe and I were discussing Tyr's history with droids' rights, and I figured we could do it here just the same as in your cargo hold." She makes a face. "Which, by the way, smells funny."

Wil snaps his attention to Bennie, who holds up both hands in front of him.

CLASSY NEIGHBORHOODS

"Independent transport *Ghost*, you're cleared to land. Welcome to Lirole."

"Copy that, space control. Thanks," Cynthia says from behind Wil, a hand to one of her ears, the commset sticking out slightly.

The *Ghost* is cruising through the wispy cirrus clouds over the capitol region of Tyr Prime. The city of Lirole is every bit as massive as every other city Wil has seen on highly advanced worlds. A core that is several miles of skyscrapers gradually tapers off into lower rise buildings and suburban sprawl. Several spaceports, their distinctive open ring shapes obvious at any height, dot the landscape.

The ghostly green guidance arrows shift on the main display. Wil follows them toward a spaceport nestled among the outskirts of the miles-wide high-rise district. "Fancy."

"He says that every time we land anywhere even moderately civilized," Bennie says, looking sideways at Wil, who picks up what looks like a small blue bear peering through an imaginary window, causing the Brailack hacker to flinch and grumble, "Drennog."

Maxim says, "I looked up directions from the spaceport to a bar." He looks over to Mress, standing near the bridge hatch. "After we escort you to Tralgot HQ, of course." The woman smiles at him.

"Hold on," Wil says, both hands on the flight control. The earlier wispy clouds are gone, and the sky ahead of the ship is clear. The spaceport ahead is growing in size rapidly.

"Be a shame if we crashed," Bennie quips. "I mean, talk about embarrassing." He looks over at Wil and winks.

"Asshole," Wil grumbles, never taking his eyes off the primary display and the various sub windows showing things like airspeed, wind speed and direction, sensor plots of nearby traffic, and a dozen other things Wil has never really gotten the hang of paying attention to while flying.

The *Ghost* is floating on her repulsorlifts, the atmospheric engines roaring, pushing her forward. Wil eases the power levels for the repulsors down as the *Ghost* clears the ring wall of the large spaceport. A flick of a switch, and the twin landing gear deploy, unfolding from compartments where the wings meet the main fuselage. Pulling back on the flight controls and flaring the repulsors, Wil slows the ship, then lowers her to the duracrete. The landing gear touches down, groaning as the full weight of the *Ghost* settles on them.

"Touch—" The ship rattles and tilts. Bennie barks a laugh. The ship settles further. "Down," Wil says, his cheeks burning. He turns his chair around to face aft. "Welcome home, Babs." He sets about flipping a few switches, powering down primary systems and placing the ship into standby.

Stepping off the boarding ramp, Wil looks around, one of Barbara Mress' suitcases in each hand. "So, a car gonna meet us, or...?" He looks around. The *Ghost* is the only ship for four or five landing pads in any direction.

Mress joins him at the foot of the ramp with the rest of Rogue Enterprises. Wil still feels weird thinking about them having an honest-to-God team name. He follows the Tygran woman, nods, and points to a large vehicle access portal in the spaceport wall. A matte black hover car soundlessly glides toward them.

"Thank you all. I would say it was a wonderful trip, but well, it wasn't. Or, well...you know what I mean." Barbara Mress is standing at the door to her office on the top floor of a skyscraper that dwarfs anything on Earth. "Thanks for the company."

Wil smiles, inclining his head. "It was our pleasure. Or, well...you know."

Cynthia elbows him aside. "It was nice to see you again."

Mress dips her head, then looks at Maxim and Zephyr. "Be well, all of you." She looks past the group to Gabe. "Gabe, if you have nothing more pressing, I'd like to show you around the building, share with you some of Tyr's history with artificial intelligences and sapience. I didn't know you when you were here last. I'd love to show you some of Tralgot's archives on the subject."

The tall droid bows at the waist. "Thank you." He turns to Wil, who shrugs and nods. "It would be my pleasure."

"We'll keep you posted on where we end up, big guy," Wil says as Gabe follows Mress into the office.

Maxim grunts. "I'd suspect something was going on between the two of them, but," he hunches his shoulders, "how would that even work?"

Bennie waves a dismissive hand. "It can work." He pulls the hood of his cloak up onto his head and heads toward the elevators. "Come on, losers. I spotted a Gibnit's a block or two up."

"Great. Space Applebee's," Wil says. He consults his wristcomm. "Guess it's early for stronger drinks. We can pre-game." He offers his arm to Cynthia, who slides her hand through.

Maxim puts an arm around Zephyr's shoulder and follows. The trip to the base of the building is fast, and stepping out onto the sidewalk, the team smiles up at the sun.

Gibnit's is not even in the top ten of Wil's favorite places to eat or drink in the GC. Its locations are always brightly lit and staffed by entirely too perky young beings. Bennie pushes the period specific double doors open. Gibnit's bills itself as an eatery out of time. Whatever the hell that means.

A young Kilden greets them. "Hi there!" She waves both hands in giant arcs. "Five of you?"

"We'll sit at the bar," Bennie says, waving her away.

"Oh, yes, of course. It's open seating—" Bennie gets far enough away he can't hear her, and the others follow him. "Have a wonderful day," she murmurs to their backs.

Bennie hops into the tall seat and flags down the bartender, a Stilten, their shell adorned with several decorative stickers and painted on images. "Five grums!" he shouts over the nameless tune being pumped out of the ceiling speakers.

"They always play the music so loud in the bar," Zephyr complains. Nods all around.

The bartender arrives, a platter balanced on one clawed hand. As they distribute the frosted mugs, they say, "Anything to eat? Fried zerglings are on—"

"Two orders," Bennie interrupts. "Extra crispy." The insectoid bartender clacks their mandibles and retreats.

Zephyr sets her mug down. "I forgot to tell you all. I got the business flexies. They're at the office, arrived two days ago."

Wil sets his own mug down and nods. "Cool. Name over the door and business cards. It's official now."

Bennie turns from whatever he was just staring at. "What?"

Cynthia rolls her eyes. "Nothing. Oh, by the way, congratulations."

The other three non-Brailack turn their attention to Bennie. Maxim tilts his head. "Congratulations?"

Bennie's cheeks turn a slightly darker shade of green. He turns to Cynthia, glaring. "I was made a full Knight."

"The fuck?" Wil says.

"Get out of here!" Maxim shouts, leaning back in his chair.

"That's wonderful!" Zephyr says. She flags down the bartender. "Shots, please. Dwejure Reserve, if you have it."

Wil is beaming. He's loath to admit it, but he's proud of his friend for finding something he's passionate about, especially if it's something other than helping rig elections for the highest bidder. "Dude, that's awesome. Congrats. Why didn't you tell us?"

Bennie shrugs. "I dunno. Seemed a bit... braggadocio."

"So, on brand, then." Wil smiles.

Bennie makes a rude gesture. "There's really not much to it. I'm the only one, after all."

The bartender delivers the small glasses of light purple liquid. Everyone raises theirs and downs the drink in a single gulp. Bennie looks at Cynthia. "How did you know?"

She winks. "You're not the only one good at finding out secrets."

Bennie's eyes narrow to slits as he slowly nods. "Okay, I see you now." Cynthia smiles, purring.

SPACE KARAOKE?

After a few more mugs of grum and one more shot in Bennie's honor, Wil pays the tab, and the group heads out, everyone agreeing that while Gibnit's fried zerglings were acceptable, they needed food and better drinks from somewhere else.

Walking down the street, Wil's wristcomm vibrates. He raises his arm. "Hey, buddy."

Gabe's face is looking back at him. Since Gabe does not wear a wristcomm, Gabe's internal communications suite renders the representation. Wil has gotten used to it. "Hello. I am done at Tralgot."

"We're walking toward someplace with better food and drink than Gibnit's..." He lets the invite hang in the air.

"I am returning to the *Ghost*. Enjoy yourselves, and feel free to comm me when you need to be bailed out." The screen flicks back to the screen saver Wil has set up on it.

Cynthia, on his arm, watched the conversation. "Life of the party, Gabe."

Wil laughs. "I can't say I blame him. It's gotta be boring watching us eat and drink." He looks at Bennie, leading their procession. "Dude, you know where we're going? We've been walking like ten minutes now."

From his place at the lead, the small Brailack raises a tiny green hand, the sleeve of his robe sliding to his elbow. One narrow finger raises. Before Wil can reply, the arm drops and points.

Wil squints. "I don't know what that means." He gestures to the holographic sign over the door of the establishment. "Noise With Friends?"

Maxim groans. "Oh, come on, really?"

"What? We've never done it before," Bennie says, waiting for a delivery vehicle to pass so he can lead them across the street.

"What is this?" Wil presses.

Cynthia hums, then says, "Singing. In front of people."

Wil grunts. "Space karaoke?" He glances at Zephyr in time to see her shoulders bunch.

Wil sighs. "I'm gonna need a lot more alcohol."

Bennie presses the control to open the door. "I've heard of this chain. They're supposed to have top-notch food and drink, plus a great selection of music from across the GC." He holds the door open as the rest of the team files in.

Inside the establishment, Wil feels like he's on Earth. At the back of the building is a stage, currently occupied by a Trollack couple belting out some kind of pop song he's never heard, their catfish-like whiskers twitching in time with the music. In the middle of the space is a circular bar operated by two multi-limbed droids. Tables fill the rest of the space, about half of them occupied.

A droid standing off to the side of the stage appears to be the emcee. Bennie finds a table big enough for their group and tosses his cloak over the back on his way to the stage.

"He doesn't waste any time," Wil says as the rest of the team takes their seats.

A small cylinder rises from the center of the table and projects a holographic menu of food and drinks. Everyone enters their selections. Wil picks something he knows Bennie will complain about.

"I had no idea space karaoke was a thing," Wil says, winking at Zephyr when she turns a scowl on him. The bartender arrives, hovering on a glowing repulsor lift emitter. Wil thanks the droid and says, "Go ahead and get another round in the queue." He slams back almost the entire mug of grum, wiping his mouth on the back of his hand. "I'll need a few more before I'm ready to sing."

"I'll need a few more before I'm ready to hear you sing," Maxim says, following Wil's lead with his own mug.

CHAPTER THREE

SING A LITTLE SONG

AFTER SPENDING a few minutes interfacing his wristcomm with the bar's sound system, and figuring out how to display the stored lyrics in the music player, Wil treats the space karaoke bar patrons first to "Girls Just Want to Have Fun," then "Gangsta's Paradise."

As the various beings around the space clap politely, Bennie and Zephyr move to replace Wil on stage. The Brailack hacker looks at his friend as they pass. "Not bad."

Wil makes a face and continues on. Back at the table, Maxim and Cynthia are talking about something he can't hear yet. Reaching the table, he grabs his mug and empties it. The bartender looks at him from behind the bar, across the room, and nods. A minute later, a small hovering drone arrives with a tray suspended underneath it.

"What're you two talking about?" Wil asks.

Maxim turns. "Well, we started with a discussion of how to keep you from singing at your wedding." Wil sticks his tongue out. Maxim continues, "Then we moved on to actual wedding planning. I'm so excited about this." The big Palorian man rubs his hands together.

While Wil and Maxim chat, Cynthia's gaze drifts over Wil's shoulder at one of the entertainment displays mounted over the bar.

Wil finally notices that Cynthia hasn't said anything in a few minutes. "Babe?"

Wil and Maxim follow her gaze to the screen over the bar. On it, a GNO journalist is reporting on some type of museum gala or something that is coming up on a planet Wil has never heard of. He pokes Cynthia's arm. "Earth to Cynthia. Sweetie, what's up? You know that place?"

Cynthia's attention snaps back to her tablemates. "Oh. What?" She looks at Wil, then Maxim. "Sorry."

Bennie and Zephyr, having finished their Durbrillian duet, arrive at the table. The much shorter Bennie reaches up and feels around the table for a mug and grabs the first one he comes across. Wil watches as his new mug of grum vanishes. When it returns, he can spot things floating in the bubbly brew.

Cynthia says, "Sorry, that news blurb jarred a memory loose. I did a job that ended at that museum."

Bennie, now in his seat, able to see the others and the tops of the tables, rummages in one of the appetizer baskets. "What kind of job? Killed some folks? Like a Xarrix job or secret ninja school job?" He finds a greasy something and pops it into his mouth.

Wil stifles his gag reflex and turns slightly. "When was this?"

"Before I met any of you. Before Xarrix and Lorath even. When I was still living here on Tyr. I was an operative for Yadro." She shudders, recalling the time.

Wil puts a hand on hers. "That Xavier school for ninjas?" Cynthia nods. He inhales.

Maxim offers Zephyr a sip of his drink as he holds up two fingers for the bartender droid.

Cynthia says, "That museum, in Mo Wumpla on Nom Clamma—"

"Mouthful," Wil interrupts.

Cynthia makes a face and continues, "The museum curator was a friend of someone high up in Yadro. They wanted to do this big exhibit of some Stilten artist, but most of the works were privately owned by a wealthy Malkorite woman on Cleblon Three."

The small hover drone arrives, depositing two fresh mugs of grum. Wil takes his and stares at Bennie coldly. Everyone places empty glassware and food containers on the tray. The drone vanishes overhead.

Cynthia continues, "They sent me to get the collection, no matter what."

"Does that mean...?" Maxim asks.

Cynthia nods. "I broke into her house and killed her. Packed up the art plus a few pieces I thought were pretty and escorted them all to Nom Clamma." She looks past her friends to the bar. "The museum owner didn't care how I got them. Barely even acknowledged me beyond telling me to tell his contact thank you."

SOMEONE THAT I USED TO KNOW

AT A TABLE across the building from where the Rogue Enterprises team is sitting, a lone Tygran woman is sipping something bright green and fizzy from a tall fluted glass. Her fur is jet black, other than a single patch of white between her eyes.

The Brailack and Palorian woman just returned from singing some awful Durbrillian song and Cynthia is telling a story.

The woman watching them stares over the top of her glass. One of the two droid bartenders comes over. "Would you care for another?" it asks.

She nods, and before the droid can drift away on its circular repulsorlift pad, puts a hand on one of the arms. "Who are those people?"

The droid pauses. "I am sorry, I—"

She points, keeping the gesture between her and droid. "The group over there: two Palorians, a Brailack, a Tygran, and I guess a Multonae."

The droid's head turns, then turns back to the Tygran woman. "I—"

Again, she interrupts, this time holding up a credit chit.

The droid's optic sensors tilt down to the hard currency. It snatches the chit and says, "Accessing." What looks like lines of code flash across the three optic sensors as it accesses the bar's central computer. It looks at her. "The tab is under one Wil Calder, Rogue Enterprises."

When the droid says nothing further, she presses. "And?"

"There is not much else attached to the record. The bank data on file indicates a branch on Fury."

Across the bar, Cynthia stops telling her story to stare across the room.

"Cyn?" Wil asks, turning to follow her gaze.

One of the bartenders is at a table, its back to them. The droid turns and drifts to another table. The table it was at is empty.

Cynthia blinks. "I thought I saw someone familiar."

Bennie says, "Well, this is your home planet, and the capital."

Cynthia shakes her head. "Anyway. The Malkorite woman apparently had rebuffed repeated offers from the museum owner, some rich Quillant man, multiple times. The Quillant was friends with one of the directors of Yadro and asked a favor."

"So, you just killed her?" Zephyr asks.

Cynthia inclines her head. "From the moment we entered the program, it was non-stop training and, well, brainwashing. The board knew she'd never part with the collection, and I couldn't just steal it because she'd report it."

"But not if she was dead," Bennie says.

Cynthia nods. "Yeah. During the flight to Nom Clamma, I doctored up some sales records from a half cycle back so that if anyone came looking, there'd be a paper trail of sorts." She looks across the room again at the empty table, her gaze drifting from table to table. She turns back to the group. "My understanding was that the owner of that museum," she points to the display, "offered her a hefty sum, but she wouldn't have it. She was rich already. Money didn't do much for her, and she insisted that the collection had been gifted by the artist, long dead, who on their deathbed asked that she keep the collection to herself."

"Why would the bug do that?" Bennie demands. He takes a sip of Wil's—now his—grum. "I mean, for one thing, the bug—"

"Stilten," Zephyr interrupts.

Bennie sighs. "Fine. The Stilten was dead. Who cares what it wanted? Plus, to be clear, should it ever come up, you can never be too rich."

Wil looks at his friend. "Aren't Knights of Plentallus supposed to live simple lives, spreading justice and living off the goodwill of others?"

Bennie waves a hand. "Bah, maybe in the old days. I get to make the rules now. Remember, full Knighthood."

Maxim shudders. "Terrifying."

Cynthia looks at her friends. "At any rate, the Stilten didn't like the direction their art was being taken, as I understood it, and the Malkorite woman was a trusted patron."

"And..." Zephyr says.

"And my orders were to get the art."

Wil leans forward. "Then what?"

Bennie tuts. "What you do think, drennog? She killed the woman and took her art."

Cynthia nods. "Yeah."

"Then what? Just...came home and took a shower?" Wil presses.

Cynthia looks at him. "Yeah."

Maxim leans back. "I knew you had a past, but wow." Zephyr elbows him, hard. "Ouch. I mean, no judgment, Cyn. We've all done some dark stuff before." He tilts his head. "But damn. Killing a woman for her art collection..."

Cynthia's facial fur ripples, Tygran blushing. Wil puts his hand on hers and smiles.

The Tygran woman smiles at her friends. "Thanks. I had kinda put it all behind me. This is the first time I've thought about Yadro, or any of those jobs, in cycles." She hugs herself as a shudder passes over her. She glances once again at the empty table across the room.

The story on the entertainment display flashes the museum one more time before moving onto a story about a racing event that looks oddly like motorized chariots with jet engines attached to them. Wil says, "So, pretty good odds the new exhibit they're talking about..."

"Stolen. Yeah, good odds." Cynthia nods.

THE WOMAN who has been watching the Rogue Enterprises team is now at the bar, sidled up next to one of the pillars that supports entertainment displays. She's next to a trio of Multonae men laughing and enjoying a night out.

Looking at her wristcomm, she places a call. A Tygran man appears on the small screen. "I've got eyes on Cynthia Luar."

"What? Where?" the small image asks.

"A Noise With Friends bar in Lirole." She glances up to make sure her quarry is still sitting with her friends.

"Lirole? She's here, on Tyr?" The man leans closer to his own communications device.

The woman nods. "Yeah. That tap in the local security feed paid off, finally. Complete coincidence. I was here finishing a job and got a ping from that automated system we installed a few cycles ago. The Gods smile on me for sure."

"Can you get to her?"

The woman shakes her head. "No. She's with people. I could probably take some of them, but it's two Palorians—look like PKs—a Multonae that doesn't look like a threat, and a weirdly dressed Brailack. Maybe a monk or something." Before the man on the wristcomm screen can say anything, she continues, "I have some intel for you to run down." She recites what the bartender droid told her.

The man nods. "I'll see what I can find." The screen goes dark.

The woman looks over at Cynthia and the group. "Retribution is coming."

One of the Multonae men looks over his shoulder. "I'm sorry, what?"

She looks up. "Nothing, never mind. Mind your business." She slides off the barstool and moves to a darker corner of the bar, her festive, colored drink clutched in her hand.

CHAPTER FOUR

Cynthia looks over to the bar where a group of Multonae men are talking. There's an empty seat next to one of them. She can't shake the sensation that someone is watching her.

"So, why don't we call the authorities?" Maxim offers. "We can alert the local PKs on Nom Clamma, as well as their own authorities. Get the museum shut down."

Wil looks at his friend. "Or..." He smiles. "We could rob the museum, take back the stuff Cynthia brought, return it to the artist's family or hive or whatever Stilten have."

Bennie shrugs. "I could do some crime."

"Good crime," Wil offers.

"Whatever." Bennie shrugs.

Zephyr says, "I don't know. Surely if we alert the authorities that the artwork is stolen, they can track down the Malkorite woman's heirs or the artist's."

Cynthia raises a hand. "I don't think the pieces I delivered are still on display, certainly not prominently. That was a while ago now."

Wil reaches for his grum only to remember that it's been taken by

Bennie. His hand falls back to his lap. "Doesn't matter. Whatever is in that museum is stolen. We can grab it and return it to where it belongs and who it belongs to."

Cynthia tilts her head. "I mean..."

"I like the crime idea," Bennie says. "We don't have anything else booked."

Wil nods vigorously.

Maxim looks at Zephyr. Both Palorians sigh.

"No killing," Zephyr says.

"No taking anything other than the stolen art," Maxim adds.

"Boring," Bennie says.

Wil looks at Cynthia, who nods, smiling. "Deal," he says. He rubs his hands together. "This is exciting. We haven't crimed in a while."

"Yeah, it was nice while it lasted," Zephyr quips.

Wil waves her away. "Oh, come on. It's fun."

"We robbed that prince. Where was that? Maldo?" Bennie says, his voice higher than normal with excitement.

Maxim chuckles. "That was fun. He actually bought that Wil was an executive at a space frame manufacturer."

"Hey, I could be an executive."

Bennie, taking a drink, spits back into the mug. He looks at Wil. "No."

"What do you mean, no?" He leans in. "I can look business-y." He runs a hand through his hair.

Cynthia waves both hands. "Anyway. If we're gonna do this, we've got a time constraint. According to the news show, the exhibit opens in a few days."

Wil flags down the bartender. "One more round, and then we'll cash out." He stands. "I've got one more song in me." He heads up to the stage.

The others watch him, then Bennie says, "I can't wait to rob someone. I didn't realize until now how much I missed it."

Maxim turns to him. "You know it's not like a blanket thing, right? We're not robbing random someones."

"One particular someone," Cynthia says, pointing at the screen. It is showing an ad for a new personal yacht developed by Lorem Shipworks.

On stage, the driving beats of Salt-N-Pepa's "Push It" start pulsing out of the speakers.

ONE TOO MANY

"I AM DRUNKER...WHAT?" Wil slurs. His one more song turned into three more drinks. The crew is at the bar, having abandoned the stage an hour ago.

Bennie raises a hand. "High threeeee," he slurs before falling over.

Cynthia looks at the two, then turns to the Palorian couple. "This is gonna be messy."

Wil moves around Bennie, not offering a high five. His shoulder slams into a hulking being that he's never seen the species of before. "Watch the fuck out," he drawls.

The being he collided with is two and a half meters tall, if it's a centimeter. Skin like gravel, massive hunched shoulders. The massive being turns, its face a scowl. The quartet of gems that must serve as eyes are squinting, the stonelike skin grinding. "Please, excuse me. I'm so sorry. Please excuse me." It holds up both three-fingered hands, palms out. "Apologies."

Bennie steps up. "Who the...Wait? What?" He leans closer to peer at the rocky knee of the apologizing bar patron. Reaching out, he pokes the thick skin.

The massive pebble-skinned being shuffles out of Wil and

40

Bennie's way. "Please accept my humblest apologies. I'll scoot down a bit."

From a few feet away, Maxim leans down to Zephyr. "That didn't go the way I was expecting." Zephyr looks up at him and nods.

Wil waves absently at the massive polite rock person. "S'okay." He takes three steps and bumps into another patron, this one an Olop man in a bespoke suit.

The small man turns. "The grolack is wrong with you?" He doesn't even wait for Wil to reply, leaping straight up onto Wil's head, blows raining down.

Bennie swears and rushes toward Wil but falls down two steps into his charge.

Zephyr shrugs. "And here we go." Maxim and Cynthia nod.

Wil is screaming and flailing as the small furry man bites his ear.

WIL OPENS HIS EYES SLOWLY. It feels like someone is jabbing ice picks into his brain through his eyes.

"Guuuh." His mouth feels like it's full of cotton. He puts his hand on Cynthia, lying next to him. "What?"

Raising his head, he spies a hairless green body curled up next to him, a thin arm draped over his chest. "The fuck!?" He flails, sending Bennie flying out of the bed. The groggy Brailack slams into the bulkhead, making a wheezy screech like noise. "Why are you in my bed?" Wil screams.

Bennie sits up. "What?" He looks around. "Why am I naked?"

Wil looks down. "Why am I naked?" He looks up and meets Bennie's gaze. His gaze darts to the ceiling as he shouts, "No eye contact!"

Bennie scrambles up, grabbing some of the sheet, pulling it away from Wil, who pulls it back. Bennie, still groggy, trips and falls to the deck again.

Wil looks around the room. It's definitely his berth aboard the

Ghost. Where is Cynthia? Why is Bennie in the room with him? Where are their clothes? What the hell happened last night?

Bennie pokes his head up over the edge of the bed. "What's going on?"

Wil is about to answer, then hears something. He holds up a finger. From outside the hatch, he hears it. Laughter. He rubs his temples. "I'm not drinking with you anymore."

Bennie stands, swaying slightly. He jabs a finger. "Don't blame me."

Wil holds a hand out in front of him to cover Bennie's nakedness. "You can come in now," he shouts.

The door opens. Cynthia, Zephyr, and Maxim walk in. Gabe is standing in the corridor. He raises a hand. "For the record, I was not in favor of this."

Bennie picks up a shoe and hurls it. "What the wurrin, you guys! Why are we naked? This isn't funny!"

Zephyr ducks the shoe, careful to avert her eyes from the small naked, angry Brailack.

Cynthia tuts and holds up a finger. "One, it's hilarious. Two, you two were in rough shape last night. That Olop guy did a number on you two before we could subdue him."

Wil nods slowly. "I kinda remember being attacked by tribbles. I thought it was a dream." He reaches up and touches his ear.

Maxim shakes his head. "He bit your ear, gave you a black eye, and bruised a rib." He points to Bennie, still trying to cover himself up with the end of the bedsheet. "You broke your arm when you fell trying to rush into the fight."

Bennie blushes. "That's undignified."

Cynthia nods. "Agreed. We finally convinced that big rock guy to sit on the Olop until security arrived."

Wil grunts. "And our being naked? In bed together?"

Cynthia beams. "Oh, that was just payback for having to carry you both back to the ship and get you into and out of the autodoc and up here. Our room was closer than Bennie's, so..." She shrugs.

"By a few steps," Bennie protests.

Wil nods again, then snaps his fingers at Bennie. "Get out." He turns to the others. "I hate you all." He glares at Cynthia. "Even you. I'm rethinking marriage."

Bennie snatches the sheet, leaving Wil with nothing but a pillow that he quickly moves in front of himself. Wrapping the sheet around his tiny body several times, Bennie marches into the corridor, saying, "You're all going to pay." He stomps out of sight.

Cynthia ushers everyone out of the room, closing the hatch. "It was funny." Wil scowls and scoots off the bed, clutching the pillow, still looking for his clothes. "You know, while you're here and, you know, naked..." She wiggles both eyebrows.

Wil stares at her. "You're still on my shit list." He scoots back onto the bed.

"We'll see about that," she replies.

NOW DEPARTING

THE BRIDGE HATCH OPENS, allowing Wil and Cynthia to enter. Bennie looks up from his console. "Hard time finding your clothes?"

Cynthia drops into her seat. "Something like that." She winks.

Bennie's face wrinkles.

Zephyr says, "We're clear for departure." She looks to Cynthia. "If you two are ready."

Cynthia shrugs. "I'm good." She purrs. Her Palorian friend smiles and shakes her head.

Wil consults his console, then looks at the ceiling. "Gabe, all set down there?"

The ceiling replies, "Affirmative, Captain. Reactor is at one hundred percent. Atmospheric engines are ready."

Wil turns to Zephyr. "Why don't you all get breakfast going?"

Zephyr nods and stands, poking Maxim's shoulder as she does.

Standing, the big Palorian looks at Wil, then Cynthia. "Not on the bridge." He points at each of them in turn.

Wil chuckles, turning his attention back to his console. "Here we go." He works the flight controls. Engine nacelle-mounted repulsorlifts power up, lifting the *Ghost* up off the ground. The small ship rises higher and higher into the air. The powerful lifts at the forward ends of the nacelles are perfectly placed for the ship to balance on.

The bridge hatch shuts behind the Palorian couple as the *Ghost* clears the ring wall of the spaceport.

Looking over his shoulder, Wil asks, "Gonna miss Tyr? We didn't get to see much of it."

Cynthia shakes her head. "Not even a little." She shrugs. "Plus, I've had this nagging feeling like we're being watched since we got here. I can't shake it."

Bennie turns in his seat. "Want me to access the local security feeds? See if I can spot anyone?"

Cynthia shakes her head. "No, it'd be a sewing implement in a grain pile, at best. I'm happy enough to just put some distance between us and my home planet." She looks at Wil. "Let's blow this... pipcycle vendor?"

Wil doesn't turn around. On the main display, the spaceport is no longer visible. He presses the ignition control for the atmospheric thrusters. A thundering boom pushes the *Ghost* forward. He says, "Close. Popsicle stand."

"Aah." She snaps her fingers. "Anyway. Let's just go home." She grins. "We've got crime to plan."

Bennie hops out of his seat. "I'm really excited about this job." He rubs his hands together.

On the primary display, the sprawling city of Lirole has dropped from view already. The view is shifting from blue to black as the *Ghost* pushes up and out of the atmosphere.

Wil spares his little friend a glance. "Shouldn't a Knight of Plentallus be, you know, against crime?"

Bennie shrugs. "I won't tell if you don't."

Cynthia's mouth hangs open as Bennie walks around the edge of the bridge toward the hatch. He looks up. "Close your mouth, you'll catch flies."

Cynthia closes her mouth and flicks Bennie between the eyes, eliciting an indignant squeak.

Wil looks over his shoulder. "Damn."

Cynthia grabs the back of Brailack hacker's shirt with one hand, opening the bridge hatch with the other. "Come on, drennog." She looks at Wil. "I'll have a cup of chlormax waiting for you."

Wil nods. "Sounds good to me." He looks at the console. "Ten minutes to FTL."

From the spaceport's administrative office on the top floor of the ring, below the squat tower that serves as space control, the woman from the space karaoke bar watches the Ankarran Raptor lift off and head into the clouds.

She turns to a younger man sitting at a console. "And you're certain that they're heading to Fury?"

The younger man nods. "Yes, ma'am. At least according to their flight plan."

The woman nods. "Find me a seat on the fastest shuttle on the planet. Redirect one if you have to. I need to be on Fury. Fast." The man nods and gets to work. Outside the window, the *Ghost* is nothing more than a speck.

NEWSCAST

"Good morning. I'm Megan, and this is your GNO Morning Briefing. The Rit Sohj Grand Prix has concluded with only three casualties. That sets a record for lowest number of deaths at the event in the last fifty cycles." She smiles. "The winner is a Trollack woman named Lbeella Fontot. This was her third Grand Prix, and she won it without having to destroy or otherwise incapacitate any of her competitors."

The blonde-haired journalist turns to a different camera. "In other news, the upcoming exhibit at the Dre Toma Museum of Exotic Art on Nom Clamma is attracting quite the buzz. The owner and curator, known for hosting lavish receptions to unveil new collections, has promised something truly amazing with his latest acquisitions."

PART 2

CHAPTER FIVE

THE CONFERENCE ROOM on the ground floor of Rogue Enterprises is, not surprisingly, Zephyr's domain. Shortly after taking possession of the building, Wil tried to decorate the room and was threatened with bodily violence if he ever set foot in the room for any purpose other than a meeting.

Zephyr taps the controls set into the table to activate the holoprojector in the center of the long meal oval. Bennie wanted polished wood but was ignored. Looking around, she says, "Okay, we don't have a lot of time. Let's get to it." She turns to Cynthia. "Why don't you walk us through what you remember of the museum and its owner?"

Cynthia nods, standing. "Keep in mind this is all several cycles old now." She manipulates the hologram, focusing on the first floor. The image zooms, the other floors fading. "The first floor is mostly small galleries. The main lobby," she points to a section with floor-to-ceiling sliding transparent doors, "is entirely functional. There's a reception desk, seating, that sort of thing. When I was there, they had stuff on the walls but nothing on pedestals or freestanding."

"Makes sense," Bennie says. "Allows 'em to focus security efforts there." He stands up on his seat. "I bet there are sensors: here, here, and here." He points to various parts of the holographic lobby.

Maxim nods and points. "Weapons, probably pacification style: there and there. They can have a perfect cross fire." Zephyr nods her agreement.

Cynthia nods and continues, shifting the hologram around to a wider view of the ground floor. "These smaller galleries were just local artists and such. Nothing too valuable or interesting. I think they mostly serve to cover his more illicit activities. No one wants to take down a supporter of local artists." She works the image again. "This grand staircase goes all the way up all four floors."

"Four stories?" Wil interrupts. "That's a big ass museum."

Bennie looks at Wil, one eyebrow ridge quirked. "You don't get out much, do you?" Wil makes a rude gesture.

Maxim leans in. "I'm guessing each landing of that stairway can be reinforced with additional security measures." Nods all around.

Cynthia looks at the two of them. "Anyway," she says. The image twists around the wide staircase. The first floor fades away, the pixels of light shifting to the layout of the second floor. "Here's where the good stuff starts." She smiles. "The pieces I delivered were exhibited here." She points to one corner of the floor. Unlike the first floor, the second is one large open floor plan with a few dividing walls but no distinct rooms.

Wil says, "But you think that stuff's moved on."

She nods. "Yeah. I can't imagine Sclaro hasn't replaced most of the stuff in there twice over." She scowls. "He gets bored easily and likes to keep things changing so he can keep people coming. Fancies himself something of a cultural icon on Nom Clamma."

Zephyr points to Bennie. "Speaking of, let's take a break from the museum. You have the précis on our museum owner?"

Bennie bows. "Of course, I do." He swipes on his PADD and the museum layout vanishes to be replaced by a well-dressed Malkorite. Each fanlike ear is adorned with various earrings encrusted with all manner of precious gemstones. Chains of equally precious metals connect various pieces. "This is our mark. Sclaro Hunflim. Malkorite. He's lived on Nom Clamma for the better part of twenty cycles. A few minor run-ins with law enforcement early on. Nothing that ever bubbled up enough for PKs to get involved. I found a few old entries that indicate he might have left Malkor under duress. I found a few smuggling and art theft reports. None stuck, but guessing he wanted a clean start."

Wil raises a hand. "Is he a known scumbag, or is all this on the DL?"

Bennie shakes his head. "Not really. Well, sorta. He's got a rep among people like, well, us. But at the upper crust levels, he's an upstanding citizen. Donates to causes, especially political ones. Feeds orphans, that kind of crap. Since arriving on Nom Clamma, all the shady stuff he was into on Malkor either ended or went deep underground. Clearly the latter."

Zephyr nods to Cynthia. "Okay, walk us through the rest of the layout." She turns to Bennie. "You can fill the gaps around the top floor?" The hacker nods.

ONCE CYNTHIA FINISHES GOING over the rest of the building, what she remembers about the surrounding neighborhood, and more, Wil says, "Okay. We're gonna need supplies. We haven't done a job like this—"

"Crime," Bennie interrupts.

Wil glowers. "A job—"

"It's crime. We're doing crime, just say 'crime,'" Bennie says. "No one will know or judge you."

Wil makes a rude gesture and continues. "We haven't done a crime like this in a while. We need gear and other supplies." Everyone nods their agreement while Bennie beams.

After Wil doles out assignments, Bennie says, "You know, if we ever add someone to the team, we'll have an odd number. Bad luck."

Wil doesn't blink. "We'd just kill you to keep it even."

Bennie leans back. "Rude." He points to the door. "I'll grab some stuff and we can head out."

Everyone breaks into their assigned pairs and filters out of the conference room toward the stairs to the living levels above to get gear before heading out. Cynthia pulls Wil aside. "Why'd you pair up with Bennie after, you know?" She grins.

Wil shrugs. "Figured I should make sure things are cool with him. Plus, he seems really fired up about this and I want to make sure he understands this isn't the start of some new criminal endeavor."

She nods. They climb the stairs. The elevator on the opposite side of the building doesn't get a lot of use. "He does seem pretty excited."

"He used to do all kinds of side jobs back in the day. I never said much most of the time because it was mostly harmless and never blew back on us." They reach the second floor, which is a space Bennie took over as a lab, plus Maxim's sparring area and some still unused rooms. "When he got into the whole Jedi thing, I thought he'd turned over a new leaf, but now I'm not sure."

Bennie rounds a corner up ahead. Cynthia leans in to give Wil a kiss on the cheek. "Well, have fun." She continues up the stairs to the living quarters.

He smiles. "Barrel of monkeys."

"That doesn't sound fun. Monkeys are those winged things? The leathery wings? Screeching and such?"

"Those are bats. Monkeys are like the cute little fury guy that hung out with Ross on *Friends*, the show about—"

Cynthia snaps her fingers. "Oh, the show with the attractive unemployed young people living impossible lives in that ritzy city."

Wil smiles. "Yeah." He turns to Bennie. "You ready, Tiny?"

Bennie smirks. "It's Sir Tiny, to you." He doesn't slow down, heading down the stairs to the first floor.

As the pairs of Rogue Enterprises team members head out on their tasks, a Tygran woman steps off a shuttle. She looks around. This is the second spaceport on Fury she's forced the shuttle to take her to. The first, a smaller one on the outskirts of Lwath, had been a dead end. The spaceport operator had no record of Rogue Enterprises or of an Ankarran Raptor ever landing there.

Her initial feeling that tracking her quarry would be easy has been stymied at every turn, thanks to Fury's relaxed space control policies and almost non-existent planetary business or citizen's registry. Hopefully this spaceport, the largest in the area, will be the one. She looks over her shoulder at the pilot of the shuttle. "Wait here."

MAX & CYNTHIA

Max and Cynthia walk out of the Rogue Enterprises building and flag down a hover cab. The market Cynthia has in mind isn't the one near the spaceport, meaning it isn't within walking distance.

"Where are we going?" Maxim asks.

"You'll see." She grins as the vehicle speeds up, merging into the light traffic that fills the streets of Lwath. Despite being the unofficial capitol of Fury, Lwath isn't that much different than most of the small settlements on the dusty brown and darker brown planet.

A few minutes into the trip, Maxim turns. "So. You've picked colors for your attendants' dresses?"

Cynthia, focused on her wristcomm, looks up. "What now?"

"Based on Wil's media archive, Earth women have anywhere from three to twelve attendants. They seem to mostly prefer dressing them in garish outfits, I think to further highlight the beauty of the woman getting joined."

"That's ludicrous."

"You've seen his shows. It must be the norm. They all do it."

Cynthia shakes her head. "I will not."

"I think it's part of the ceremony." The big Palorian man shrugs.

"They stand at the front of the room with you, opposite him and his team."

"For one thing, I don't have that many friends." She shifts to not have to turn her head to look at him. "All women, I assume?"

Maxim tilts his head. "Seems like. On one show—I can't remember the name—that bride had a male in her party. In the show it caused quite a stir, but I would guess it's not unheard of."

Cynthia grunts. "Well, there's Zephyr." She ticks a finger. "And, well, that's it, unless we start counting Jussip and his Buttoxian helpers and maybe your friends from when you dealt with that automated dreadnaught."

Maxim shakes his head. "I think Bennie broke it off with Xan in a, well, typically Bennie way. She might try to murder him if she saw him."

"Shocker." She shrugs, moving to face forward again. "Maybe I can convince him to do a more traditional GC nondenominational ceremony?"

Before Maxim can answer, the vehicle pulls over, the sliding door opening. Cynthia swipes the payment on her wristcomm. The driving system beeps happily.

Walking toward the entrance to what looks like a rundown warehouse, Cynthia says, "So, I found this place a few months back. Don't freak out or anything."

They reach the corrugated metal sheet that serves as a door. Maxim reaches up to pull it aside. "Why would I freak out?"

"I'm just saying."

He pulls aside the metal sheet and the first thing they see are two Brailack in a cage, fighting. Each has a blade as long as their arm. Cheering crowds surround the three-meter square cage. The light blue skinned fighter dodges an attack and slices downward, severing the arm of his opponent to the excitement of the crowd. The dark green Brailack falls to his knees, cradling the stump. He looks up in time to see his opponent's blade before it cleaves his skull. The crowd goes wild as several bookmakers start doling out winnings. An industrial mover droid trundles into the cage, scooping up the corpse and its arm.

Maxim's mouth is hanging open. The victor is dancing around the small cage, soaking up the cheers of the crowd. "The grolacking wurrin?" he whispers.

Cynthia grabs ahold of his elbow and guides him past the miniature fighting pit. "Come on, big guy."

"This is...That..." He turns his head to stare at the fighting pit as they work their way deeper into the warehouse. The winning fighter is on someone's shoulders, waving at the crowd.

"I know. Like I said, don't freak out." Cynthia is moving with purpose.

"There's a PK garrison, such as it is, less than a plorith from here. How is this place here?"

Cynthia turns right at another cage, much larger than the previous one, with three Ruknak in loincloths, trying to hack each other to pieces with heavy axes taller than Maxim. She gestures to a Palorian man in a Peacekeeper subcommander's uniform. "Because they're paid to look the other way." The subcommander is browsing the wares at a shop that looks like it sells illicit pornographic holos. Cynthia takes a left at a stall selling personal energy shield emitters, military grade, so says the sign.

"Where is Rogue Enterprises?" the Tygran woman asks, for the third time. She's in the main administrative office of the spaceport. She's definitely been in dingier places, but not by much.

The Vokamian Spaceport manager, currently pinned to his desk by her hand clasping his throat, wheezes, "I don't know who that is." The overwhelming odor coming off the squat being is turning her stomach.

She lifts him slightly, then slams him back to the desktop. "They fly in an old Ankarran Raptor. A Multonae man, two Palorians, a—"

"Oh, them!" he croaks. When her grip doesn't loosen, he slaps at her arm. Once free, he sits up. "They used to pay for a pad here. They got their own place a half plorith or so from here. Some dingy old warehouse. I haven't seen them since."

"Address?" she growls.

The smelly little spaceport manager shakes his head. "No idea. When they cancelled their lease—without proper notice, I should add—they didn't leave a forwarding address."

"Sir?" says one of Buttoxian underlings that the Tygran woman tossed around the room when she entered. "I believe their new office is on Durntelp Street."

The Tygran woman drops the little foreman and turns to the assistant. "Tell me more."

The small woman flinches. "I don't know the address, but I think it's a bluish building with a gray trim. It looks a bit run down." She holds up a hand in front of her face.

The woman looks around. "If they know I'm coming before I get there, I'll hunt you and your families down." She growls, and everyone in the room ducks their heads.

Jussip sits up. "Don't worry about that. Screw them." He brushes off his shirt.

The Tygran woman nods. "Good. Thank you." She departs, letting the door slide closed behind her, her tail swishing out of the way just in time.

CHAPTER SIX

"So, how come you never filled us all in on the whole droid politics thing?" Zephyr asks. She and Gabe are in the principal market outside the spaceport. While still offering plenty of illicit wares, this market caters to the more mainstream needs of a spacer.

Gabe shrugs. "I worried you would mock me."

"Me?"

He looks down. "No. Wil and Bennie." A pause. "Mostly Wil."

The Palorian woman half shrugs. "You probably weren't wrong." She points toward a section of the market. "Still, we would support you no matter what. You must know how proud of you all of us are."

Gabe stops in his tracks. "I do not understand."

Resting a hand on the taller droid's arm, Zephyr says, "You started life as a basic engineering droid, locked in a crate—"

Gabe interrupts. "I served the Peacekeepers for twenty-one cycles before the crate incident."

Zephyr rocks back. "That long? Wow. Anyway, your life with us started on the station in the Barsoom sector." Gabe nods his agreement. She continues, "You've gone on countless adventures with us as an equal, then led the effort to bring civil rights to all droids throughout the GC, succeeding in that mission with little initial support." She smiles. "That's impressive, then add on helping find your people a planet to call their own. And now, being a part of the fledgling government, invited by your peers to lead..." She shrugs and continues toward their destination. "Impressive."

Gabe remains motionless a moment, watching his friend head into the foodstuff and general goods section of the open-air market. He finally moves to follow Zephyr. He catches up to her a few stalls into the market, a small cargo bot already dutifully following behind her.

"What do you think?" She holds up a box claiming to contain enough emergency rations to feed a crew of twelve for five days.

"I think that everyone will complain," he offers. A quick scan of the nearby stalls, and he points to a stall three down on the opposite side of the aisle. "That vendor has emergency meal kits of a higher caliber and wider variety."

"Excuse me?" the Multonae man behind the counter says. "My ration packs are top quality!"

Zephyr pats the air in front of her. "Okay, calm down." She points to a shelf behind the man. "We'll take two of those."

The man turns. "Oh, this is one of my most popular products." He reaches up and pulls two medium-sized boxes off the shelf. "High grade chlormax."

Zephyr nods.

Gabe watches the transaction silently. The vendor offers him the two boxes, which he places into the cargo area of the bot behind Zephyr.

After purchasing the higher-grade ration packs from the vendor across the way, they move further into the market.

"I'd like to get a few pieces of Jerlack and maybe a few units of doorip," Zephyr says, putting a pouch of dehydrated something or other back down on a shelf.

Gabe nods, saying nothing. He has picked up a weird transmission. Anonymous packets are flooding the local wireless network.

Looking around, he spots a utility pole. About two meters up, someone has affixed a device he isn't familiar with.

"Excuse me. I will be right back," he says. He doesn't wait for Zephyr's reply. She is busy haggling with a vendor over the price of ploth cubes.

The device is a handmade network device. Someone has spliced a data cable from the municipal unit further up the pole into the mystery device.

Gabe looks around. No one appears to be monitoring the device. He raises a hand, data tendrils slithering out of his fingertips.

He remains motionless next to the utility pole for a minute or two. The data tendrils withdraw and he turns. Zephyr is loading the cargo bot with a bag of ploth cubes. She turns. "You okay? What's up?" She cranes her neck. "What's that?"

He nods. "I am fine. It is nothing." He holds an arm out so that she can head toward the next aisle. As he falls in behind her, he hears the sound of several Peacekeepers shouting orders at someone in a stall two aisles over. He's a bit surprised that the Peacekeepers moved on the hackers as quickly as they seem to have. There must have been a patrol in the market already.

"Wonder what's going on over there?" Zephyr asks, her head inclined in the direction of the shouting. The Peacekeepers are shouting about skimming the network for payment details.

WIL & BENNIE

"Do you have a shopping list or anything?" Wil asks as they exit the hover cab.

They're on the far side of Lwath from the market Gabe and Zephyr are shopping in, near the outskirts of town. Known for illicit tech from around the GC, the market doesn't have a name or even an address.

Bennie shrugs. "Nope. I figure I'll know what I need when I see it."

"Uh. No." Wil shakes his head. He's certain he's never been to this part of town before. The only sign they aren't in an abandoned commercial district is the wholly out of place Ruknak in a bespoke suit, standing next to a wooden door. He points. "How do you even know about this place?"

Bennie looks up, waves a hand. "You don't want to know."

Wil kicks him, eliciting a yelp. "You're not a Jedi. Cut that shit out."

Bennie frowns. "Grolack you. My old crew used to work out of a unit here."

As they approach, the Ruknak smiles. "Hello Ben-Ari. I haven't seen you in a while. Why are you dressed funny?"

Bennie is wearing his Knight of Plentallus uniform, as Wil calls it. Basic earth tone tunic and boots with a slightly lighter colored overshirt. He left the cloak at the office. He smiles. "Hi, Gurber. Yeah, I got a new crew. We're more legit."

The massive rocky face crinkles. "Legit?"

Bennie waves his hand. "Not that legit." He grins. The other man chuckles, like someone is gargling with pebbles. A thick fingered hand pushes the door open.

The inside of the building turns out to be the inside of five buildings. Light strips, bars, and bare bulbs are strung around the ceiling in what Wil has to assume is a haphazard way. Along the edge of the massive space, another level has been assembled with vendor stalls lining it.

Wil looks down at his friend. "Other crew?"

Bennie doesn't look up. He shrugs. "You thought I was some sad sack loner until you bozos found me?" He raises a finger. "Found me and totally destroyed my workshop, I might add."

Wil rolls his shoulders. "Well, for one thing, it was the PKs that destroyed your workshop. For another, yeah, you're not exactly easy to live with. I assumed you had been thrown out of your home and been alone ever since."

Bennie makes a rude gesture, then points seemingly at random down an aisle. "This way."

Wil follows. "So, what were they like? What happened to them?"

They stop at a booth selling stuff Wil can't identify beyond knowing it's mostly all computer equipment. Bennie haggles over the price of a few things, then moves on. "I mean, they were a lot like you all, I guess. Gokil was Multonae." He looks up, eyeing Wil. "I assume you were the first one out here, right?" He doesn't wait for Wil to answer. "Flon and Dur'vol were Malkorites." He rubs his chin. "I actually don't know what Scil was. She was so modified by the time I met her."

"That's a lot of past tense," Wil says.

Bennie ignores him. He stops at a stall lined with circuit boards of various shapes and sizes and entirely unknown functions. "Ohh." He rubs his hands together. "We'll definitely want some of those modular interphase units."

Wil looks over the top of Bennie's head. "For what?"

Bennie looks up. "Like you'd understand." He turns to the vendor. "Three." Turning to Wil, the Brailack hacker and Knight of Plentallus says, "Oh, yeah. They're all dead." When he sees the expression on Wil's face, he pats the air. "Calm down. I didn't kill 'em." He looks to the vendor swiping on his wristcomm. "Send them there."

Wil rocks back. "Uh, I didn't think you killed them." Squinting. "Why would I think you killed them?"

Bennie turns. "Anyway. We were doing a job on Palor and things went a little sideways. Gokil was supposed to boost a hover speeder so we could make our getaway. That dummy attracted the attention of some PKs. We didn't know he had gotten himself shot. We were standing around waiting for him when the PK garrison arrived." He shook his head. "I barely got away."

"Aren't we all lucky," Wil drawls as they make their way to a vendor with a stall full of PADDs of all shapes and sizes.

BREAKING AND ENTERING

THIS PLACE IS A DREN HEAP. The Tygran woman looks it up and down. She consults her wristcomm, looking over the schematics on file with the city's real estate database, such as it is. Not much detail other than the official Peacekeeper notice about slavers. The sales record has the transaction details and names, that's all.

Sighing, she looks around, then moves to the side of the building, staying out of range of the myriad scanners and cameras that someone has placed around the perimeter.

"Impressive," she says. She looks at the building next door. Abandoned, as far as she can tell. "Let's see how clever you are."

The building next to Rogue Enterprises looks deserted but most definitely is not. The Tygran woman immediately finds several covert sensors and cameras rigged throughout. Tapping her chin, she looks around. "Can't go around. Which means I can't go over." She spies a sewer access cover. "Guess I'm going under."

She's been to Fury only once before. That job didn't bring her to Lwath, but she's realizing that the entire planet is poorly managed. The sewer access cover isn't secured and easily allows her into the sewers that run under the building.

Within minutes, she's crawling up through the grate in the hangar bay, having swiftly bypassed the security measures she found.

Looking up at the *Ghost,* she murmurs, "Cynthia, who the wurrin are you associating with? This place is a dump, and this thing looks like an old piece of dren." She produces a small device from the slim backpack strapped to her back. She walks around the ship a few times before deciding on an out of the way place to secure the device.

Once her primary objective is complete, she decides to explore the building. The first-floor conference room and lobby are like any other. The second floor isn't very interesting; some sort of lab or tinkering space for someone into computers and such. A workout area with sparring mat and various practice weapons. Several empty rooms, full of boxes and what she assumes must be trash.

The third floor proves more intriguing: the living spaces. She finds the room that smells most like Cynthia and discovers she's cohabitating with that Multonae man she spied at the bar on Tyr. "Disgusting." She shakes her head.

She pokes around a bit longer, exploring each of the sleeping rooms, the kitchen, and the lounge space. Bored, she heads back to the hangar and the ship, figuring the more she knows about it and its capabilities, the better.

She is walking down the ship's cargo ramp just as she hears the front of the building come alive. The crew are returning from wherever they've been. She ducks back down the sewer access grate, making sure to slide it back into place, exactly where it was. Re-enabling the security features as she retreats is child's play.

By the time the crew of the *Ghost* makes it into the hangar, the Tygran woman is back on the street outside, walking away.

CHAPTER SEVEN

FINAL PREP

"Okay, Max and Gabe, you okay loading all this onto the ship?"

"No," Maxim says.

Wil talks over him. "We'll get the gear together upstairs and then we can regroup and go over things one last time before we leave."

Up on the second floor, Wil and Cynthia walk into one of the rooms full of storage modules. He looks at her. "One of these?"

She looks over and nods. "Yeah, I think that yellow-sided one."

Wil unlatches the lid to look inside. "Uh, no, this looks like something Bennie would own."

She peers over his shoulder. "Oh, yeah, that's a Brailack nest starter." She looks at Wil. "He planning to start a family?"

Wil shivers, remembering the countless times Bennie has tried to explain Brailack procreation to him. "God, I hope not." He replaces the lid, snapping the latches down. He spies a similarly covered crate further back in the room. "Oh, maybe that one?"

Cynthia nods. "Oh yeah, that's it. Been a while since I've looked at it."

Wil smiles. "While it's hot as hell that you're some type of super ninja assassin lady, I'm pretty okay with this part of your life being a bit of a mystery."

Cynthia removes the lid and reveals what has to be a skin tight piece of clothing, matte black with a cutout on one arm for a wrist-comm and several built-in hard points that allow armor and weaponry to attach directly to it.

"Okay, that can make its way to our room," he quips.

She places the garment aside and withdraws several things Wil can't identify but assumes must attach to the outfit. She pulls out what looks like a shoulder-attaching blaster cannon. After examining it, she places it on the pile of other gear she has removed. "Okay. This all seems to be in good order still." She grins. "I kinda thought Bennie woulda rooted around in here."

Wil points to a case nearby: brown with a black lid, probably Maxim's. "That mark in the corner." He points. On the side of the lid, too small to notice if you didn't know to look, is a circle with a line bisecting it horizontally. "He hasn't gotten to your stuff yet."

Cynthia leans down. "That little drennog. He marks the ones he's been in?" Straightening. "How did you know about this?" His finger hovers over the mark.

Wil shrugs. "I've lived with him for a bit now. He thinks he's slick, but I've been spying on him for a few years now. Mostly in self-defense." He rubs the mark off. "This is the best way to stymie him."

Maxim and Gabe are at the foot of the cargo ramp. The big Palorian looks at his mechanical friend. "So. Governor Gabe? Does have a nice ring to it."

"No. It does not," the droid says. He grabs a crate and places it on the gravsled. "I did not do this for power."

Maxim picks up one of the crates that Bennie loaded up. There's a sticker on it that reads, *Bennie*. "Understood, but it's not a bad side effect. Your people could benefit from your experiences." He shrugs. "And leaders that don't seek to lead often are the best at it."

Gabe takes the crate, placing it on the sled. "They could. They have. I will continue to provide my guidance and insight as needed." He gives the crates a shove, the sled registering the movement and beginning to climb the ramp. "However, my place is here. With my friends. My people will figure it out."

OFF WE GO

The *Ghost* roars up and out of the wide hangar doors in the side of the Rogue Enterprises building. As the small warship drives higher and higher, the thick doors slide closed.

"I really am loving this," Wil says. On the forward display, the thin, wispy clouds of Fury are passing by. The sky ahead is darkening as the ship gains altitude. Her atmospheric thrusters are roaring.

"The crime?" Bennie asks, turning in his seat.

"What? No. The being able to come and go without negotiating with spaceport control and Jussip's little annoying lackies."

Bennie shrugs, turning to face the main display. "Yeah, I guess that's cool, too."

Cynthia tuts. "As if it was you that had to talk to them all the time."

Wil doesn't turn. He shrugs. "Details." The view ahead is now almost entirely black. The brightest stars are twinkling in the last of the atmosphere. He pushes the throttle a bit, then twists the flight controls, sending the ship into a corkscrew. "Woo!" he shouts.

"Captain, please stop that," the ceiling says. "I would prefer to not stress the newest repairs to the port repulsorlift power coupling," Gabe admonishes.

As the sky goes completely black and fills with stars, Wil straightens out their flight and cuts in the sub-light engines. The roar of the atmospheric engines dies out, followed by a few dull thudding echoes as the thrust ports cool.

The *Ghost* pushes up and out of orbit, her sub-light engines fighting against gravity. Fury never has much orbital traffic. Being a backwater keeps freighter traffic light, and the last tourist was the first, a few hundred years in the past.

"Okay. Off we go," Wil says, putting the flight controls on automatic. He looks at the ceiling. "Computer, let us know when we're clear for FTL." The reply that comes back is unintelligible gibberish. Wil snaps his gaze to Bennie. "Bennie?"

Bennie hunches his shoulders. "Oh. I forgot about that." He turns his chair. "I was working on the computer last week. I found an operating system update on an old Ankarran Spaceworks server." He shrugs. "I think it might have been corrupt." Everyone on the bridge turns to stare at him, mouths all hanging open. "What?"

Wil shakes his head. "What do you mean, what? We're flying through space in a ship with a corrupted OS?"

"That doesn't seem safe," Maxim says.

"Like, super not safe," Zephyr adds.

Bennie pats the air in front of him. "I'm sure it's fine. We're still alive."

"Not. The. Point," Wil says.

Bennie says, "Okay, fine. I need to make a pit stop anyway to forge up some documents for Nom Clamma. I can restore from backup there."

Wil takes a deep breath in through his nose, then releases it. "How long?"

"Not long. Here." He pushes something on his console, and a sub monitor on Wil's lights up. "I can do what I need, there."

"We kinda have a timetable," Cynthia reminds the hacker.

"I know that. Once we dock, I'll restore from a local backup, then get to work on the documents."

"Why didn't you do the documents at home?" Maxim asks.

"Or do a restore?" Zephyr adds.

"I forgot." Bennie waves a hand.

"I swear to God, you're like ten seconds from being tossed out an airlock," Wil growls.

"Just get us there. It'll be fine." Bennie points at Wil's flight console. "I'll be fast."

Wil checks the coordinates against the nav database. "Croixa station. It is on the way, at least."

"Duh." Bennie turns back to his console.

Wil focuses on his station, grumbling under his breath. Zephyr continues to stare at Bennie, then looks at Maxim, who shrugs.

SPACE TRUCK STOPS

Eight hours later, the *Ghost* clunks against a docking arm. "Welcome to Croixa station," the overhead speaker crackles.

The station has three bulk freighters docked at various docking arms. A two-story holograph sign is projected over the top of the station, slowly rotating.

Wil reads, "Jizz Stop?" He looks around the bridge. "Nobody?"

Blank expressions are all he gets back. Maxim shakes his head slowly. Then, "Oh!" Bennie claps. "I know this one. It's from the stuff Wil used to keep in an encrypted part of his archive."

Wil turns. "I'm sorry, what?"

Bennie's smiles fades, and he turns back to his station.

Wil looks at the team hacker. "You got an hour."

"What if it takes longer?" the little being asks.

Wil stands. "It better not. We're pushing our timetable enough." Bennie opens his mouth. Wil holds up a finger. "I'll murder you. Swear to all the things. I. Will. Kill. You. Violently." Bennie closes his mouth.

Bennie turns back to his console. "I'll start the restore. Gabe can monitor it. I need to access the data link on the station for the Nom Clamma docs. I don't want to use our comm node for this."

Wil looks at the ceiling. "Gabe, can you come babysit Jedi Master Kermit?"

The ceiling makes an exasperated noise. "I will be right there."

Zephyr stifles a laugh.

Cynthia pushes open the bridge hatch. "Let's go explore this place. I've never been here."

"You're not missing much," Maxim says. "It's a Multonae-run station. A bunch of Wils everywhere."

"You say that like it's a bad thing." Wil smiles.

Zephyr shudders. She looks over her shoulder. "One tock." She holds two fingers to her eyes, then points them at Bennie. He makes a rude gesture in return.

They pass Gabe in the neck, the corridor that connects the forward and much larger aft sections of the ship together. Wil holds a hand up to stop the droid. "Once he's done, he's planning to come aboard the station to do some hacking. You mind shadowing him? I assume you can monitor the ship's OS restore remotely?"

The droid nods. "I do not mind, and I can."

Wil nods. "Thanks, pal." He follows the others through the far hatch into the ship's lounge area.

Gabe enters the bridge. "Hello."

Bennie turns. "Oh, good. I need your help. I don't actually have a backup of the ship's OS."

Gabe tilts his head to the side. "I do not understand. I was under the impression that you were restoring a local backup."

Bennie shrugs. "That's what I told them. I didn't think the upgrade was suspect, so I didn't bother with a backup."

"Do you not run a backup of the operating system regularly?" The noise Bennie makes is answer enough. "I see." Gabe moves to Bennie's station. "We do not have long."

Bennie nods his agreement.

THE RECEPTION AREA of Croixa station is about twice the size of the *Ghost*'s cargo hold. Posters cover every vertical surface, both animated and of the more Earthlike paper and glue variety. The station itself is only about twenty decks in all. Each of the eight docking arms empties into the reception area with four large open frame freight lifts in the middle. Next to them, a bored looking red-haired woman is sitting at a circular desk answering questions and directing people.

Wil approaches. "Hi. This is our first time here. Anything we should make sure to see?"

She looks up from the PADD she's reading. "This is a trade station. Bars, shipping, and storage are all there is to see. Hope one of those tickles your fancy." She doesn't wait for his reply, returning to her reading. She looks up. "The History of Jizz Museum is on Deck 19."

Wil shakes his head. "Pass."

Cynthia pushes him toward one of the waiting lifts. As they board, another lift is rumbling its way down.

The interior of Croixa station isn't at all what Wil expected. The remaining dozen-plus decks of the station aren't separate decks but assorted mezzanines. You can't see from the bottom to the top, but from any level you can gaze up at least three to four decks before the various offsets obscure the view.

"Neat," he says.

Maxim points to a directory.

MISTAKEN IDENTITY

"Space truck stops," Wil says as they walk up the ramp that connects. "How have I never been to one of these?"

"Because they suck," Zephyr replies. "The company that ran them, as far as I know, went bankrupt...I don't know," she looks at Cynthia and Maxim, "ten cycles or more ago?"

Maxim nods. "Yeah, I'm guessing someone managed to buy this one out when the company was liquidating." He looks around. "Still looks like a Jizz Stop."

"Can we—? We have to stop saying that." Wil holds up a hand. "How about truck stop?" He looks at Zephyr. "I'll leave the 'space' part out."

Zephyr sighs. "Sure. Truck stop."

"What's a truck?" Maxim asks.

They reach the level they want and look around. "There," Cynthia says.

"Looks appropriately seedy," Wil agrees. Their destination is a bar that, to Wil, looks very much like a tiki bar he frequented in Florida during spring break. "Pilfroggy's Place? Has a nice ring to it. Think ol' Pilfroggy is here?"

Everyone shakes their head. There is no host station. Tables litter the space, most of them occupied.

"Little busy for this time of day," Zephyr says, checking her wristcomm.

Pilfroggy's Place seems to cater to mostly Multonae. It's the most Wil has felt like home since leaving Earth. In the corner, a being with three limbs is playing some type of musical instrument, either from his or her home planet or custom designed. To Wil, the music sounds like jazz and mariachi music playing from competing speakers, overlapping into a tangled jarring mess.

They find a table with four mostly clean chairs.

"Okay, this isn't going how I'd expected." Bennie exhales.

"I am curious how you expected it to go," Gabe says.

Bennie looks up from one of his displays. "That felt judgey."

"That was the intention."

He grunts. "I figured I could find a clean copy and download it."

Gabe tilts his head. "While risky, that does not seem to be an unreasonable idea. There are several repositories for ship operating systems."

Bennie nods. "Right? Except for whatever reason, the OS we need isn't on any of them."

"Did the Ankarrans release a new version?"

Bennie rubs his chin. "Uh, I don't know. That would explain why everyone has taken down the current one."

"Yes, it would."

Bennie sets about tapping at his console. "Well, dren." He looks up at Gabe. "This is embarrassing."

"Indeed."

Bennie works for a few minutes, then looks at the main display. The large screen flickers, then goes black, lines of code scrolling down. "There we go."

"That does look promising," Gabe agrees.

Bennie checks the time on his wristcomm. "You okay making sure this finishes? I gotta get onto the station, find a terminal, hack the Nom Clamma internex exchange, and get us some tickets to an ultra-exclusive reception."

"It seems like that is something you could have done at home."

Bennie hops out of his seat. "I forgot. I had a date." He heads for the bridge hatch. "You good?"

Gabe makes a noise. "Yes."

"WHAT KIND of bar doesn't have grum?" Wil complains. "I mean, it's like, ubiquitous."

"Clearly not," Maxim says. He changes the topic. "I have some ideas for your bachelor party, by the way."

Wil swirls the little metal stick in his glass, mixing the multi-colored drink before him. "Oh, uh...Sure, what ya got?" He glances at Cynthia, who is smiling but says nothing.

"I figure staying on Fury is out. I mean, it's Fury." Maxim takes a sip of something that is a cloudy, swirling mix of purple and pink liquors. "So, then I was thinking about that place we partied at after that job on the ice planet. On Cuhn Faro Two."

"The place with the, uh..." Wil says. He looks at Cynthia, blushing deep crimson.

She leans forward. "The what?" Her drink, something blue that the dark-haired bartender with a cybernetic arm called a Plasma Filament, swishes in one hand.

Maxim coughs. "Oh, yeah. Maybe not." He looks at his wristcomm, swiping on the screen. He looks up. "How about Durbril Two?" Wil wobbles a hand. "They remind me too much of mogwai." He smiles. "We do have the vouchers for pleasure station Moklan..." Wil arches an eyebrow.

Maxim smiles. "I'll reach out and see what they've got." He turns to Cynthia. "You could probably do your bachelorette there as well."

She blinks. "My what now?"

Zephyr elbows her. "Remember, the women of the joining get together and pay a man to undress."

Wil raises a hand. "Woah w—"

"Jamo?" someone says, loudly, behind Wil. Wil opens his mouth to continue his comment. When the same voice says, "Jamo, it is you!" a hand drops onto Wil's shoulder.

Wil turns. "Look, pal." Before he can say anything further, a fist slams into his nose, driving him backward to tip out of his chair to the floor.

"Hey!" Zephyr and Cynthia shout in unison, rising from their seats. Maxim is out of his seat and on top of the attacker before the man can even draw his hand back to strike at Wil again. "What the wurrin do you think you're doing?"

Two other Multonae men are moving in. A blonde-haired man with a bushy beard, wearing what looks like a flannel and blue jeans, says, "Jamo stiffed us on a job!" He rushes in to kick Wil, only to be tackled by Cynthia.

The other man, a red-head, ducks under Zephyr's reach to land on Wil and begin pummeling him.

"You should fight back!" Maxim shouts.

Wil, protecting his face with both arms, while he remains curled in a fetal position on the floor, shouts back, "Oh, you think? Ow! Stop it!" The man continues to swing wildly, connecting with Wil more often than not. "I'm not Jimbo!"

The man under Cynthia gets free. "You shouldn't screw people on jobs, Jamo!" He lunges to dive onto Wil and the man still pummeling. "It comes back to bite you!"

"Help me out, for crying out loud!" Wil screams between punches and kicks. A foot sweeps in and he's able to catch it and twist, sending the owner toppling to the ground. Rolling on his hands and knees, he kicks out at someone, eliciting a scream. "This is crazy!"

Zephyr leaps onto someone's back. Two quick blows, and her opponent crumples to the deck like a sack of stones.

The cybernetically enhanced bartender steps up and grabs one of the attackers. She punches him in the face once. When the man opens his mouth to exclaim something, she punches him again.

Wil gets to his feet just in time to dodge to the side as the drink Cynthia was drinking sails through the air.

The bartender and Zephyr have the first man to attack Wil, each holding an arm. The other woman shouts, "Darren! Darren, that's not Jamo. Look at him, you drennog!"

Bennie exits the docking arm connected to the *Ghost*. The reception area is busier than when the others came through. One of the larger freighters is preparing to depart. Its crew is filtering back to depart, most of them deeply inebriated.

"Hey."

The red-haired Multonae woman looks up, then back at her PADD.

"Down here, Red."

She stands. "Oh. What can I do for you?"

"What deck are your public data terminals on?"

"Seven." She sits back down.

Deck 7 is almost entirely cubicles. Bennie can't fathom whom the creators of the station thought would be using it, that it needs this many public internex terminals. Each terminal has a large display and simple computing core on the desk. Bennie finds one far from the entrance and the few other patrons in the space. Dropping his backpack, he hops into the seat.

Powering up the terminal, Bennie tuts. "Good grief. This is embarrassing for them." He unspools a few data cables from his wristcomm, connecting them to the back of the computing core. "Making people use such outdated tech."

He reaches into the backpack and pulls out a PADD. Tapping the screen a few times, he grins. "This won't take long." He accesses the station's public network, blowing right past the meager firewalls. He's snooping around the station's systems when he spots a security alert at a bar a few levels away. Pulling up the security feed, he groans. "Those drennogs." He shakes his head, closing the security feed.

The station has a reasonably good internex access. Bennie is in the municipal network of Nom Clamma in microtocks.

The Dre Toma Museum of Exotic Art's network security is suspiciously advanced. Bennie hums a song to himself, one he found on Wil's archive and likes a lot. Something about waterfalls.

By the time he's done humming the song to himself, he has the forged gala invites created. No one will be able to tell they were added remotely. He unplugs his wristcomm and slips the PADD back into his backpack. He heads for the exit, starting his humming over again, adding, "Don't go chasing..."

PART 3

CHAPTER EIGHT

THINGS COST (A LOT OF) MONEY

The *Ghost* drops out of FTL near the outskirts of the Clammat system. Consoles around the bridge flash new information as the system's space control system detects the ship and immediately begins both querying for information and sending instructions.

Wil looks over his console. "Wow. Chatty space control system." He swipes an ad aside to see the navigational beacon data for Nom Clamma, their destination.

"The Ficu outsource a lot," Zephyr offers, "including the entire space control operation." She rubs the two thumbs of her left hand together. "I think it's a Juniper Collective setup."

Bennie nods. "Yeah, easily hackable." An ad for a sporting event appears on the main display. He points to it. "Very easily."

"And they just leave it like that?" Wil asks. He swipes two more ads from his display, as well as the one on the main display at the front of the bridge.

Zephyr shrugs. "The Ficu view everything in terms of personal effort. Since the space control system still does the job they installed it to do, they don't mind that someone has hacked it. Or rather, no one yet has minded enough for the effort to be worth it."

Maxim closes his station down. The ads are annoying him, and they won't need weapons this close to the core of the Commonwealth. Turning, he says, "Plus, the ads don't bother them. Most local traffic doesn't use the public system."

An ad appears on the main display for an adult entertainment district in one of the smaller cities near the large central desert. The animated Ficu is using two of their three tentacles to pleasure a Malkorite woman.

Wil swipes the ad away, then turns to Bennie. "Okay, that's quite enough of that. Can you do something about this?"

Bennie turns. "Magic word?"

"Now, or I'll shoot you."

"That's more of a phrase, but whatever." He turns to his console, nimble green fingers a blur. The ads on Wil's command console, as well as the primary and secondary displays at the front of the bridge, vanish.

"Thank you," Wil says.

Zephyr clears her throat. "Now that that's settled...Thoughts?" She consults her console. "We'll be in orbit in three tocks." She presses a control and half the primary display updates to show a pricing sheet. "I found the pricing for the spaceports near our destination."

"What the hell?" Wil leans forward in his seat. "Why is Mo Talla so much?"

Cynthia says, "It is the planetary capital."

He shrugs. "I mean, I don't think it cost us that much to land on Tarsis."

"Technically, we didn't pay to land on Tarsis," Maxim points out.

Wil waves him off. He points. "What about that one? Is Mo Wumpla close to Mo Talla?"

Zephyr looks at her console, then back to the group. "It's the neighboring city, about three-quarters of a tock public transit ride away."

Wil nods. "Okay, it's half the cost. We'll take the bus."

Zephyr nods. "Booking now." She looks up as the pricing sheet vanishes from the forward display. "Done. We're booked at the Vel Roa Spaceport. Pretty sure, features-wise, it'll be on par with Fury." Ghostly green arrows appear on the main display, guiding the ship to their destination.

Back at Croixa station, a speedy personal shuttle is docked at one of the small craft docking arms. The Tygran woman steps out into the main reception area, a PADD clutched in one hand. She consults the device and hisses. "Dren. They stopped here. But why?"

She reaches the welcome desk, holding her PADD screen out. "Seen them?" On the screen is a picture of the crew of the *Ghost* taken sometime after their job escorting Barbara Mress to the Corporate Congress Summit.

The woman behind the desk looks up. "Probably not." She looks back down.

The other woman leans down, extending a finger under the receptionist's chin, a claw sliding out as she does. "Maybe one more look."

The red-haired Multonae woman gulps and looks again. "Oh, them. Yeah, the brown-haired guy asked some dumb questions, then they went up into the station." She tries to smile.

"How long were they here?"

After swiping closed the book she's reading, the receptionist says, "Just...just over a tock. They caused a ruckus in one of the bars and were asked to leave."

The Tygran eases her claw back into the muscle sheath in her fingertip. "This was how long ago?"

"Uh, yesterday."

Turning, the woman says, "Thank you." Reaching the hatch to her docking arm, she taps her wristcomm, raising it to her face. "They stopped at Croixa station. I don't know why. They're on the move again. I'll wait for the tracer to stop, then follow."

WELCOME TO NOM CLAMMA

Nom Clamma turns out to be pretty, as far as Wil is concerned. Kind of Earthlike, at least insofar as the ground is mostly green, the clouds white, the water blue. The nearly continent-sized desert in the middle of the primary landmass is the big outlier in that comparison.

"Busy place," Wil says. He guides the *Ghost* underneath a bulk freighter that is towing a cargo train two kilometers long if it's a meter. Three similar cargo haulers are lumbering nearby, just beyond the planet's gravitational reach.

Cynthia says, "They get a fair bit of shipping traffic here." She closes her eyes as Wil brings them closer than she's comfortable with past a cargo station, its spindly arms loaded with in- and outbound cargo modules.

A bulbous luxury cruiser is burning hard to leave orbit ahead of them. "Oh, hey, is that the...?" Wil squints. "Nope."

In the distance, a Peacekeeper Command Carrier leisurely hangs near Nom Clamma's third and smallest moon.

"Surprised to see a PK carrier here," Bennie says.

Cynthia purrs absently. "Yeah, I don't remember them having that big a presence here when I was here last."

Maxim says, "Mress mentioned to me that she'd heard the Admiralty was planning some PR tours to show that, despite their recent losses, the Peacekeepers are still around and powerful. The GC council needs to keep peace and order now more than ever."

"Makes sense, I guess. Crappy timing, that's for sure," Wil agrees. "They got their asses kicked in a big way. Probably more than a few systems thinking that they can go it alone, their dues and taxes alone likely enough to build their own military."

Zephyr nods. "I've heard those rumors."

Wil's console beeps angrily at him. On the forward display, a small ship has drifted from its flight path, directly into the *Ghost*'s path. Wil pulls the controls over. "Hey, asshole! Watch out!"

As the invading ship slides off the main display, a window appears. "So sorry, dearie!" a disheveled Trollack woman says. "Got lost in the view." The window closes.

Wil looks around. "What the fuck? What view?" Cynthia nods back to the screen at the front of the bridge. He turns. "Oh..." The massive desert is moving into the nightside, and as it does, a spectacular borealis is forming, covering the continent in blues, purples, greens, and yellows. "Okay, that's cool."

"Right?" Bennie whispers.

"Wow," Maxim says.

The Vel Roa spaceport matches up with everyone's expectations.

"This is a dump," Bennie says as the *Ghost* drifts toward her designated landing pad.

"Told you," Zephyr says. "I booked umbilicals for power and sanitation."

Wil nods. "Still cheaper than landing in Mo Talla."

The bridge hatch opens, allowing Gabe in. "I have prepared our gear in the cargo hold."

Zephyr snaps her fingers. "Dren. Forgot to book transport. Will do that now."

Gabe tilts his head. "Unless you would like me to carry everything."

She looks up. "That's an option?"

"It is not."

The *Ghost* roars as Wil flares the repulsorlifts, bringing the ship's forward movement to a complete stop, hovering over their designated landing pad.

Reducing the power to the repulsorlifts, Wil guides the ship down until the landing legs thump down on the permacrete. He kills the power, and the ship settles into its resting position, balanced on the powerful legs.

Wil puts his station into standby and turns in his seat. "Welcome to Nom Clamma."

TOUCHDOWN

THE CARGO RAMP clangs down onto the pitted and cracked duracrete. Wil is the first to step off the ramp. "Wow." He looks around. "The whole of their society really is driven by 'what's in it for me?'"

Cynthia joins him, sighing. "Yeah. In a lot of ways, it kinda works." She points over the wall to the downtown region of Mo Wumpla. From this distance, the high-rise buildings look shiny and new. "Want to impress someone? Build a shiny high-rise. No one else will."

"Like society by lowest level of effort," Maxim grunts.

A gravsled drifts down the ramp, followed by another, followed by Gabe. "Is our ground transportation here?"

Zephyr points. "Looks like it's on its way." In the distance, at the arched vehicle passage through the spaceport's ring wall, a matte black hover van is trundling toward them on what looks like three out of four functioning repulsorlift pads.

"Indeed," Gabe says, turning to head back up into the ship.

By the time the hover van arrives, the *Ghost* is sealed and everyone is waiting on the duracrete.

The Ficu driver leans out. "Which one of you is Zeefer?"

Wil purses his lips and looks anywhere but toward Zephyr.

"Zephyr," the Palorian woman corrects.

The van driver frowns, his bulging half-sphere eyes blinking several times. "No, I'm pretty sure it's Zeefer." He blinks more. "Maybe they're parked somewhere else?" A three-fingered hand rubs his forked chin. "Well, finding Zeefer sounds like a lot of effort. Where are you all going?"

Zephyr looks up at the sky, taking a deep breath. Maxim puts a reassuring and restraining hand on her shoulder. She says, "The Super Nova Lodge."

The driver beams, his flat teeth gleaming. "Well, my day is getting better and better. That's where Zeefer was going. No extra work on my end." He slaps the door. "Load up." The back of the van drops to form a ramp.

Bennie walks past Zephyr. "Come on, Zeefer, let's get going." He ducks, just avoiding a swipe at the back of his head.

Maxim turns to Gabe. "I'll help you load up." He pats Zephyr's shoulder.

Wil and the others board the passenger compartment of the van. Wil leans forward. "So, what's your name?" One of the driver's tentacles reaches up to flip down a visor in the middle of the driver's area. Wil squints. "Zirt..." He stretches out the *t* sound.

"That's me." The Ficu smiles and clacks his teeth.

From the back of the van comes a thud, then the sound of the ramp locking back into place. Maxim and Gabe join the others. The droid says, "This vehicle is in poor shape."

Zirt makes a hissing noise as two of his tentacles wave anxiously. "Lucile—"

"Lucile?" Wil interrupts.

The Ficu man ignores him. "—Is in adequate condition."

Maxim's eyebrows raise, his brow ridges furrow. "Adequate?"

"I do not agree," Gabe says, his body shifting and compressing to allow him to take a seat in the passenger compartment. "This is not adequate."

SPACE BED BUGS

THE SUPER NOVA Lodge is a motel, sort of. The van glides away, a three-fingered hand waving from the driving compartment. Wil looks around. "Uh..." The holosign planted at the corner of the property where vehicles enter is malfunctioning. Only the letters *Su N ge* are active.

The L-shaped building is three floors with exposed stairwells. It looks like any other run-down, seedy motel you'd see in the outskirts of any major city in America. The few vehicles in the lot don't appear to function. One is even sitting on duracrete blocks, its gravpads long gone.

"Well, this is possibly the worst place we've ever stayed," Bennie says, taking a few steps toward the lobby. He makes a slow circle. "Bets on whether there's a body in one of our rooms?"

"Sucker bet," Cynthia says under her breath.

Gabe guides one of the gravsleds toward the lobby. "We should get the equipment set up."

Wil turns. "Let's go, Zeefer. We'll get everyone checked in."

"I can kill you." She points at the ground. "From right here, without leaving this spot. Dead." Wil opens his mouth. "Three ways. No, four—four ways, dead."

Wil takes a step back, hands up, palms out. "Okay, okay."

Zephyr follows.

Bennie looks at the others. "I'm thinking of having the computer call her Zeefer for a while."

Maxim looks the Brailack up and down. "She'll kill you."

Bennie tuts. "Oh, come on."

Maxim shakes his head. "She. Will. Kill. You." He looks Bennie in the eye. "Not kidding."

Cynthia makes a face and moves next to Gabe. "Come on. Let's get groceries."

"That seems like the least dangerous thing to do," the droid agrees. He turns to Maxim. "Please be careful of the equipment."

Maxim smiles. "Have fun."

Wil and Zephyr walk out. "All set." He holds up three physical access cards, pointing to the far side of the lot. "Those're us."

The door, on hinges, swings open.

"Nope!" Wil shouts, pulling the door closed.

At the room next door, Maxim and Zephyr both turn to look at Wil, the latter with her hand on the doorknob. On the other side of them, Bennie steps backward out of the room he and Gabe will share, his beam saber drawn and activated. "I'll sleep in the *Ghost*."

"You're being ridiculous," Zephyr says, pushing the door open. "Oh, shit ass!" She leans in and pulls the door shut. She turns to Wil. "I'll book us something else."

Bennie closes down his beam saber. "What makes you think we'd trust you to book the next place?"

Zephyr makes a face. "You think you can do better with the budget constraints? By all means."

Bennie shrugs and raises his arm, looking at his wristcomm. He hums as he taps at the device's screen.

Wil leans over. "Is that...'Waterfalls' by TLC?"

Bennie looks up, his finger jabbing an icon on the screen. "And, done."

An alarm sounds on Wil's wristcomm.

Zephyr leans over. "How'd you find us a better place on our budget so fast?"

Bennie opens his mouth but is cut off by Wil. "Because the little shit spent nearly three times the budget!" He turns to the Brailack, growling.

Bennie grins, bearing his tiny pointed teeth, one hand moving to rest on the hilt of his beam saber. "No time for dicky dacking. We're burning tocks we don't have."

Wil growls again. "Hours you wasted!" He throws his arms in the air. "Let's go!" He snaps his fingers at Bennie. "Send us the details and summon a van. Maybe not the one that brought us here. Oh, and it's dilly dally." He sighs and mumbles, "Dicky dacky?"

"Okay, this is definitely nicer," Wil says, walking into the suite. "I don't know if it's three-times-our-budget nice, but nothing is crawling on the walls, so there's that." He moves further inside and drops his duffel bag on the floor.

Bennie follows, the others on his heels. "You doubted me?"

"Knight of the Word, or whatever, or not. Yeah. I always doubt you." Wil looks over his shoulder at the team hacker making himself comfortable on one of the two sofas in the recessed conversation lounge.

"That's cruel," Bennie replies.

Gabe and Maxim guide the gravsleds into the suite, the former saying, "I am pleased that this hotel has a freight elevator." Maxim grunts his agreement, guiding the unwieldy cargo crate through the space.

Zephyr helps Maxim open the crate he brought in. As she removes bits and pieces of technology and other equipment, she says, "Okay, let's get this all set up. We don't have a lot of time." Nods all around.

Wil and Maxim are lifting one of the sofas up and out of the conversation pit when Wil says, "Oh. Did you all know that Little Green had a team before us?" He looks at Maxim. "Pivot!"

Bennie looks up from the folding table they've set up with a few computer cores on it, where the other sofa had been. "What? I told you already. They were long before you all."

Wil ignores him. "Like that episode of *Seinfeld*. He had a bizarro version of us."

Cynthia's nose twitches. She and Zephyr are pushing the other couch into a more usable position. "How do you know we're not the bizarro version of them?"

"What?" Wil almost drops his end of the couch. He and Maxim are trying to negotiate the narrow door to one of the smaller bedrooms. "Pivot!" He turns his head. "No way. They're the bizarro ones."

"You're the bizarro one," Bennie retorts. He looks over at Gabe. "How's it coming? Need any help?"

Gabe, standing next to a wall panel that has been pried from the wall, says, "I believe I am almost through the final firewall. This hotel has impressive anti-intrusion software."

"Wonder why?" Bennie says absently. He shrugs as one of the computer cores in front of him comes to life.

Wil and Maxim return from the side bedroom, the former saying, "So, anyway, this bizarro team of his. They're literally like us. There was a me." He points to Maxim and Zephyr. "A couple, I think he said Trollack." He looks at Gabe, then Cynthia. "Might have been before you two counted."

Gabe turns, a hand still deep inside the wall and its circuitry, data tendrils snaking all over. "I have been here since the beginning."

Wil shrugs.

Bennie sighs. "They were just the crew I ran with before you. When you all are killed or caught or arrested or whatever, I'll find a new crew." He shrugs. "Maybe I'll go full time Knight of Plentallus and do a recruiting tour."

"That sounds rather ominous," Maxim says.

Zephyr adds, "Yeah, you seem rather sure we'll meet an end that won't include you." Her eyes are narrowed.

Bennie shrugs, turning his attention back to the array of displays before him. "I'm slippery. You lot, well?" He points to the coffee table, still in the conversation pit. "Gabe, can you put the holoprojector there? I think that'll give us our best angle."

Gabe's data tendrils slither back into his fingertips. Closing the access panel as best he can, he says, "If it helps, I would be okay going offline with you all."

"Sellout," Bennie hisses.

CHAPTER NINE

THE NEXT MORNING, the team is in the hotel restaurant having breakfast. Bennie returns with his third plate. "So where were we?" he asks, hopping up into his chair.

Wil makes a face. "We were talking about the job. You know, the one we do tonight. The one we have exactly a day to iron out because we had to stop at that dingy space truck stop." He glances at Zephyr.

Bennie pops something greasy into his mouth. Around it, he says, "You worry too much. We get in, steal some art, get out. Then return art to those that it rightfully belongs to."

Zephyr reaches over for something on his plate only to have a small green hand smack hers. Rubbing the back of her hand, she says, "Simple, yeah. The hard part will only be making our way to the secure floors, getting in, scanning the works there in real time, picking what to take, getting it out, getting us out." She stares flatly at Bennie. "Peasy sleazy."

"Easy peasy," Wil corrects without looking up from stabbing something on his plate with a fork.

Cynthia pushes her plate toward the center of the table. "The hard part is that I can't go in."

Maxim nods slowly. "He might recognize you." She nods back.

Wil turns to Bennie. "You're gonna have to go in. Cyn can be overwatch."

The Brailack nods. "That's fine." He shoves his plate into the center. "We should get going."

Zephyr nods her agreement. "It's a two-plorith walk from here."

Bennie raises a hand. "I think there's a bus."

Wil looks at him. "It's not that long of a walk."

"Says the drennog with legs twice as long as mine."

Bennie turns to Gabe, who is standing next to the table. The tall droid isn't looking at them, watching something in the distance. He doesn't look at Bennie. "No."

"But."

"No."

Wil stands. "We can see if this place has rental strollers. Dress you up like a child." Bennie makes a rude gesture and hops out of the chair.

The hotel Bennie picked is not just nice and outrageously expensive. It is on the edge of the upscale neighborhood that the Dre Toma Museum of Exotic Art is in. The streets of Nom Clamma are immaculate. Wil notices an automated cleaner turning the corner up the street. The hotel is surrounded by similar high-rise buildings made of polished metal and a transparent material like glass.

Wil looks around, turning right as he says, "Nice day." Overhead, the sky is clear. Pale sunlight is just creeping over the tops of the buildings.

"I think the public transportation terminal is this way," Bennie says, turning left.

"We're walking," Wil says.

"We already talked about this," Bennie says, holding out one leg and shaking it. "Short legs."

"We did. You'll live. We're walking."

"I hate you."

"I'll live." Wil waves. "Come on. The museum opens in an hour. Maybe we'll find a cafe, grab a chlormax."

Cynthia slips her arm through Wil's. "What's going on with you and Little Green?"

Wil shrugs. "I dunno. Since going all Luke Skywalker, he's been getting a bit annoying. Figured he needed a little push back, keep him grounded."

"Maybe we let me do the child rearing."

Wil stumbles. "What? Kids?" He looks down. "Are you…?"

Cynthia grunts. "What? No. Slow down there, champ." She raises an eyebrow.

"Used it right," he concedes.

The group rounds a corner a block from the museum. "Yes!" Wil pumps a fist in the air. He points to a table. "I'll grab us some drinks." Consulting his wristcomm, he adds, "We've got about fifteen minutes or so before the museum opens." He heads inside.

Maxim holds out a seat for Zephyr and Cynthia. Gabe's body shifts and clanks as his body compresses to be closer to Wil's size. "I am detecting significant post-construction modifications to the building."

Everyone turns in their seats to look at the four-story museum across the street. Maxim says, "Can you tell what's changed?" He looks at Bennie. "Your plans didn't mention any changes."

Bennie dips his head. "Yeah, he must have paid to keep the modifications off the official record."

THE SPACEPORT FEES might be too rich for Wil's blood, but the fast shuttle rented by the Tygran woman pursuing the crew of the *Ghost* has no such constraints. Walking off the shuttle as its engines vent and hiss, she consults her wristcomm. "So, your gravsled is here?" She heads for the pedestrian exit of the spaceport, following the duracrete's painted lines, designed to keep people from being landed on or knocked over by engine wash.

WIL & CYNTHIA

"We'll scope out the exterior. I don't want Cyn on any internal cameras or sensors," Wil says as the team leaves the cafe. He points. "Max and Gabe, see if you can get in through the back, the employees-only sections. Zee and Bennie, take the interior." Everyone nods and heads off toward the museum, angling toward their destinations.

Cynthia looks up. "He hasn't changed much on the outside that I can see." They cross the street, and as Zephyr and Bennie mount the steps to the main entrance, they continue along the busy road. The building sits between two other buildings: a bank, as far as Wil can tell, and a department store. Whether by design or not, there's a significant amount of distance between each building and the museum, making any rooftop crossing tricky and obvious.

"So, I was thinking. Maybe we keep Moklan station in our pocket for a honeymoon," Wil says, keeping his eyes forward.

Cynthia's eyes dart to the side to look at him. "That's the part after the wedding where we—"

"Stay naked most of the time, yeah," Wil interrupts, grinning.

Cynthia tuts. "So then, where would we do the pre-joining party things? We'd cancel that?" she asks hopefully. The sheer volume of human customs around two people joining is overwhelming and annoying to her. On Tyr, when a couple wishes to move their relationship beyond casual, they announce their intent, then submit two forms to the local governmental office. Dissolution is equally easy with simple amendments to the forms. She has no idea why humans make it so complicated.

"I was thinking of Duch's island."

She stops in her tracks, pulling Wil to a stop, as well. After making a face, she says, "You know, that's not at all a terrible idea."

"Thanks," he deadpans.

She waves her free hand. "I'm serious. It's secure. Out of the way and not flashy. It's pretty. I wouldn't mind another meal at that restaurant in town, either."

Wil nods. "That was good. Yeah, I figure his folks can help with planning and anyone we want to invite will get screened. He'll probably do it for free."

They resume walking, reaching the gap between the museum and the department store. It's wide enough for a hover van to enter the alley in back and probably come out the other side. "I wonder if there's an actual alley running the length of the street," Wil says. He tilts his head and they continue toward the department store.

"I don't recall," Cynthia says. "I came in the front door to avoid anyone wondering how I'd gotten in, if they saw me." She rubs her chin. "I'd guess, yes. The streets we passed on our way here had alleys. Probably a citywide design."

"What was it like? You've never really talked to me about that," Wil says.

She looks over. "What? Alleys?" She sees the face he makes. "Aah, being an assassin."

"Said so nonchalantly," Wil quips. He shrugs. "Yeah. I get the impression Zee knows some of the story. I've never wanted to press."

She shrugs. "It's not that interesting of a story. I was an orphan. Got recruited into an organization that trained kids to be killers and spies. I did that until I could find a way out."

"Xarrix," Wil adds.

"Lorath, actually. Then, yeah, Xarrix." She nods. "The stuff before was stuff like this. I'd be told who to kill or spy on, or what to steal, and where to go, if needed."

"Pretty screwed up."

"That's why Tyr is never high on my list of places to visit. There are no good memories, and Yadro taints everything around it."

They reach the street corner and turn to follow the department store. Reaching the alley entrance behind the department store, Cynthia puts a hand on Wil's chest and points with her other hand. Tucked up under the roof three floors up, a small sensor unit and camera are mounted with a view of the opening of the alley the buildings share.

"That answers that. I wonder how well monitored it is?" He makes a note on his wristcomm. He looks up and down the alley, past the department store building to the broad back wall of the museum. "Let's go see if there's an easy rooftop access inside Space Macy's."

She nods, one eyebrow arched questioningly. "Good idea."

MAX & GABE

"Copy that, Wil." Max turns to Gabe. "Thoughts?" Wil just let them know about the cameras on the roofline of the department store.

Gabe and Max have reached the back alley via the access way between the museum and the bank. "I suspect this side will be even more heavily monitored." He points to the building next to them. "Bank."

Maxim nods as he thinks. "Yeah. Think you can get us inside still?"

Gabe looks up. "There is a sensor emplacement at the corner of the building." He points up to the eave over the fourth-floor windows. He raises a hand, finger pointed at the sensor cluster. Maxim watches. Lowering his hand, Gabe says, "We have a microtock or two before the sensors reset." He heads around the corner of the museum toward the loading bay doors.

Following, Maxim asks, "What did you do?"

"Targeted micro pulse EMP," the droid replies, reaching the personnel hatch. "I do not detect anyone within the immediate proximity of the loading area." He reaches for the control panel next to the door, data tendrils snaking out of his fingertips.

"Never not creepy," Maxim whispers, watching.

"Intriguing." Gabe looks over his shoulder. "The security system is considerably more advanced than I would expect for a building like this. In fact, I would be surprised to see as advanced a system as this next door."

Maxim shifts his weight from foot to foot. "You mentioned only having a microtock or two on those sensors," he prods.

"I am well aware of our time constraints," Gabe snaps.

"Sorry," Maxim says.

The door clicks and slides open. Gabe rushes in, Maxim on his heels.

The shipping and receiving section on the ground floor of the museum is about what Maxim expects. Crates of various sizes and shapes fill the space, ready to leave the museum or waiting to be unpacked and put on display.

"Are there any—" Maxim starts.

"Sensors? Yes." He points over their heads. "I am currently emitting a jamming signal. Unfortunately, it is not foolproof. We should move along before someone comes to investigate."

Maxim nods, and they head off deeper into the receiving area. As they move, Maxim notes locations of sensor packages on his wrist-comm. Gabe is almost certainly doing the same, but years of training have drilled the value of redundancy into him.

"According to the schematics that Bennie acquired, the security section should be this way," Gabe says, pointing to a secure hatch on the far wall. The security door is two meters from the door that leads to the corridor as well as the museum lobby and exhibit space on the same floor.

The security door slides open to reveal a Palorian man easily equal in mass to Maxim, wearing a dark blue bespoke suit.

Gabe and Maxim lower themselves behind a crate. Maxim whispers, "If he has a hand scanner—"

Gabe holds up his hand. His voice is barely audible. "The jamming field I am emitting will hide us from scanners, so long as we are close to each other."

Maxim nods, scooting fractionally closer to his friend.

The security man makes a slow circuit around the shipping and receiving area, ending at the door Maxim and Gabe entered through. He does indeed have a hand scanner. Studying the door and the readout on his scanner, he puts a hand to his ear. "Must have been a surge. Nothing weird out here." He listens to someone, then says, "Since I'm up, I'll do a loop around the first floor." Placing the scanner back into the pocket of his jacket, he moves to the hatch leading out of the loading area.

Once the door slides closed, Maxim says, "Okay, these guys are definitely pros." He looks at Gabe. "Did you get a scan of the interior of the security section when the door opened?"

"I am afraid not. My own sensors are rather limited when my jamming field is active."

Maxim nods. "Well, at least we have an idea of response times now."

Gabe nods his agreement. "We also know that there are likely always at least two people in the security office."

THE LOBBY SPACE of the Dre Toma Museum of Exotic Art is just as stunning as Zephyr expects. As they walk in, a friendly faced and well-built woman in a tailored suit ushers her and Bennie to a security scanner.

At the scanner, another well-dressed security man, a Palorian, says, "Any sensitive electronics, please place them in the bin. Wrist-comms are okay through the scanners."

Even before the security checkpoint, Zephyr notices several works of art on the walls. She nods to them as they move through the scanners. "Pretty confident in his security, having pieces this close to the door."

Bennie walks through the scanner and says, "Yeah. Wonder if that's bravado or an earned smugness. Cynthia said the lobby didn't have any displays when she was here."

"Let's find out," Zephyr whispers as she joins him on the other side of the walk-through scanner array. She notes the scanners, as well as the three sensor and camera emplacements in the corners of the ceiling.

The reception desk is manned by a bright platinum-plated droid. "Greetings. Welcome to the Dre Toma Museum of Exotic Art. Two tickets?" The droid's voice and chassis are distinctly feminine. Almost garishly so.

"Yes, please," Zephyr says.

Bennie stands on the tips of his toes to see over the top of the desk. "You have a big show here tonight?"

The bright blue optic sensors whir, focusing on the barely visible Brailack. "We do, indeed. The gala begins at sundown. The museum is showcasing a new exhibit by several artists from less developed worlds of the GC." After a pause, "I am afraid your ticket does not include access to the gala. However, there are a limited number of VIP tickets still available if you'd like to add any to your purchase?"

Zephyr waves a hand. "We're just passing through town and wanted to check out the museum. Thank you, though."

The droid nods and holds a device up for each of them to pass their wristcomm near. Zephyr leans down to hoist Bennie up high enough to reach the device with his arm.

Walking into the first room, he says, "Insulting to build that desk so tall."

Zephyr smiles and says nothing.

They pass a group of Ficu looking at a series of paintings, each standing on their trio of tentacles. The paintings are abstract, each depicting what look like figures at war with each other, or dancing— Zephyr can't tell. The small displays underneath show the name of the piece and artists, first in Ficunan, then in galactic standard.

Continuing on, they move through the small galleries on the main level to the wide central atrium and its circular staircase. The museum has become more crowded as Ficu and other beings have entered, moving floor to floor, looking at the various exhibits. Several young Ficu are clustered on the staircase using their wristcomms to take image and video of their visit.

Reaching the second floor, Bennie says, "Oooh, Brailack fire sculpture."

Zephyr follows him into a gallery. Pedestals line the walls, a few standing alone with enough space to move around them. On each a flame burns, twisting and curling into recognizable shapes.

Bennie gestures to one of the sculptures. "Sel-Kii the Noble."

Zephyr looks at the shape. It is vaguely humanoid shaped, with a familiar large head and thin limbs. "Looks like you," she quips. "Come on." She glances at the ceiling, making a note of the sensor emplacements in its corners, each with clear views in all directions. She notes that there are a few moving walls that could provide cover, if needed.

They make their way around the large open floor, reaching the staircase again. There's a velvet rope across the staircase entry leading up to the fourth floor. A heavily muscled Multonae man holds up a hand. "Sorry, folks. The third and fourth floors are closed for tonight's gala."

"Not a problem," Zephyr says. "Must be quite the event, the gala tonight."

The man nods. "All I know is that it's a who's who of Mo Talla and the surrounding cities. Some sort of unveiling of a new collection." He smiles.

Bennie grins. "Bet that'll be a party."

CHAPTER TEN

WHAT DID WE LEARN?

WIL SETS HIS GLASS DOWN. "So, you're confident?" He looks at Cynthia, then Bennie and the rest of the team. "All of you?"

Zephyr nods. "Yeah. Bennie and I got a good look at the first two floors and mapped the locations of the security features. Third and fourth are a bit of a mystery beyond the public plans, though." She looks at Cynthia. "I think we can adapt a lot of what Cyn brought to my gear." Cynthia nods.

Maxim scoops up a handful of crunchy tidbits from the bowl in the center of the table. After popping a few into his mouth, he says, "Gabe and I have a rough layout for some of the internal service corridors."

Gabe says, "I do not believe the security system will pose a significant threat."

Cynthia leans back. "That's not the same as no threat."

"You are correct." Gabe tilts his head to the side. "The security system in place is quite advanced. With Bennie's help, I should be able to stay ahead of it enough to accomplish the mission."

Bennie puts his empty mug down. "When we get back to the hotel, I'll set it all up and give Cynthia a crash course on the systems. I won't be much use once inside the building."

Cynthia smiles and salutes. "Hacker Apprentice Luar, checking in." She grins and takes a drink of her grum, then adds, "Wil and I mapped out the department store next door. It should be closed by the time the gala is underway. Would make a good secondary exfil." Nods all around.

Wil taps his wristcomm to pay the bill and stands. "Okay, let's get back to the hotel and get ready." He looks at the time on his wristcomm. "We've got three hours before the gala kicks off. Assuming we can do this in an hour, that gives us two to prep and get back here."

"Math for the win," Bennie quips, then quickly ducks out of range of Wil's arm.

Everyone heads out, this time taking one of the mass transit people movers to save time.

BACK IN THE SUITE, Bennie and Cynthia are at the makeshift command center that Bennie set up earlier. "Okay, this is the interface for the scanner. You'll need to be quick on this since we won't have a lot of time, and the more, the better. It's tied into as many databases as I could access without drawing too much attention."

Cynthia nods along. "Okay, seems straightforward. You'll scan the art, and I'll figure out where it comes from."

Bennie nods. "Yup, then we'll print out the replacement." He points to a backpack-like contraption. "Sucks to be Maxim." The backpack-like device has a meter-long tube on one side that folds in half. The smaller, flatter piece is a high-end processor tied to the rapid fabricator in the meter-long tube. While not tested, Bennie assures everyone that the fabricator, in a microtock, can spit out a canvas that would fool an art critic.

Wil walks out of the room he and Cynthia share. He's in a tailored suit and pointing to Bennie. "You better go get changed."

Bennie stands. "Still think it's dren that I can't just wear my uniform."

Wil sighs. "Because, dummy, a..." he chokes a little on what's next, "...rich Brailack philanthropist and his Multonae assistant don't stand out at all. A Knight of Plentallus kinda does." He winks. "And I don't have a laser sword."

Bennie waves a dismissive hand as the door to his room slides closed. "You'd poke your eye out."

Wil joins Cynthia at the overwatch station. "You good? I know this is a bit outside your comfort zone."

She shrugs. "Can't be helped. If there's even the slightest chance that Sclaro recognizes me, we're blown." Wil nods his agreement.

Maxim and Zephyr walk out of their shared room, both in form fitting matte black skin suits. Each has small bits of armor and padding here and there: places to attach weapons and equipment. Zephyr's has a few of the bits Wil and Cynthia retrieved from the storage room back home.

Wil whistles. "Ninja suits."

Maxim holds his arms out, examining each. "Glad we finally get to use these, if I'm being honest."

Wil smiles. "And they do the stealth thing?" Zephyr touches a control on her wristcomm. Her body wavers into invisibility, leaving only her head floating there. He shudders. "Okay, creepy. You two better get going."

Zephyr's body returns to visibility. She nods and reaches for a pair of cloaks hanging near the front door. Maxim grabs the portable art fabricator. "We'll see you there," Zephyr says as she and Maxim throw the cloaks on and vanish down the hallway.

Wil looks at Gabe, who has been standing near the window since they returned. "How you doing, big guy? Ready to do this?"

Gabe turns, his uncanny valley smile on full display. "I am ready. I do have reservations, however."

Cynthia turns to stare. "Why?"

"We have, mostly, moved on from crime. I was...happy with that." He shrugs. "This feels like a step backward."

Wil moves next to him. "I get that. I won't lie: I missed this. But, I understand your concerns. If it helps, we're breaking the law to punish a scumbag and hopefully return a lot of artwork to those who created it, or to their families."

Gabe inclines his head. "That does help, Captain." He presses his mouth into a line, then says, "I will help right this wrong as best I can."

Wil smiles. "Don't worry. We're still good guys."

T-MINUS 1 TOCK

STANDING on the opposite side of the street from the Dre Toma Museum of Exotic Art, Maxim checks his wristcomm. He opens the shared comm channel. "T-minus 65 microtocks."

Zephyr adds, "Looks like the staff are still setting up outside. A small gaggle of journalists, that's it. Shouldn't be hard to get past." She looks up at Maxim, who nods his agreement. They both pull flexible head coverings up and over their heads, thin visors deploying over their eyes. Nano material gloves deploy, covering their hands.

Nodding to each other, they toss off the cloaks as the stealth suits activate, bending light around them. Unlike the Peacekeeper Infiltration suits they wore on the criminal storage facility way back when, these are off-the-shelf models. No armor or counter surveillance tech outside the active stealthing. It took Bennie and Gabe a good portion of the trip from the space truck stop to modify a third suit to cover Maxim's semi-bulky portable fabricator rig.

Maxim wasn't thrilled about using off-the-shelf gear when they have a perfectly good, and more advanced, kit aboard the *Ghost*. Wil's argument was that if they had to ditch gear, it wouldn't link back to them. Maxim admitted it made sense, but this stealth suit itches and bunches in awkward places, and the backpack fab bites into his shoulders.

"Ready?" Zephyr asks. She's nothing more than a ghostly green outline on his visor.

"Let's do this."

They stride across the street, dodging journalists waiting for celebrities to arrive and museum staffers scrambling to erect last minute decorations and security features.

The security foyer is busier than it was earlier in the day. Two burly Palorian men are standing on either side of the entry scanner, each clearly armed. In front of them is a Ficu woman giving orders to the staff. Next to the sensor arch, two museum staffers, also Ficu, in matching uniforms are preparing to usher guests through as quickly as possible; they practice handing off bins of sensitive devices that won't be scanned and guiding people into the larger space beyond the lobby where the party will start for everyone.

One new addition to the foyer is an actual metal fence forcing all guests through the security arch. Zephyr looks at Maxim. "Guess we see how good Bennie is."

"Is there any doubt?" the Brailack asks over the comms.

"Yes," both Palorians answer in unison, voices low despite their garments' purported ability to fully block all sounds. The Brailack hacker makes a rude noise.

Zephyr removes from a thigh pouch a small device no bigger than the palm of her hand, careful to keep it cradled in her hand so that it doesn't appear to be floating in midair. She creeps as close to the sensor arch as possible, angling between one of the big Palorians and the angry Ficu woman, still shouting orders, and sliding the device on the floor to land next to one of the arch's supports. The moment the small device slides to a stop, a light comes on at the top of it, blinking twice before remaining solidly lit.

"Strong signal. Ready?" Bennie asks.

"Yup," Zephyr answers.

The light on the device flashes twice. At first Zephyr isn't sure it worked. Then the security men and museum staffers burst into motion as the archway beeps angrily, lights on the control panel flashing.

The two cloaked Palorians slip through the archway between security men and move into the main first-floor gallery. As she passes through the opening, Zephyr jumps up, slapping a small device no bigger than her thumbnail against the wall.

Wil comes out of his and Cynthia's room as Bennie is saying, "Is there any doubt?" He looks at Cynthia, who shrugs. "You ready, green bean?"

Bennie looks up. "You clean up pretty okay." He turns to Cynthia. "Questions?"

She shakes her head. "No, I think I got it."

Bennie nods. "Let's go, then." He grabs a tailored blazer from the back of the chair he was sitting in, putting it on in a flourishing over-the-head maneuver.

Wil whistles appreciatively. He moves to let Bennie pass, then leans down to kiss Cynthia, whispering, "We'll be back."

"You'd better be. I'll be here waiting." She winks. "Good hunting."

Bennie is at the door. "Well, come on, assistant."

Stepping off the hover bus, Wil looks up the street. The crowd outside the museum is sizable now. The journalists that had been milling about more or less aimlessly when Maxim and Zephyr arrived are now formed up along the roped off line of hundreds of guests waiting to be let into the museum.

"Quite the crowd," Wil says.

Bennie nods. "Yeah. Let's wait over here until they open the doors."

Wil looks down. "Why?"

Bennie looks up, a disconcerting grin splitting his face. "Because Lan'Do Ca-lrissian doesn't wait in lines."

Wil's eyes go wide. "If Earth stuff ever gets mainstream out here, there are gonna be a lot of confused people and records."

Bennie shrugs. "Until then, it's fun." He grins. "You should see the backstory I put together for this."

Wil sighs.

INSIDE THE MUSEUM, Maxim and Zephyr are slipping from display to display, placing sensor patches wherever they can. As they move to the second floor, Cynthia asks, "How's it coming?"

Maxim places another of the small sensors on the wall below one of the museum's existing sensor clusters. "We're on the second floor. I'm about to place the signal booster."

Bennie chimes in, "Remember to keep an eye on the signal scanner on your wristcomm. The booster is designed to piggyback on existing signals if it can."

Maxim looks around. "Meaning?"

The sigh on the other side of the channel is loud. "Meaning, placing it on its own will make it stand out like a sore thumb if they're running signal scans, and they almost certainly are."

Zephyr replies before Maxim can, "So, where should we put it?" She's on the opposite side of the floor, placing a sensor patch under a sensor cluster in the corner of the ceiling.

After a pause, Bennie says, "Find the tech on the floor, probably in a closet or maybe under the stairs."

"Maybe?" Maxim quips.

"I was busy when I was there earlier."

Gabe says, "The museum's tech is localized on each floor to a small alcove in the north corner, next to the restrooms."

"Thanks, Gabe," Maxim says, making his way to the north corner of the building.

Zephyr looks at the staircase. "We've got another issue."

"What's up?" Wil asks.

"The staircase. Third and fourth floors are not just roped off this time. They installed an actual floor-to-ceiling barrier."

"Shit," Wil hisses. "Can you bypass it?"

Zephyr looks at the bored-looking security man, a hulking Multonae man with pale white hair. "Negative. Lot of outsourced security."

Gabe says, "I am working my way there now. I should be able to assist shortly."

"Copy that," Zephyr replies.

T-MINUS 10 MICROTOCKS

"Watch out! Get out of my way!" a voice screeches from the rear of the line, awaiting their turn to enter the Dre Toma Museum of Exotic Art Gala.

A Ficu couple jump as if they received a shock, parting to allow a well-dressed Brailack to move that much closer to the front. Behind him, an embarrassed Multonae man is apologizing as he follows his diminutive employer.

"I don't know who you are, but I bet you know me!" Bennie hollers at the Trollack woman in front of him. She turns, looking like she's just eaten something sour, shaking her head. "Well, you will. Move it, loser." She steps back, aghast.

Wil slides in behind Bennie. "I'm so sorry, he hasn't eaten yet." She starts to ask who Bennie is supposed to be, but Wil is already two more people further up in line, and Bennie is three.

At the head of the line is the massive wall of muscle that Gabe and Maxim spied earlier. He lowers the PADD he's holding in a meaty paw of a hand. "Who're you supposed to be?" His jet-black hair is pulled into a tight top-knot.

Bennie looks up, squinting. "I'm Lan'Do Ca-Lrissian."

"Never heard of you."

"Your loss, man-bun. Move aside." Bennie moves to step past the big security man, who drops a big hand on top of Bennie's head.

Bennie growls. "Unhand me, you ruffian!"

"Ruffian?" Wil says. He turns to the crowd behind him. "Our apologies. My employer is eccentric." Turning back to the security man, he presents his wristcomm.

The other man glares at Bennie, then checks his PADD, glancing at Wil's wristcomm and back a few times. He looks down at Bennie, exhaling. "My apologies, Mr. Ca-Lrissian." He moves aside a stanchion.

Bennie walks past. "I could buy and sell your whole family. Twice!" He holds up two fingers.

Wil passes the security man. "He's just hungry." The other man glares but says nothing.

Inside the lobby, Wil leans down. "Laying it on a bit thick, no?"

Bennie looks up. "The more they're watching us, the less they're likely to notice our friends."

Wil can't argue with that.

GABE STEPS up to the door to the shipping and receiving area, his jamming field shielding him from the sensors outside the door. The access panel beeps and the door slides aside. Gabe's previous intrusion hasn't been detected. *That is a good sign*, he thinks.

The inside of the loading area is nearly the same as it was when he and Maxim were there earlier in the day. The most notable exception is the pile of empty storage crates, likely for the newly installed fencing and security features.

I am inside, Gabe sends over the team comms. The door to the security office is closed. With his jamming field active, his scanners are limited. It is impossible to determine how many security staff are in the office or out on the floor. Gabe moves to the door that he and Maxim believe leads to the service corridors. Sliding the door open, he looks around. The corridor is empty and clearly not meant for public viewing. The ceiling is conduits and pipes, and the floor, bare duracrete.

Gabe moves along the corridor quickly, looking for some place to set up.

"Gabe, you ready?" Zephyr asks over the team channel.

No, he sends back a moment before finding a small metal door. Sliding it aside, he spies what he has been hoping to find: a network wiring closet, bundles of wires running floor to ceiling, branching into conduits.

Update. I am plugging in, he sends. Closing the door behind him, he reaches for several bundles of wires, data tendrils snaking from the fingertips of each hand.

Over the team channel, Cynthia says, "Okay. Data coming in. Good job, Max. Data stream is strong."

"Good to hear," the big man replies.

Cynthia adds, "Sensor patches are beginning to ping as well. I should have a good picture in another microtock or two."

Gabe nods, data pulsing through the data tendrils. *I am masking my presence now.* He lowers his jamming field, his sensors flooding with data.

CHAPTER ELEVEN

T-PLUS 10 MICROTOCKS

CYNTHIA LEANS BACK in her chair. The myriad displays on the table are populating with data now that the device Maxim placed is linked to the museum's network, thanks to Gabe. The first few sensor patches come online, giving her a grainy view of the lobby of the museum just in time to see Bennie and Wil walk through the security checkpoint.

Muting her comm, she leans over and grabs the in-suite PADD, pulling up the room service menu. On a window that just came to life, Bennie is shoving some sort of appetizer into his mouth as Wil looks at the ceiling uncomfortably. She taps a few things on the PADD and submits her order.

Cynthia looks back at the displays, now populated with significantly more views from the sensor patches the Palorian couple has been planting. "Everything is looking good here. Sensor patches are sending fine." She looks at a smaller monitor. "Data throughput looks acceptable." She activates the art scanning program, getting ready for the next step in the plan.

Wil is following Bennie around the first floor, now much more crowded than it was a few minutes ago. Guests are flowing in freely now, moving through security quickly, finding their way to the roving appetizer and drink peddlers. He's impressed at how well the Ficu staff move; balancing a tray on each hand, their three locomotive tentacles allow them to glide through the crowd.

"I do say, Charles!" Bennie exclaims. He points to a piece of art on a pedestal near the staircase. "If this isn't one of the most amazing things I've seen."

Wil smiles. "Indeed, sir." He leans down. "What're you doing? Now you're a southern fried chicken mascot?"

Bennie shrugs. "All your Earth media runs together." He pushes Wil's face up and away from him.

In both of their ears, Cynthia says, "Sclaro just came in. He's moving into the gallery you just left."

Wil nods and looks at Bennie. "Ready."

Bennie takes a deep breath, running a hand down his face. "Ready." Wil makes a face and extends an arm back the way they came.

"I do say! Is that Sclaro Hunflim?" Bennie says loud enough to cause those nearest to turn and look at the well-dressed Brailack like he has two heads. Wil sighs and smiles, following along behind him.

The Malkorite museum owner turns, his jewelry laden ears jangling in a metallic symphony. His coppery skin is smooth, and to Wil, well oiled. "Hello there. You must be Lan'Do Ca-Lrissian! I saw your name on my guest list." He bows. "I'm honored to have such a patron of the arts at my humble establishment."

Wil raises an eyebrow.

Bennie grins, offering his arm. "How could I pass up such an event? This exhibit sounds absolutely wonderful! Undiscovered artists from around the GC? I mean, really. How could I miss it?"

The museum owner smiles, taking Bennie's arm in his. "I look forward to hearing your thoughts when we move up to the special exhibit floors. Perhaps, if you have the time, I can show you my private collection?"

Bennie returns the smile. "I look forward to it."

The museum owner nods and moves to engage a Burzzad couple that is approaching from behind Wil and Bennie.

A server walks past, a tray full of drink balanced in his hand. Wil motions him to slow down, extracting two fluted glasses with pale blue liquid in them. Handing one to Bennie, he says, "Well done."

Bennie accepts the drink. "You doubted me?" He takes a sip.

Wil smirks. "Yes, a lot."

LONG TIME, NO SEE

CYNTHIA IS WATCHING Sclaro Hunflim address his audience from the steps of the grand central staircase, working them into a frenzy for when the bidding starts later in the evening. She smiles. He's good, she'll give him that. The guests haven't even gone up to the second floor, which is more of the same at the moment.

They'll spend a half tock or so there, eating a bit more and drinking a lot more. He'll probably address them one more time from the steps to the third floor before flinging up the flimsy security gate he had installed. The guests will rush to the third-floor gallery to ooh and aah over art from unknown artists that Hunflim robbed and likely had killed to make their work even more valuable. She can't wait to see the look on his face when the team's plan comes down on him.

The announcer panel next to the door to the suite beeps twice, followed by a tinny voice. "Room service."

Cynthia taps the mute button on the control console and gets up, and with a last glance to make sure nothing is wrong on the various little windows arrayed across the myriad displays attached to the table, heads to the door.

The door hasn't finished sliding out of the way when a powerful kick lands square in Cynthia's midsection, launching her off her feet to sail backwards, crashing against one of the dining area tables that was sitting homeless in the middle of the kitchenette area after the furniture shuffling of the previous day.

The door to the suite slides shut behind the tall Tygran woman that has been dogging the team, unbeknownst to them, for almost two weeks. She's got a tight-fitting matte black body suit on underneath what looks like stolen laundry: mismatched pants and blouse with a scarf that clashes against both pieces of clothing it is meant to accentuate.

Cynthia rolls over, flipping back on to her feet, moving toward the conversation pit and overwatch station. She looks at her attacker and stops dead in her tracks. "Margo?" She looks down at her wristcomm for the "Emergency Abort" macro everyone on the team has on the device's home screen during missions.

Her attacker cocks her head, bearing her sharp incisors. "I wasn't sure you'd remember me." She inclines her head. "Don't bother. You've forgotten standard procedure?"

Cynthia scowls. On her wristcomm screen, a small alert is flashing "NO SIGNAL." Placing a localized signal jammer near your target before making your first move is right near the top of the field manual. Margo probably stuck hers to the wall just outside the door. Right now, anyone in the rooms immediately around the one the team booked is wondering why their PADDs and wristcomms have lost local network access.

Margo leaps at Cynthia, claws extended out of her fingertips. Cynthia dodges, landing a powerful uppercut into the other woman's stomach as she passes overhead. The punch sends Margo to the opposite side of the room.

Cynthia lunges for the computer station and the PADD she was reading on. Her hand closes around the PADD just as hand closes on her leg, pulling her off balance. Her face slams into the table, bouncing up as she is dragged clear of it.

She swings the PADD at Margo, clipping the woman's knee, eliciting a yelp as she backs off. Before the other woman can move in again, she hurls the PADD at her, striking her shoulder. The PADD clatters to the floor.

Cynthia flips over backward, gaining her feet. "What the wurrin is this?" she demands, adopting a fighting stance. "What are you doing here?"

The other woman takes up a matching stance. She tilts her head. "You have much to answer for." She doesn't wait for Cynthia to reply, lunging in with two quick jabs and a savage spin kick that drives her opponent against the makeshift workstation, knocking over monitors and computer cores. Two miles away, several earpieces erupt in static.

Getting back to her feet, her tail ramrod straight behind her, Cynthia says, "I left the program. I did the job I was contracted and just never came back. There's nothing more to say. Certainly nothing to answer for." She dives in with a powerful jab followed by a more powerful right hook. Not giving Margo a chance to stagger, she grabs the other woman's head with both hands, driving it down to meet an up-thrusting knee.

Margo staggers back, shaking her head to clear the stars before her eyes. While she's rapidly blinking, Cynthia leaps past her, grabbing the PADD she threw moments before. She presses a button on the device's screen just as a powerful hand grabs the back of her shirt and hurls her back toward the table of monitors.

This time, her impact is enough to topple the table. The few remaining monitors and processing cores clatter to the carpeted floor, erupting in sparks and a few small bursts of flame as they do. Cynthia drops the tablet before rolling over to face her onetime friend. "This makes no sense. Why now? After all this time?"

"I saw you on Tyr. Did you think you could just come back like nothing had changed? That you had a place on our world after you abandoned it, and us? That there wouldn't be a conclave?"

Cynthia looks her in the eye. "I mean, it's a big planet." When her opponent only stares at her, she adds, "Margo, I abandoned no one," punctuating it with a low growl.

"Lies!" Margo screams.

Cynthia raises her hands in a defensive posture. "How did you even know where to find me?"

The other woman's eyes dart around the room, landing on the two gravsleds pushed against the far wall, one powered down and sitting atop the other.

Cynthia's gaze follows. "What? You put a tracker on us? How'd you even...? You tracked us to Fury." It isn't a question. "How did you get into the office? Why didn't you attack me there?"

Margo snarls. "I owe you nothing." She leaps to tackle Cynthia. More sparks erupt from damaged equipment as the two women fall into the pile of broken gear, raining blows on each other.

Margo is able to get the upper hand, straddling Cynthia, punching her in the face repeatedly.

"Stop!" Cynthia shouts, albeit weakly, through more than a few busted teeth. She turns her head and spits blood. Breathing hard, she says, "You...went through...all this, just...to kill... me?"

Standing, Margo produces a small pistol. "No." She fires once.

A blue bolt leaps out to strike Cynthia, wrapping her in angry blue electricity that makes every fiber of her body scream in agony, before shutting down and rendering her unconscious.

Sliding the pistol back into a holster in the small of her back, Margo says, "Your debt is to more than just me and for more than just answers." She moves to scoop up Cynthia's unconscious form.

CHANGE OF PLANS

Bennie and Wil are standing in the crowd of wealthy art snobs at the base of the staircase. Sclaro Hunflim is three steps up, high enough to look out onto the gathered crowd of wealthy socialites from over a dozen different worlds.

"My friends, thank you for coming out tonight." He pauses as polite applause starts. Once the last clap echoes, the grinning Malkorite continues, "Tonight, in just a bit, you'll be treated to something truly unique. I've spent a great deal of time—and, well, a great deal of money— acquiring art from lesser-known worlds across the GC." He grins, a gleam in his eye. "And from a few worlds beyond the GC."

Several polite oohs and aahs come from the crowd. Wil looks around, wondering how many of these people know that the art in this building is largely stolen. He shrugs. More than he's comfortable thinking about, probably.

"You may not know these artists or the worlds they call home yet. But after tonight, you will, and better yet, the highest bidders will have a piece of art that will be beyond priceless in no time." More oohs and aahs.

Over the shared comm channel, a burst of static causes everyone to flinch. Maxim and Zephyr—still cloaked on the third floor, having found the service lift used by the catering staff— flinch, the latter almost knocking a piece of ceramic art off its pedestal.

Bennie and Wil, surrounded by a hundred-plus wealthy art patrons, draw some startled stares as each of them winces and rubs his ears.

Down in the wiring alcove, Gabe says, "I am no long receiving downstream data from overwatch."

"What do you mean?" Maxim asks. He has the specially designed fabricator unfolded before him.

Zephyr is standing in front of a piece of art that looks like a Multonae woman placidly sitting for a portrait, a knowing half smile on her face. She slowly passes the hand scanner device in front of the painting. "Overwatch? Sending first scan. How do you copy?" No reply.

Wil moves as casually as he can toward the rear of the crowd gathered around the steps. "Overwatch? Cyn? Come on, what's going on over there?" he whispers.

Bennie joins him. "This can't be good."

Wil nods his agreement. "I'm calling it."

"What? Really?" Maxim says.

"Are you sure?" Zephyr asks. "She didn't trigger the call-back. It could just be an issue with the local internex."

Bennie pulls up the sleeve of his jacket to reveal his wristcomm. Sighing, he says, "No, the local net looks fine." He looks up at Wil. "This was so much fun."

"Gabe?" Wil says.

"I am on it."

Wil clears his throat. "Ladies, gentlemen, non-binary beings." He waves his arms as he makes his way toward the stairs, Bennie trailing behind him.

"Excuse me?" Sclaro Hunflim stammers. "Mr. Ca-Lrissian, what's the meaning of this?"

Bennie steps up the stairs, pushing the Malkorite man aside.

Wil takes two more steps and turns to look at the group, mostly all gaping at this sudden change in the expected programming. "This guy—" he points to Hunflim "—this guy hires thugs and assassins to kill artists and collectors in order to take their works. In the case of artists, he knows that dead artists' works sell for more coin. Dead collectors can't file complaints."

Oohs and aahs rise up from the crowd, mixed with a lot of gasps. Unlike the last time, these noises are laced with shock and a little anger. Maybe fewer than Wil thought know the truth of things.

One of the security men starts to move in from the side. Bennie turns toward the man, still across the room. He takes a step closer to Hunflim. "I wouldn't, big man. I can snap his neck before you get halfway across the room."

Several people in the crowd scream.

Wil sighs, looking down at Bennie. The Brailack shrugs. "What? You wouldn't let me bring my saber, and that guy can snap us both in half if he gets over here."

Wil looks at the scowling Multonae man, who bears more than a passing resemblance to a young Arnold Schwarzenegger, and nods his agreement to Bennie. He turns back to the crowd. "I know you all didn't know this, but you do now. It's up to you to shut this monster down. Ensure the works on this and the floors above are returned to the artists or collectors. Trace the provenances of each piece in this building."

"This is outrageous!" a now thoroughly worked up and indignant Sclaro Hunflim screams. He stamps a foot, causing his jewelry-laden ears to erupt in a chorus of tinkling metal and gems. He motions to the security man still standing off across the room. "Secure the building!"

The lights go out. For a brief second, the room is silent before screams punctuate the silence. Emergency lighting kicks on just as the Multonae security man reaches Hunflim. Wil and Bennie are nowhere to be seen, but the recently installed security gate closing the stairs to the third and fourth floors is open.

SCRAMBLE

Gabe is watching Wil and Bennie address the crowd, while simultaneously opening dozens of data connections to news networks off-world. According to their telemetry, the two Palorians have moved to the rooftop via the small service lift in the building's corner.

He is also doing everything he can think of to access their suite at the hotel. Whatever has happened, it seems to have cut all data connections between them and Cynthia. Something is definitely not right back at the hotel.

In one of the floating video windows in his field of vision, he sees Wil and Bennie on the stairs. The museum owner is flailing and shouting. As he shouts, Wil looks up and winks. Gabe cuts all power to the building.

The sensor patches are too low-powered to offer multiple image processing capabilities, so he is forced to hope and wait for Wil and Bennie to reach the service lift.

Disconnecting his data tendrils from the bundles of wires, he steps out of the cramped space into the slightly less cramped corridor. At the far end, opposite the door leading into the loading dock area, is a small hatch halfway up the wall.

Gabe makes his way to the hatch, arriving moments before it

slides up to reveal an incredibly uncomfortable Wil with a possibly even more uncomfortable Bennie folded up in his lap. Both grunt and squint against the light pouring from two small LEDs deployed in Gabe's shoulders.

"Apologies," the droid says, lowering the power of the lights, and offering his hand to Bennie to help extricate him from the small space.

Once free of his Brailack friend, Wil exhales and asks, "The others make it out?" He holds out a hand to Gabe.

Pulling Wil out of the cramped lift, Gabe says, "Maxim and Zephyr are on the roof, making their way to the department store next door." He lets go of Wil's arm and adds, "I was able to find several off-world news outlets to upload the feed to, GNO chief among them. The feed will be active until discovered." He smiles. It still creeps Wil out.

From a few feet away, toward the exit, Bennie says, "Best we can do."

Gabe nods. "Yes. I was able to add images of several pieces in range of the sensor patches; however, their resolution is not great."

"Fingers crossed," Wil says. He points Gabe toward Bennie and the exit. "Best we can do right now. Were you able to get anything on overwatch?"

The trio exits into the loading dock to find two startled security officers. Bennie wastes no time leaping on to the chest of the nearest, raining blows on the man's face while bellowing some type of war cry.

Before Wil can react, Gabe's right arm transforms into the familiar double barreled blaster configuration. Two bright blue bolts of energy drill into the second security man, dropping him to the floor. One shot has struck his shoulder, the other his thigh. Gabe turns to Wil. "I see no reason to kill these men."

Wil nods and turns in time to see Bennie's opponent fall to the ground under his attacker. "Huh," he says as he and Gabe join Bennie. A distinct bite mark that looks about the size and shape of the

Brailack hacker's mouth is on the man's neck. Wil looks down. "Did you—"

"Let's move," Bennie interrupts, wiping his mouth.

Wil looks at Gabe. The droid makes a shrugging motion.

On the roof of the museum, Maxim deactivates his stealth suit. The hood and visor retract, folding back against his neck. "This thing is so itchy," he complains. He shrugs off the portable fabricator, dropping it to the ground. "Next time, Wil carries the tech." He kneels and presses a button on the side of the unit. Something inside emits an electronic pop. Faint whispers of smoke drift up from the now ruined device.

Zephyr appears next to him. "Maybe you should have bought a larger size." She pats his stomach. "We don't train as hard as when we were in the service."

Maxim's face turns dead serious. "That was mean." A heartbeat later, his expression cracks into a wide grin. "Let's go find out what's going on with Cynthia." He turns and walks to the edge of the building. "Long jump," he says.

Zephyr joins him, holding up a small spool of ultra-lightweight filament. "Hope you haven't put on too many gembs." She kneels down to attach one end of the thin cable to a piece of equipment.

"I love that you come prepared."

"One of us has to." She grins.

PART 4

CHAPTER TWELVE

BROKEN

WHEN MAXIM and Zephyr reach the rendezvous location, a block from the museum, Wil is fidgeting, moving from foot to foot. He sees the two Palorians and turns to Gabe and Bennie. "Okay, let's go. Gabe, can you score us a ride?"

Gabe nods, stepping into traffic directly in front of an oncoming hover car. The vehicle's anti-collision systems kick in, swerving the vehicle to avoid the droid-shaped obstacle. The vehicle comes to a stop just past him.

"What the wurrin is wrong with you?" an irate Ficu shouts, free hand waving.

"Please forgive me," Gabe says, moving around the rear of the vehicle.

"Well, be more careful next time," the driver says, easing back into the driver's seat. Gabe opens the door. "Hey! What're you doing, crazy droid!"

"I meant, I am sorry for this." He motions the others over and deposits the woman on the sidewalk.

With Wil in the driver's seat, they pull away as the irate Ficu woman flails arms and tentacles.

"I'm sure it's nothing," Zephyr offers.

Wil has both hands on the car's controls, his knuckles white. "We'll know soon enough." The vehicle's motor is whining as it picks up speed.

Bennie looks around out the windows. "Better be careful. I know it's only two ploriths, but no need to get local security involved." When Wil doesn't respond, he puts a tiny hand on Wil's shoulder.

Shrugging it off, Wil growls, "We have to get to her."

Maxim, in the passenger seat, puts a hand on his captain and friend's arm. "Wil, she's a trained assassin. She can take care of herself. You know that. Slow down. We're already almost there."

Up ahead, the hotel is just visible over the tops of the nearby buildings. Wil eases off the throttle control.

Pulling up and around the vehicle unloading area, Wil flings open the door, not slowing to close the door or wait for the others, dashing into the lobby. A hover van is pulling away at the same time. Everyone else files out of the vehicle. Maxim meets the parking attendant, a young Harrith man. "You can leave this here. It's not ours." He doesn't wait for a reply, following the others into the lobby. Wil is already in an elevator holding the doors open with one hand, waving the others on with the other.

The elevator doors part, and Wil sprints the length of their floor. The door to their suite is closed. He slows down enough to look around the door. Nothing seems out of place. Pressing his palm to the access panel, he waits for the beep, followed by the door clicking and sliding aside.

Nothing looks wrong outside; everything looks wrong inside. The room is trashed. Bennie's command station is in shambles. Displays lie shattered all over the room, the table is tipped over and bent, and the computer cores are littered around the floor of the conversation lounge.

He turns slowly, taking in the damage. The wall next to the door to Maxim and Zephyr's room is dented, the picture that was hanging there, on the ground, bent.

"Oh, dren," Zephyr whispers as the rest of the team arrives.

"My gear!" Bennie shouts, pushing past Wil then skidding to a halt to look up at his friend. "Oh, sorry."

Wil is standing motionless in the center of the space. One of the kitchenette cupboard doors is ripped from its hinges. There's a burn mark near the overturned chair Cynthia was using at the homemade command center. There are splatters of blood in several places.

Maxim reaches for Wil's shoulder only to have his hand batted aside. "Where? What?" He takes a few steps toward the most ruined part of the room before falling to his knees and screaming. Maxim kneels next to him.

Zephyr looks at Gabe. "Ca—"

"I am already scanning the room," the droid assures her.

SHOCK

GABE KNEELS DOWN NEXT to one of the blood splatters, pressing a finger into the sticky carpet.

Maxim pulls Wil up and guides him to the remaining sofa opposite the ruined command center setup. "We'll figure this out. It's what we do." He assures his friend. Wil doesn't respond. His eyes are open but unfocused, staring out the window at the city beyond.

Gabe stands. "This is not Cynthia's blood." Everyone turns to him. "It is Tygran, but not Cynthia's."

"Who?" Wil croaks, turning slowly to look at his mechanical friend.

Gabe turns to Bennie. "I will need your help to access planetary and GC databases." Bennie nods. He turns to Wil. "We will find out."

Zephyr is picking up pieces of the ruined overwatch setup, trying to stack them out of the way. "Why would another Tygran attack her? Here, of all places?"

"I cannot say," Gabe replies.

Maxim stands and makes a slow circle, running his hands through his hair. "I need to get out of this thing," he says to no one in particular, reaching for the release on his stealth suit. He heads into his and Zephyr's room. A few minutes later, he comes out wearing a simple pair of trousers and shirt. He has a PADD in his hands. "This was in our room." He holds it up for everyone to see. The device has a sizable dent in one corner and what looks like blood splattered across its screen.

He offers the device to Gabe. Wil stands and joins them, craning his neck to see the screen. "What is it?" he whispers.

Gabe looks from the device to Wil. "I will know in a moment." He resumes his examination of the device, then says, "A recording." He presses a control on the screen. When nothing happens, several data tendrils snake out, working their way into the device. The screen flickers and begins playing the recording.

Gabe stops the playback when they hear the sound of the door closing behind Margo, whoever that is. Everyone sits and stands silently for a handful of heartbeats.

Bennie is the first to break the silence. "A grolacking tracker?" He looks around the room.

Gabe's eyes turn a light purple as he remains motionless. "Intriguing." He points to the gravsleds pushed against the corner near the kitchenette. "I believe the tracker is on the one of the gravsleds." His eyes turn back to their normal yellow.

"How?" Maxim asks, moving to look the devices over.

Gabe shrugs. "I ran through all of my sensor modes, including several I inherited from the Peacekeeper intrusion software I absorbed. Several of them are not normally used."

"That's what purple eyes mean?" Zephyr asks.

Gabe inclines his head. "I detected an unusual frequency that I would otherwise have never noticed. It is ultra-wideband. To track such a frequency would require access to planetary infrastructure."

Maxim is kneeling next to the two gravsleds. Running a hand along the bottom, where the low power repulsorlifts are housed, he withdraws his hand, a small gray square in his palm, no bigger than five credit coin.

Zephyr whistles. "Dren." She takes it from Maxim, handing it to Gabe. "Any idea the range? Can you track it back to her?"

Before Gabe can reply, Wil says, "She said something about a 'conclave' on the recording. That ring any bells?"

Gabe turns the device over in his hand, making his mechanical sigh sound. "No, I am afraid not."

Bennie shakes his head. "No. When we get to the *Ghost,* I can run it through some of my search algorithms."

Wil nods. "Add Margo to your list, too." Bennie gives him a half smile and nods.

Zephyr clears her throat. "Gabe, can you and Bennie access the local spaceport files? If this Margo woman tracked us, that means she likely was on Fury, and maybe even the truck stop. Maybe you can find any ships or shuttles with any of those points of origin."

Gabe and Bennie exchange a glance, the latter moving to the sole sofa in the room, the former moving to the wall panel with the suite's data connections hidden inside. Bennie produces a PADD from somewhere and is frenetically tapping the screen. Gabe removes the panel and sinks both hands into the bundles of wiring.

Zephyr moves into her room but shouts, "She can't be that far ahead of us. Bet she landed here in the city."

Wil runs a hand through his hair, taking a deep breath. "We gotta go. We gotta get mobile." He starts tapping and swiping on his wrist-comm. "Fuck!" He drops his arm. "Too late." He raises his arm and swipes toward Maxim.

He looks at his wristcomm, saying loud enough for Zephyr to hear in the room where she's changing out of her own stealth suit, "Local security is here."

From the bedroom, Zephyr shouts, "Guess we shoulda seen that coming. Bit faster than I expected, though."

Bennie looks up from his PADD. "They just activated a jammer. Nothing Gabe and I can do now. The whole building is dark."

Zephyr steps back into the main room. "Then it's time for us to go."

"Looks like your friends might have caused a ruckus," Margo says as several municipal security patrol vehicles race past the hover van in the opposite direction, back toward the hotel.

From the back of the van, a large piece of luggage shifts, and something or—more accurately, someone—inside shouts muffled curses.

"I'd let you out, but I don't know that I can trust you to behave yourself." She turns back to the view out the forward window. "Can I?"

A muffled answer comes back.

"No, you're right. You'd definitely make the trip to the spaceport arduous, trying to get free every chance you got. Better to leave you where you are for now." The muffled reply sounds rude. Margo smiles. "We'll be there shortly."

The van makes a turn. Margo raises her wristcomm. "I'll be there soon. Get the shuttle ready. Prep for two passengers."

"WE SHOULD'VE PAID for closer parking," Bennie says, disconnecting his wristcomm from the last of the remaining semi functional computer cores. He looks up. "Okay, these are as clean as they're gonna get." He points to two of the units that are still smoking. "I can't sanitize all of them, however."

Wil nods, shouldering his bag. He produces a pulse pistol and fires into each of the damaged units twice, melting them into molten slag.

Bennie leans back, waving both hands to clear the acrid smoke coming from the ruined computers. "Drennog!" he hisses.

"We gotta go. We've got to get out of this hotel, to the *Ghost* and back this way before this mysterious Margo chick takes off." Wil snaps his fingers. "Oh, and between those last two, actually track her down. There's more than one spaceport in this metro area."

"First things first," Zephyr says. "How do we get out of here? The security forces have absolutely locked down the lifts by now. The stairs will be swarming with armed Ficu."

Gabe opens the door. "Switch to local comms." He vanishes down the hall.

Wil makes a circle in the air with one hand. "We gotta go. What's he doing?" He taps his wristcomm, releasing an ear piece and snugging it into his ear. "Gabe, what are you doing?"

"Securing us a ride. You should all make your way to the roof."

Wil looks around the room. Everyone shrugs and resumes prepping for their departure.

Bennie grabs his small duffel bag. "Let's go already." He presses the control to open the suite door. It opens on a startled Ficu security officer. "Grolack!" Bennie shouts, pushing the startled officer back before slamming his hand on the door control. He turns. "Company."

"Fuck!" Wil growls. "We don't have time for this." A bang comes from the door. He points to the panel.

Bennie's eyes go wide. "Oh, sorry." He pulls the access panel off the wall, reaching inside. The door begins to slide open but stops and reverses itself. Bennie turns. "That won't last."

Maxim looks at the ceiling. "The bot said, roof." He nods to Bennie, who returns the gesture and makes a running leap to land on his big friend's shoulders. With a snap-hiss, his beam saber comes to life. He jabs the blade into the ceiling and begins making a slow circle.

Maxim, still holding Bennie on his shoulders, jumps aside as the circular section of the ceiling crashes to the floor. Bennie leaps off Maxim's shoulders. "Ta ka."

"Ta da," Wil corrects, moving to look up into the hole. After a few seconds, he says, "Looks clear." He looks at Maxim. "Boost."

The big man makes a face, then cups his hands. After boosting everyone up, he jumps up, grabbing Wil and Zephyr's outstretched hands.

Bennie runs to the door, opening it. He looks back. "Clear. Let's hurry." Everyone follows him into the hallway. This floor is, like every other floor in the hotel, the exact same as the one below it. The staircase nearest them is at the end of the hall.

Zephyr reaches the door first. Unlike the doors to the rooms and suites, the stairwell door is on hinges, with magnetic locking mechanisms and automatic hinges. She eases the door open, peering into the harshly lit stairwell. Holding up two fingers, she points up, then motions forward.

From somewhere below, Wil can hear the sound of tentacles slapping on metal and duracrete. He shudders. Thankfully, their suite was only four floors from the top of the building. They reach the roof without trouble, the security forces having not yet checked the top three floors that were above their suite.

Zephyr sees Gabe standing next to a communications tower, data tendrils from his hand burrowing into a small control panel at the base of the tower. "Gabe, we're here. You have a plan?"

The data tendrils withdraw. Gabe turns. "I do." He smiles his uncanny valley smile.

Maxim looks around. "Is our ride cloaked?"

"It will arrive momentarily," Gabe says, motioning to the edge of the building.

Bennie leans over the edge. The street below is awash with flashing lights. He whistles. "Wow, lotta law enforcement. Wonder why they're here and not at the museum?"

Gabe says, "The rest of the city's law enforcement is, in fact, at the museum. Sclaro Hunflim has been placed under arrest." He turns. "Aah. Our ride is here." Everyone looks around. Gabe points up.

"The hell?" Wil says.

Above them, a large dull green oval is lowering on a pair of runner-like repulsorlifts. The vehicle rotates as it lowers, the rear opening a giant toothless mouth. The front of the vehicle sports two thick arms that end in forklift-like clamps.

"A trash truck?" Wil says.

"No way," Zephyr says. She looks at Gabe. "Was a sewer too hard to find?"

Gabe tilts his head. "The sewer is forty-two floors that way." He points to the ground below.

Bennie's flat nostrils clamp shut. He points to his face, chuckling. Zephyr makes a face.

The garbage collector settles in next to the rooftop. "We should go," Gabe says, stepping aboard the craft. It dips slightly, repulsorlifts shifting to keep the vehicle level.

Wil sighs and steps into the back of the vehicle. "Oh, God." He looks around. "I'm gonna hurl."

Maxim helps Zephyr in as Bennie leaps into the hold. Landing, he slips on something and falls into a pile of trash bags, half of which are ripped open and spilling their contents around the floor. He holds up a hand for someone to help him up, but when they see it's covered in grime, everyone turns away, resulting in more expletives.

Gabe's arms extend with a few whirs and clicks to brace himself in the center of the trash area. "This is Waltern," he says.

"Who's Waltern?" Bennie says, then looks around. "Aah. Trash droid."

"That is correct. I am happy to assist Gabe the—"

"Gabe is fine," Gabe interrupts. He looks around. "I was able to use the comm tower to reach out for help. Waltern is broadcasting an emergency code that will allow him to travel much faster than normal, in spaces that would normally be restricted."

"We should arrive at your destination in ten microtocks," the cheerful voice says from all around them.

Wil whistles. "Damn. You go, Waltern." He looks at Gabe. "We need to nail Margo's departure down. I have an idea. Can you mask a call?"

CHAPTER THIRTEEN

"Yes, hello. I'd like to let you know that I've planted several explosive devices throughout the spaceport," Wil says. He looks at the others and shrugs hopefully. He shakes his head. "No, no, I'm not on property. Why would I be? Well, why would I want to be in the danger zone? Clear the port or blow up, doesn't matter to me."

Bennie looks at Zephyr. "His people do this all the time?"

Wil taps the mute icon on his wristcomm. "All the time. Did it once to get out of a chemistry midterm. I was so hungover from a party the night before. I couldn't remember a damn thing." His eyes lose focus. "Yes, that's right. Several explosives. Uh huh. All over the port."

Zephyr shakes her head. "I don't like the panic this will cause, assuming they believe him." She shrugs. "But I don't have a better idea."

"Why?" Wil says into his wristcomm. "Because the docking fees are outrageous. Turn on your local news broadcast. The group that caused the ruckus at the Dre Toma Museum and the Galaxy Palace Hotel—yeah, that's us."

Maxim, leaning against the least gross part of the interior of the garbage collector, wishing he had left the stealth suit on, says, "As far as plans go, I guess this might be a new low." He waves his hands in front of him to clear a cloud of gnats away from him, albeit briefly.

"That's right, you charge far too much to land. Maybe when I blow up your spaceport, the next one will charge reasonable rates," Wil says. He mutes the channel. "I might have underestimated this whole Ficu personal effort thing. This guy isn't convinced it's worth his time to sound the alarm."

Gabe says, "He may not be convinced that he needs to sound the alarm, but he is attempting to back trace the call."

Wil nods. "Look, dummy. I'm done talking to you. The explosives will go off in one tock. Alarm the authorities or don't. Clear the port or don't. The deaths will be on your head." He disconnects the call. "It worked better back home." He looks at Zephyr. "Two more?" She nods.

"Your people are stupid," Bennie says.

"We are nearing your spaceport," Waltern says. "Two micro-tocks. I will need to land outside the facility, I'm afraid."

"That is acceptable. Thank you, Waltern," Gabe replies.

The entire vehicle jostles a bit, then the back yawns open. "It has been my pleasure to assist Gabe the—"

"We appreciate it," Gabe interrupts, looking pained.

Bennie laughs as he hops out of the trash hauler. "It's never going away. Get used to it."

Gabe looks at Bennie but says nothing. Turning to Wil, he says, "It appears your efforts were successful." He inclines his head to Wil's arm.

Everyone looks at their wristcomms to see a newscast Gabe is forwarding to them. The main spaceport in Mo Talla, as well as two smaller ports, has been shut down while authorities investigate bomb threats.

"Yes!" Wil pumps a fist into the air. "Let's get going." He heads for the pedestrian entrance to the Vel Roa spaceport and the waiting *Ghost*.

"Dren!" Margo hisses. "What do you mean, closed?"

The Ficu woman in the small freestanding guard shack shrugs. "Are you unfamiliar with the word? The spaceport is closed, the opposite of open. Someone claims to have planted explosives because our prices are too high. Security needs to clear the facility before we can let anyone in."

Margo growls. "What am I supposed to do now? I have places to be."

The other woman makes a face. "Try to contact flight control. They're letting ships out one at a time, based on need, to help clear the field."

"Why didn't you lead with that?" Margo shouts. When the disinterested Ficu just stares at her, she puts the hover van into drive mode and pulls away from the closed vehicle entrance.

Once out of the flow of traffic trying to get into the spaceport, she calls the shuttle pilot. "Patch me through to flight ops." She adds, "Then be ready to lift off."

NEEDLES, HAYSTACKS

"I'll get the preflight started. You two get to work. We have her face, find her," Wil says as he drops into his command station. He wastes no time flipping switches and pressing buttons, waking the small warship up after it had been sitting on the duracrete landing pad for a few days.

Bennie nods. "We'll find her." He motions for Gabe to follow him to the hacker's bridge station. The myriad screens welded and epoxied to the hull spring to life as the two get to work.

Zephyr sits down at her station. The screens and console come to life. "Pulling comms over to my station," she says. "I'll get us cleared."

Wil nods, watching his console. "Reactor is warming up."

Maxim turns and heads for the hatch. "I'm taking a shower."

Wil looks over his shoulder. He's about to complain that none of them get to shower but realizes that if they need Max, things are really, really bad. He turns back to his console. The reactor display is in the orange zone. Enough power to lift off but not yet enough for weapons, FTL, or much more than coasting on the repulsorlifts. Thankfully, the atmospheric engines run on a different system and can be lit off at almost any time.

"Up we go," Wil announces a minute later, choosing to give the reactor a little more time to power up. He eases the repulsorlift power lever up with one hand, while keeping the other on the flight controls to keep the nimble ship balanced as she rises off of duracrete.

Bennie turns around, pushing against Gabe's hip so that he can see Wil. "I think we have her."

THE SHUTTLE DESCENDS to the impromptu alternate landing area. A quartet of Ficu ground crew guide the ship down. Margo, standing off to the side with a large rolling suitcase, is tapping her foot as the shuttle slowly rotates and touches down. One of the Ficu looks over and waves her in.

The spaceport managers have set aside a small parcel of land beyond the ring wall, allowing one ship at a time to lift out of the spaceport and land outside to pick up whatever passengers, crew, or cargo they need before lifting off again to depart the planet.

The rolling luggage rattles and starts making noise. Margo kicks it, looking at the Ficu ground crew operator nearest her. "Left the batteries in." She smiles.

Aboard the shuttle, she pushes the suitcase in and lets it roll toward the back. She knocks on the hatch to the forward section. "Let's go!"

The floor shifts underfoot as the shuttle rises off the ground. Opening the oversized luggage, Margo says, "If you behave, you can make the trip like a civilized being. If not, I'll knock your ass out and leave you in the luggage."

Cynthia looks up at her, murder in her eyes. She takes a deep breath through her nose, her mouth covered in adhesive. She nods.

Pulling the strip of adhesive material from Cynthia's mouth, Margo smiles. "Good. We can catch up."

Cynthia doesn't smile. "Looking forward to it."

A speaker in the ceiling announces, "We'll be leaving atmosphere in five microtocks. One tock to FTL."

Cynthia unfolds from the suitcase gingerly, her muscles aching loudly from the tocks spent folded up in the large bag. "I'm hungry."

Margo checks her wristcomm, pressing an icon. "Me too."

THE GHOST IS APPROACHING Mo Talla proper. The airspace is crowded and chaotic. Wil's bomb threat has clearly had the desired effect, mostly. He leans forward in his seat. "Are they..."

"Letting ships leave the spaceport? Yes," Zephyr says, looking up from her screen. "Dren. I assumed they'd keep everyone locked down."

"Me too," Wil agrees. He turns to Bennie and Gabe, still at the Brailack hacker's station. "Anything?"

Gabe answers, "We have been able to track her departure from the spaceport. She came in a class two private rental shuttle."

Bennie waves a hand. "I'm accessing the spaceport traffic management system now."

"We're getting yelled at," Zephyr says. "Space control is waving off incoming traffic." She grins. "They definitely bought your story."

Maxim, now clean and sitting at his weapons control station, adds, "Looks like they pushed almost everyone out already." Inside the ring wall of the kilometer-plus diameter spaceport, the duracrete landing area is almost completely empty of ships.

"Damnit," Wil says, eyeing the main display and the largely empty spaceport on it.

Wil looks at Gabe and Bennie. "Anything?"

"Bad news," Bennie says.

"No," Wil says.

"Sorry, Wil," Bennie says, the sadness written across his green face. "According to the traffic management system, the shuttle left orbit almost ten microtocks ago. It's currently burning hard to escape the gravity well."

"Can we—"

Bennie shakes his head. "I'm sorry."

"Fuck that." Wil pushes the atmospheric thrusters to full power. Taken by surprise, everyone is pushed into their seat backs. Over Bennie's screaming, Zephyr says, "They're too far ahead. You're just causing problems down below and making sure we're never welcome here." The *Ghost* is now roaring over the city, causing alarms to go off in the streets below. Zephyr's console comes alive with complaints from space control.

"Fuck this place," Wil grates.

"Wil..." Zephyr says, softer.

Easing the thrust control lever back toward safer levels, Wil slams his other fist on the arm of his chair. "Did they log a flight plan?"

Gabe puts a hand on Bennie's shoulder. "Yes, but it is suspect.

According to the traffic management system, the shuttle is bound for Malkor."

"They have to be going to Tyr," Maxim says. "This Margo woman was able to best Cynthia in hand-to-hand combat. She mentioned that conclave thing. This has to be related to the assassin orphanage, or whatever, that she grew up in."

Wil nods. "Yeah, probably." He adjusts their course, pushing a bit more power to the atmospheric engines now that they've reached a safer altitude. The deck tilts as the nimble ship burns for orbit.

The *Ghost* reaches orbit. Her atmospheric engines cut out as the sub-light engines power up. Somewhere too far ahead to reach, a shuttle is preparing to jump to FTL.

Bennie and Zephyr both leave the bridge to take showers. Wil is sitting numbly at his station, the *Ghost* burning away from the planet and its gravity shadow. Gabe excuses himself to check on engineering.

The only sounds on the bridge are the various beeps and chirps that come from the audio file Wil likes to have play on repeat whenever the bridge is manned. It irritates Zephyr to no end, but she has decided she has other battles to fight.

Maxim clears his throat. "You know we'll get her back, right?"

Wil doesn't respond for a beat, then turns. "What?"

"Cynthia. We'll get her back," Maxim repeats.

Wil nods. "Yeah."

Maxim gets up and walks to the center of the roughly oval-shaped bridge, putting a hand on his friend's shoulder. "I mean it. Don't get lost in your head. We'll get her back."

Wil shakes his head, turning to look up at his friend. "Yeah, I know. It's just..."

Maxim nods. "I understand." He squeezes Wil's shoulder. "She's tough. She's been through a lot and this will be just another story we can all laugh about over drinks later." He takes a deep breath. "You stink."

That takes Wil by surprise. He blinks twice. "What?"

"You smell like, well, the inside of the trash hauler. Go shower." He looks at Wil's console. "We've got half a tock before we can jump to FTL."

STEPPING out of the small refresher, Wil looks around the quarters he shares with Cynthia. It looks exactly like it did when they arrived on Nom Clamma. Cynthia's nightshirt is in a crumpled heap near her pillow. He pads over to her side of the bed, picking up the garment and raising it to his nose. It smells like her. He closes his eyes.

The ceiling speaker beeps. "Wil, we're almost to FTL distance." It is Zephyr. Everyone is back on the bridge.

Wil looks up. How long was he sitting there? "Be right there." He moves to the small dresser affixed to the bulkhead, fishing out clean clothes. He gets dressed, throwing his dirty street clothes into the small clothing refresher.

He takes his time moving through the ship. The level below the crew berths and brig is quiet. The lounge area is empty. Gabe is somewhere aft in the engineering spaces. Wil looks around the area: the overstuffed sofa and chair in front of the large bulkhead-mounted display, the triangle-shaped dining table in the kitchenette area.

The hatch to the bridge, as usual, is closed. Opening it, he looks down the long corridor to the hatch at the very end. One of the lighting elements flickers. "Huh," he says, looking at it.

The bridge hatch opens, and Wil walks in. Zephyr looks up. "We can jump to FTL at any time."

Wil nods. He drops into his command chair. "Course plotted," he says after double checking the navigation screen. He's about to push the power lever for the FTL engines all the way forward when Zephyr shouts, "Incoming!"

CHAPTER FOURTEEN

SNEAK ATTACK

"These are fancy," Cynthia says, holding up both hands, turning them palms out, then palms in. The gray gloves that go just past her wrists, ending in a thick bracelet with blinking lights, are snug.

"A little something the tech team worked up." Margo smiles. "Not only do they keep your claws in," she holds up her wristcomm, showing an icon on the screen, "they can lock your hands together in the blink of an eye." Smirking, she says, "Cuffs that the public never notices." Nodding to the plates before them, she asks, "Enjoying?"

Cynthia nods. "Yes. I haven't had Lolop in a long time." She eyes the other woman's wristcomm. "What's that other icon? You did something before we left orbit." On Margo's wristcomm, next to the icon for the cuff gloves on Cynthia's hands, is another icon, blinking red.

Margo looks at her wristcomm, then up to Cynthia. "Oh, that. I blew up your ship." She takes a bite of her meal, chewing slowly.

Cynthia's mouth hangs open a moment. "What?"

"When I planted the tracker on your gravsled, I also planted a small explosive on the reactor." She takes another bite. "Can't be too safe."

"You're lying." Cynthia places both hands flat on the table, a low growl building in her throat.

"What possible reason would I have for lying? They mean nothing to me or the organization. You're never going to see them again, might as well erase anyone that knew you." Tilting her head, she adds, "You know the procedure. Don't leave witnesses." She nods to Cynthia's plate. "Don't let it get cold." She grins.

THE *GHOST* LURCHES as something above Wil overloads raining sparks. He pushes the flight controls forward, putting the *Ghost* into a corkscrew dive. The main display crackles with static. The hull groans.

"What the—who the hell?" Wil shouts, waving smoke away.

"Weapons hot," Maxim calmly says. "Two targets. Modified light freighter and a gunboat of some type."

"They came out from behind the smaller moon," Zephyr says.

The ship rattles again. The sound of the ball turret mounted behind the bridge echoes, tracking one of the attackers as it passes overhead.

Wil turns slightly. "Like what? Just hanging out, out here? Pirates?"

Zephyr shakes her head. "They came right at us, like they were waiting." On her screen she can see three other vessels that were on outbound trajectories with the *Ghost* scrambling clear of the battle. The *Ghost* is obviously the target.

"Where the hell are those PKs?" Wil says.

"Scanning..." Zephyr consults her screens. "Looks like the PR tour wrapped up. No sign of them."

The ship shudders. Wil pushes the controls over, putting the *Ghost* into a spin.

"They're good," Maxim says. He's hunched over his console, trying to his best to lock onto the two attacking craft.

Wil pulls the sub-light throttle control all the way back toward him, cutting their forward thrust, letting their momentum carry them. The larger of the two attacking vessels flies by overhead. Green energy bolts from the ball turret and nacelle-mounted disrupters lance out, tracking the ship. Its shields light up with each impact.

Maxim turns, smiling. "That helped. Thanks."

Before Wil can answer, the lights flicker. Something under his command console sparks. He pushes the throttle back to full power.

Down in engineering, Gabe is moving between two consoles, adjusting power flow. On the large master status display, the starboard engine nacelle is blinking orange. He turns, grabbing a tool case near the door, and heads into the ship.

The access panel to the ship's nacelles is in the cargo hold. It takes him less than a minute to descend the stairs and cross the mostly empty hold. From the staircase he can see smoke wafting up through the seams in the access hatch. The lights blink as the deck shudders.

Inside the narrow service corridor, several power junctions are glowing white hot, nearing overload, and potentially, meltdown.

Over the years, Gabe has gotten used to keeping the *Ghost* in the fight, as it were. Spare parts are in bins bolted to the deck of the service corridors where they will be needed. This has the added benefit of keeping spare parts out of engineering.

He sets to work, replacing power mux interlinks and about to melt power couplers.

CHASING

"I'M LOSING power in the starboard disruptor," Maxim reports, several sections of his console blinking.

At the same time, a pair of missiles streaks up from the bottom of the main display, racing toward the larger of the two attackers to explode against its shields. The vessel onscreen rocks, the protective bubble of energy flickering wildly.

"These assholes are tough," Wil says, watching the ship on the screen shrug off the missile attack.

Zephyr says, "Nom Clamma Space Control, unsurprisingly, isn't that interested in sending aid. The last freighter that was in the area just jumped to FTL. It's just us."

Bennie looks up from his console. "I feel like it's worth pointing out that if we're dead, we can't save Cynthia." Wil glares at him until he turns back around. "Just sayin'."

"We gotta get clear of these guys. Zee, find me a destination, somewhere close by that we can get our bearings."

The ship rattles again. Something in the neck of the ship shrieks loudly enough to be heard through the sealed bridge hatch. Zephyr looks up from her station, then returns her attention to the sensors. The two ships, while neither would pose a threat separately, are doing an exceptional job of outflying Wil and, in many cases, outshooting Maxim. Neither should be happening.

"Something is weird," Wil says to no one in particular.

"We're getting our asses kicked, but that's fairly normal," Bennie says, then yelps as the ship takes a hit that causes one of his monitors to break from its mounting and fall to the deck, showering him first in sparks, then in broken electronic components.

Wil curses and works the flight controls, forcing the ship into another twisting maneuver to buy him a few seconds of no incoming fire.

"Come to 112 by 40," Zephyr orders.

Wil doesn't hesitate bringing the *Ghost* around on the indicated heading.

"You have a clear FTL window. Punch it!" she says.

Again, Wil doesn't hesitate, pushing the FTL control lever forward. On the main display, the stars, normally pinpricks of light, stretch into rainbow-colored lines. He exhales loudly. "Shit." He looks around the small bridge. "What the hell was that?"

Maxim puts the weapons systems into standby and turns his chair. "Those weren't random raiders or pirates."

Zephyr says, "This course isn't plotted out more than a light year." She nods to the FTL control on Wil's station. He tips his head, then pulls back the slider, returning them to non-FTL speeds.

"Any thoughts?" Wil asks.

Bennie says, "Maybe that drennog Hunflim called 'em in?"

Zephyr shrugs. "Possible, but last time I saw a news bit, he was neck deep in explaining himself to the authorities."

Wil leans back in his chair, looking at the ceiling. "Yeah, I can't imagine him using his one call to call in a hit team. Plus, how could they get there so quickly? Or know when we'd be leaving?"

"One call?" Maxim asks.

Wil looks at him. "You know, you get arrested and you get one call."

The big Palorian shakes his head. "Not a thing. You've been arrested before. How do you not know that?"

"Whatever. Can't be Hunflim." He looks to the ceiling. "Gabe?"

Before the droid can answer, Zephyr shouts, "Grolack! They're here!"

"Damnit!" Wil hisses, pushing the sub-light throttle forward. On the small tactical monitor next to the main display, two red dots are bearing down on the *Ghost*'s blue dot.

"How—" Maxim starts but is interrupted by missile impacts against the aft shields.

Wil lets the smaller, faster attacker overtake them. Maxim rakes it with disruptor fire from the small ball turret. Pushing the sub-light engines back to full power, he pulls the *Ghost* in behind the other ship. "Max."

"On it." Two missiles lance out of the *Ghost*'s launchers. One strikes the other ship, rippling its shields and knocking it off course.

"Yes!" Bennie shouts.

The larger ship wastes no time opening fire on the *Ghost*. A warning light blinks to life on Wil's console: hull damage, starboard wing.

"Course?" Wil says.

"Working it," Zephyr replies.

"Break starboard!" Maxim shouts.

Wil pushes the controls over. The *Ghost* tilts, maneuvering thrusters and pushing the ship into a tight turn, the nacelles groaning loudly through the hull. A pair of missiles streaks past the ship, one passing far enough away to keep going. The other grazes the hull, exploding.

The explosion tosses the *Ghost* end over end, the gravity generators barely keeping everyone on the deck.

"Wil!" Zephyr shouts.

"Hold on!" he shouts back, fighting the controls. The main display is a swirl of stars. Slowly, the view straightens out, the stars moving less erratically on the screen. "I need a course!"

"Sending to your station," Zephyr answers.

"Going," Wil says through gritted teeth. He pushes the FTL control forward.

TRACKING

Gabe steps into the cargo hold from the access hatch. *I will need more tools*, he thinks, looking over his shoulder. The access corridor he was in now has a pair of matching holes, still glowing around the edges where a bolt of super charged plasma ripped through the wing.

He closes the service hatch and sends an instruction to the ship's computer to re-pressurize the cargo hold.

"Hey, Gabe," the captain sends through ship's comms.

"Yes, Captain."

"Are you okay? I've got a hull breach warning."

"I am fine. What is our situation?"

"Pretty fucked up, pal. Glad you're okay down there. We're FTL again, heading for..." His voice lowers. "Where? Oh. Zee found us a transfer station. In the meantime, can you work with her on scouring the ship? That Margo chick must have put a tracker on the ship as well as the gravsled."

Gabe moves across the cargo hold. "Yes, I am on my way back to engineering. I will work with Zephyr on it."

"Thanks, pal."

Turning to look first at Maxim and Zephyr, then Bennie, Wil says, "Okay, thoughts? We don't have time to play cat and mouse with those two, and God forbid if they have friends to call in."

"Think they'll follow all the way to Tyr?" Bennie asks. He has a cut on his forehead that he's gingerly poking with one finger.

Wil shrugs. "I have to assume so. I mean, they probably know where we're going. The more I think about it, it has to be this Margo chick. She tracked us down to kidnap Cynthia. It stands to reason she'd have some backup on hand to keep us busy."

"Or kill us," Maxim offers. Wil nods.

Zephyr says, "Well, based on the data I could find on the model shuttle that we saw board, we've got at most two, maybe three, days' lead time."

Wil rubs his chin. "That's a plus, at least. If we can get rid of our friends and haul ass for Tyr, I'd prefer if we could get there ahead of her, or at least around the same time. We can't let the trail get cold." Nods all around from the others.

Gabe's voice comes over the ceiling speaker. "I am about to run a resonance scan throughout the ship. Your wristcomms will be offline during the scan, as will, well, most things aboard the ship."

"How long do you need?" Zephyr asks.

"Should we drop out of FTL?" Wil adds.

"Two microtocks should be sufficient, and no, FTL systems will not be impacted. If there is a signal being emitted from inside the ship, this will reveal it," Gabe says.

Wil inhales. "Okay, do it."

"Acknowledged."

Every wristcomm on the bridge beeps, flashing a NO SIGNAL message. Zephyr's console, currently running comms in Cynthia's absence, beeps, as well.

Two minutes later, Gabe says, "There is indeed a signal coming from inside the ship."

"Can you isolate?" Maxim asks.

"I am endeavoring to do so now. Zephyr, I am sending commands to your console that I cannot execute directly."

She turns and looks down. "I see them. One millitock."

"Thank you. Please meet me in the lounge in five microtocks."

Gabe places a device no bigger than his hand on the dining table. "I found this wedged between the secondary power flow regulator and a bulkhead."

Wil reaches for the device but stops short when Bennie smacks his hand and picks up the device. He glares but then says, "Any idea whose it is, or how it works?"

"No to the first, but it is a safe assumption to say the same woman that planted the tracker on the gravsled planted this. The answer to your second question reinforces the first. This device," Gabe points to the unit in Bennie's hands, "is transmitting on the same channel as the gravsled device."

Bennie looks up. "Still is, too." He holds the device up. A single green light is blinking.

"I thought it prudent to keep the device active until we decided what to do with it," Gabe replies.

Maxim nods. "Good call. Destroying it would tell them we found it. This way, we can dictate the next engagement."

"You didn't detect it, using the same..." Zephyr points to Gabe's eyes, "...thing you did at the hotel?"

Gabe shrugs. "I apologize. I did not anticipate another tracker, so did not include that scanning range in my standard routines." Inclining his head, he adds, "I have rectified that oversight."

Zephyr puts a hand on his shoulder.

Bennie puts the tracker back down on the table. "I'm hungry."

Wil squints. "I'm beginning to think you might be a sociopath."

Bennie shrugs. "We can't strategize while we eat? I can multi-task." He taps the side of his head, where several cerebral implants are located—old tech from when he made his living being one of the best code slicers around. Turning to Zephyr, "We're, what? Another six tocks from that trade station?" She nods.

"See, plenty of time." Bennie grins.

Wil gives up, moving to the refrigeration unit. "Fine." He turns. "Pizza?" Everyone nods, so he sets about getting everything out and prepping the counter. As he works, he says, "Okay, so we're six hours from the trade station. We don't have time for a drawn-out cat-and-mouse game."

"Agree," Maxim says.

Wil continues, "Okay, so we can't just destroy that thing. They have to know where we are going, long term. We have to lead the baddies away, buy us a few days' head start, at least." He looks over his shoulder. The four crew members are staring at him. "So, uh... that's all I got."

"A recap of the obvious? Way to contribute, boss," Bennie says. He ducks a swipe from Zephyr and sticks out his tongue.

Maxim says, "We plant it on another ship."

Zephyr nods. "How, though? They're likely only a few micro-tocks behind us. When we drop out of FTL, they'll be on us in no time."

Wil finishes sprinkling the closest thing to pepperoni he's found in the GC on the pizza and slides it into the cooking unit. "Can we rig it to something? Toss it out of the airlock or fire it from the missile launcher?"

Gabe shakes his head. "The risks of missing would be high, even if I were the one throwing or otherwise launching the device. I will go EVA when we arrive."

Wil grabs bottles of grum from the refrigeration unit and sits down. "Too dangerous." He passes the bottles around. When he gets to Bennie, he sticks his tongue out and points to the chiller. "Get your own. Be nicer next time."

Bennie scowls, hopping down from his seat. Removing his own bottle from the chiller, he says, "It makes sense. Gabe's thrusters can get him around out there, and he can ramp up his jammers to keep the bad guys from detecting him."

Maxim rubs his chin. "Probably the only way this works. If we just fire the thing off, stuck to a missile, they'll know. Too fast, not enough mass, no ship silhouette to follow."

While they wait for the pizza to cook, a plan comes together. Just under six hours later, everyone but Gabe is back on the bridge, watching the rainbow lines streak past on the main display.

"Ready, big guy?" Wil asks, looking up.

"I am ready," Gabe replies from the port airlock. He has the tracker grasped in one hand; the other is resting on the airlock controls.

Wil turns to Zephyr, who nods. He pulls the FTL control slider back. The rainbow lines shrink back to pinpricks of light. Directly ahead, a small mushroom-shaped space station is growing in size.

"Scanning," Zephyr reports.

"Airlock open," Gabe reports.

"Zee..." Wil says.

"Shut up." She doesn't look up from her console. "There! Sending data." She looks up, smiling.

"Received," Gabe says.

The main display updates with a larger tactical view. The *Ghost* is a blue icon near the bottom, the trade station a dark green near the top, and the dozens of ships nearby are yellow dots of various sizes. Gabe, a lighter shade of blue, is moving toward one of the yellow dots when his icon vanishes.

"He's activated his jamming systems," Zephyr reports.

The moment they drop from FTL, Zephyr sets about finding a ship that is on an outbound vector, near enough for Gabe to make it to the ship before it jumps to FTL. The ship she targets is a medium-sized freighter, its ID beacon broadcasting a Trollack flag.

Wil is drumming his fingers on the arms of his chair. The *Ghost* is almost to the trade station, cleared to dock on the far side of the mid-sized station. The yellow icon representing their target disappears. Leaning forward, he says, "Anything?" to no one in particular.

"Nothing yet," Zephyr replies.

Too many heartbeats later, Gabe's voice comes from the ceiling speakers. "Mission accomplished."

CHAPTER FIFTEEN

OLD FRIENDS

"So, are you gonna tell me what this is all about?" Cynthia asks.

For the last day, the two women have sat at opposite ends of the shuttle. Cynthia slept in fits and starts. Her curiosity has finally gotten the better of her.

Margo looks up from the PADD she's reading something on. "I thought it was clear. You're going before the conclave."

"The Collective died cycles ago." Cynthia sits up in the seat she's been lying across.

"Rumors of the Collective's demise are...exaggerated," the other woman purrs. She waves a hand. "The Collective was forced to move...underground. For a while."

"Underground?" Cynthia repeats.

Margo nods. "Smaller, more selective in our clientele, but no less lethal. Or far reaching." She stands. "You didn't think you could escape our justice forever, did you? You know as well as I do that you don't just walk away." She smirks. "You thought you were special? Careful? That your crime bosses would protect you?" She runs a hand through her hair. "Really, the Collective was so bad, yet those two criminals were better?"

Cynthia shakes her head. "I finished the job I was given. Took nothing with me when I left. Owe nothing to anyone. I told no one, not even my subsequent employers, about the Collective." She scowls. "And no, neither of them was better, but they put a roof over my head and a place to sleep that didn't require me to sleep with one eye open."

The other woman shakes her head. "Ironic, that last bit." She points at Cynthia. "However, that's not how it works. You know that."

Cynthia shrugs. "I won't go back into the Collective. I'll die first."

"On that, we agree." Margo grins. "I'm sure the conclave will find you guilty and, well, we know the sentence." She grabs the PADD. "I'm going to the bathroom. Behave yourself." She moves past Cynthia to the refresher in the back of the shuttle.

Cynthia waits for the door to slide closed. She's already looked the shuttle cabin up and down several times but can't resist another go. As expected, Margo has made sure there isn't a stray bolt or piece of silverware anywhere in the passenger compartment.

"Dren," she hisses, standing up from inspecting the underside of the seat Margo just vacated. She hears the other woman finish up in the refresher and moves back to drop into her seat.

THERAPY

THE CREW DOESN'T HAVE to wait long. Their pursuers drop from FTL before Gabe is back aboard the ship.

"They're here," Zephyr whispers as if they might hear her. The *Ghost* docked with the trade station moments ago and activated its stealth systems to the confusion of the station space control operator.

Everyone turns to the main display out of habit. With the trade station blocking their view and the sensors set to passive, there isn't much to see. Bennie hacked the station's sensor array so they can at least see arrival and departure data. The screen shows a list of nearby vessels, with two new additions. Next to the word "UNKNOWN" are descriptions matching their two friends and range data. The range data decreases then stops, both vessels holding position several thousand kilometers from the station.

"Nothing suspicious about that," Maxim quips.

After a few minutes, the two entries marked "UNKNOWN" vanish from the list of nearby ships.

"Yes!" Bennie punches a fist into the air.

Wil smiles. "Okay, good." He turns to Zephyr. "As soon as Gabe gets aboard, let's undock and get out of here."

She nods.

"I'm worried about Wil," Bennie says, looking over to Maxim and Zephyr, both sitting on the sofa in the crew lounge. The Brailack hacker has the large overstuffed chair all to himself.

"He's worried," Maxim offers.

"And sad," Zephyr says.

Bennie nods. "Sure, I get that, but he's been in his quarters since we left the trade station."

Gabe, standing behind the chair, says, "The Captain is distressed. Seclusion and depression are typical reactions to trauma."

Zephyr says, "You know, it might not be the worst thing if you went to check on him. You two have been at each other's throats for a few weeks now."

Bennie rubs his chin, then nods. "Yeah. He needs a friend." He slides out of the much-too-large chair and heads for the staircase to the crew berths above.

"A friend, or a Bennie," Maxim says. Bennie reaches the hatch to the stairs, makes a rude gesture, then closes the heavy hatch behind him.

Gabe says, "I am not at all certain that Bennie will have the affect you are hoping for, on the Captain's mood."

Zephyr grins. "Oh, I'm sure he won't. But the two of them have been annoying me since before we decided on this little job. Maybe they'll get into it and work out whatever needs working out. Beating on Bennie might make Wil feel better."

Maxim looks at her. "You are getting ruthless."

She turns to the large entertainment screen. "I like things calm. They were messing with that."

Wil looks up when the knock sounds against the hatch to his

quarters. "Not interested," he slurs. An empty whiskey bottle from his stash is lying on the deck next to the bed.

The door slides open. "Too bad." Bennie walks in. He looks around. "Wow, you certainly don't waste time. We left the trade station five tocks ago and you're already grolacked up."

Wil glares. "Get out."

"No can do." The Brailack climbs up onto the foot of Wil's bed and says, "I get it. You're worried about her. We all are." He affects a sympathetic expression. "She's our friend, too."

Wil kicks him off the end of the bed, eliciting an angry squeak.

Climbing back up, Bennie says, "Do that again and I'll cut your foot off." He slips his beam saber hilt off the hook on his belt, resting it in his lap.

Wil stares at him. "What do you want?"

"You, at your best." He wiggles a small green hand. "Okay, actually better than your best, if you can manage it. I mean, I've seen your best, and well…" He raises his beam saber hilt when Wil raises a foot. "Kidding. I know we've been butting heads, but I'm your friend."

Wil sits up. "Dude, what if she's already dead?"

"She isn't."

"You can't know that!" Wil screams, his eyes glistening. His hands are balled into fists in his lap.

Bennie nods. "You're right. But I have to have hope. Cynthia is an ass kicker. She survived to make it into Xarrix's organization and move up the ladder. I can tell you, that ain't easy." Setting his beam saber hilt aside, he adds, "She can't be dead because I don't know what I'd do if she was." He pats Wil's foot, then wrinkles his nose. "Your feet stink."

"You stink."

"I have completed the repairs to the starboard wing," Gabe says.

Wil looks up from the PADD he has been holding tightly for several minutes, doing nothing with. "Anything too serious?"

"No. However, we should replace the shield emitter that covers the dorsal starboard wing sooner rather than later. The power coupling is prone to overheating, which reduces the shield's efficiency."

"Replace starboard shield emitters. Check," Wil says.

Gabe makes a face. He adds, "Since we are discussing ship's systems, the FTL systems are in the red. We could use a few more rest breaks."

Wil shakes his head. "Can't be helped. We have to beat Cynthia to Tyr. Being chased by whoever those two ships belonged to, plus the time you needed for repairs, cost us a lot of time. We'll get back underway now."

Gabe inclines his head. "I understand and will do what I can to ensure we do not explode before reaching Tyr." He turns and heads for the short corridor that leads to engineering.

Wil looks back to his PADD, tapping an icon. The screen goes black, then gray with the word "CONNECTING" in green text in the middle.

A moment later, Maltor Grimalkin's face appears. "Captain Calder. To what do we owe the pleasure?"

"Afraid there's no pleasure in this one." He takes a breath. "Cynthia's been kidnapped."

The other man's face falls. "What? Where? How?" He looks off screen, then turns his attention back to Wil. "What can we do to help?"

"We're en route to Tyr." He looks around. "I can't remember the city, but Gabe is certain it's a city on Tyr."

The screen updates to be split in half, Maltor on one side, Barbara Mress on the other. The older woman says, "What happened? Do you know who kidnapped her? Or why?"

Wil shakes his head. "We know her name is Margo and that she's Tygran. She mentioned taking Cynthia back for a conclave."

Mress inhales slowly. "Yadro."

Wil makes a face. "That X-Men school place? I thought she left that all behind." He cocks his head. "And that the government shut it down."

Maltor inclines his head. "Yadro was shut down. Wasn't it?"

Mress nods slowly. "Yes, as far as we knew." She focuses on Wil. "What do you know about Yadro?"

Wil shrugs. "Not much. Cyn has always been pretty mum on the topic. I know she was raised by them in a special orphanage. They trained the kids to be killers and spies and such. Real Black Widow shit."

Both Tygrans tilt their heads. Mress says, "I don't know what that means." She takes a breath. "The Yadro Collective operated for, well, no one really knows. Their history goes back hundreds of cycles, intertwined with Tygran society. They had orphanages all over the planet, looking for children with promise, and probably more importantly, children that no one would miss. For years they slipped those poor children out of the system and into their training programs."

Maltor adds, "The kids vanished, erased from the government records. They trained in secret, eventually becoming elite assassins and spies, hired out to the upper echelons of Tygran society and government."

"For what?"

"Mostly killing."

Wil looks up from the PADD. "Damn, that's dark."

The two Tygrans nod as one. Mress says, "Agreed. Rooting out the corruption and evil that the Collective wove through our society was a bloody and lengthy business."

"So, if they're gone, then who's this Margo? What's the conclave? Where are they going?"

Maltor looks off camera. "I'll do some research."

Mress smiles. "There's someone I can ask. How far out are you?"

"Another day. We're burning hard. The shuttle she's in isn't as fast. I want to beat them to Tyr. They should be two days behind us, -ish."

Mress nods. "Okay. I'll call you back shortly."

Wil nods. "Thanks." The screen of the device goes blank. He looks up. "You can come out."

Bennie's head pops up over the back of the couch. "Just making sure you're okay."

"Uh huh." Wil smirks and adjusts his position on the couch. "What'd ya think?"

Bennie climbs up onto the sofa. Once he's done getting situated, he says, "We'll get there first, but that might not do much for us if we don't know what we're looking for."

Wil nods. "Hopefully Babs and Maltor will come through for us."

Bennie nods. "I'll tell Maxim to get us back underway."

Wil nods his thanks.

"Dropping to normal space in five, four, three, two, one," Wil says, pulling back the FTL control lever. The star lines on the main display shrink back to pinpricks.

"Nothing on sensors, yet," Zephyr announces.

"We're stealthed," Bennie says.

Wil nods. "We'll have to make ourselves known in a bit, but let's see if our friends from Nom Clamma show up." He adjusts their course, setting a direct line for Tyr Prime, the homeworld of the Tygran people. The system is heavily populated, with no fewer than two other worlds and a dozen or more moons colonized. Freighters and personal craft of all shapes and sizes are busily burning between planets.

A few tense minutes later, Wil says, "Okay, think we're clear." He nods to Bennie. "Shut off the stealth system." Turning to Zee, "Can you try to raise Babs? Hopefully, she'll have something for us."

Zephyr nods and taps a few controls. She turns to Wil. "Got her." She turns to the main display as it blinks from stars and a random freighter to Barbara Mress's head and shoulders. "Captain Calder, everyone. I assume you're in-system."

Wil nods. "Just arrived a bit ago. We wanted to make sure that some friends we made over Nom Clamma weren't going to show up. We're about…" He looks down at his console. "Two hours from Tyr."

Mress nods. "Okay. I've put together what I know, but for now, head for the Dwihl Nora spaceport. I think that'll put you close to where you'll need to be." She leans in. "I can't say too much on this channel. Even with my connections, asking some of the questions I've been asking is dangerous. I will say, my earlier assessment seems to have been at least partly incorrect."

Wil nods. "Great. Okay, we'll head for Nora Roberts and set up a watch. Will look for your data packet."

Mress nods and the screen goes black before returning to normal, stars and assorted nearby ships.

Wil looks at Bennie. "Time to change our identity."

The Brailack hacker nods and taps a few commands into one of his consoles. A moment later, he looks up. "New transponder, ident codes, registry, and name. We're the *Rocinante* now." He looks at Wil. "I don't know what that means."

Wil smiles. "We'll watch one when we get Cyn back." He looks over at Zephyr and nods.

After a minute, Zephyr says, "I've got us cleared through to Dwihl Nora."

Maxim asks, "What'd she mean about being wrong earlier?"

Wil turns. "I called her the other night. Asked about Krakatoa and conclaves. Our initial assumptions were right. Whatever is going on, it's tied to Cyn's past. Mress and Maltor were both under the impression that the group she used to work for was long gone. Dismantled."

"Kalroa," Zephyr corrects.

"But they were wrong," Bennie adds.

"She looked a bit worried," Maxim says.

"If it has her scared, we should be worried," Bennie says, his face showing his concern.

Two hours later, and the *Ghost* is sandwiched between two mid-sized freighters in a parking orbit. Wil drums his fingers on the arm of his chair. Turning to Zephyr, he opens his mouth but stops short when she says, "Still no answer other than *soon*."

"We're burning time we don't have," he growls. He looks at Bennie. "Can you hack into the planetary network from up here? Start digging?"

"Digging for what?"

Wil waves his hands. "I don't know. See if you can find the records for any incoming shuttles from Nom Clamma or that match the shuttle type we gleamed from the security feeds."

"Oh, you mean look for a kormu in a pile of cuttings?" the team's hacker retorts. He sighs and waves a hand. "I'll see what I can find."

Wil pushes up out of his chair. "I'm gonna make some lunch, sandwiches. Takers?"

"I'll take one," Maxim says.

Zephyr raises a hand. "Same, thank you."

"Bennie?" Wil asks.

"Pass. Your sandwiches are always dry. I'll make something later."

Wil shakes his head and leaves the bridge.

When the hatch clanks shut, Maxim turns to look across the small bridge. "What the grolack is wrong with you?"

Bennie turns. "What? His sandwiches are as dry as a Fury back alley."

Zephyr tuts. "I know this might not make sense to you, but he's hurting."

Bennie waves her off. "I know that. You think I'm blind?"

"Insensitive," Zephyr says.

"No, just a drennog," Maxim adds.

Bennie makes a croaking sound. "Has it occurred to you that treating him like a broken toy will only make things worse? I know you met him at the end of his last bout of whatever it is that messes with Earth people's minds. I met him before that. He was a vicious drunk when he was coherent enough to function. He was a mopey, sad sack, otherwise, shuffling from one job to the next for Xarrix.

Sometimes I think he took jobs that might kill him, just because. Treating him like a widower is just going to drive him down that path that much faster."

Maxim turns to look behind him to Zephyr's station. "Damn."

She nods. "Right?"

CHAPTER SIXTEEN

WELCOME (BACK TO) TYR

The *Ghost* settles on her landing gear with a creak followed by the hiss of venting gasses from the atmospheric engines. The Dwihl Nora spaceport is nicer than Wil and the team expect. Kalroa is about two hundred plorith or so from Lirole. A city, but not a major metropolis. Still, much nicer than anything Fury offers.

Wil puts the ship into standby, flipping a few switches. The drone of the reactor fades as it settles into standby mode. He rubs his palms across his knees. "Okay. Let's go figure out our next steps."

The lounge is messier than normal. Wil's funk has resulted in some of his more slovenly habits reasserting themselves, which feed Bennie's. Maxim brushes a food wrapper off the couch and drops into the large plushy seat. "Okay," he says.

Wil nods. "Okay." He points to the large entertainment screen on the bulkhead. "I looked through Mress's data. It's on the computer. Take a look when you can, copy it to your wristcomms, too. She confirmed that we're likely in the right place." He takes a sip of his water. "If there are any lingering Yadro folks, and she's surer now than she was before that there are, they're here in Kalroa."

Bennie raises a hand from the large chair to the side. "I found your kormu. There are three shuttles scheduled to land at Dwihl Rel in the next day."

"Rel?" Wil asks.

Zephyr beats Bennie to it. "Smaller spaceport outside the metropolitan core."

"Suburbs. Cool," Wil says.

Bennie is frowning. "I can continue?" Wil makes a *go on* gesture. "That's really about the extent of the good news. Getting the schedules was easy. Getting deeper proved to be a bit troublesome. I can probably push through, but it'll likely throw up some flags. Despite being a smaller port, the space control system is planetary." He shrugs. "Given what Miss Mress told us, that's probably a bad idea. For sure, this Yadro group will be watching. I wasn't sure if we wanted to tip them off."

Wil nods. "Yeah, leave it be. We'll set up patrols or something." He turns to Gabe—as ever, standing near the side of the room. "Pal, I'd like you to lead that effort."

The droid nods. "Of course, Captain."

Maxim says, "We should find a place to set up base camp. Someplace that isn't the *Ghost*." He runs a hand over his face. "Does this port have a deep storage?"

Wil tilts his head. Bennie claps once. "That's a good idea. Margo, and likely her allies, will recognize the *Ghost* if it's just sitting out on the duracrete."

Wil leans back. "Damnit. Good call." He looks at Gabe, the question on his face.

Gabe remains motionless a moment, then says, "Yes. This spaceport has a deep storage facility. I have scheduled the *Ghost* for transfer."

Zephyr says, "Okay, that means we have to take everything we'll need with us." She gets to her feet. "We left the gravsleds on Nom Clamma, so I'll book a van."

Maxim says, "Hiding the *Ghost* and setting up shop out of the way could be our biggest asset for now. If they think we're dead, or at least busy with those two ships from Nom Clamma..." He lets the notion hang there a moment, then turns to Zephyr. "Do we know where that ship Gabe attached the tracker to was going?"

Bennie smiles. "I do, yeah. Harrith."

The big Palorian smiles. "That'll keep those two busy." Everyone nods.

LESS THAN AN HOUR LATER, a troop of squat droids on heavy treads is trundling up to the *Ghost*. The crew is standing off to the side of the landing pad, dozens of crates piled next to them.

Gabe moves toward the assemblage of droids. Each droid is almost as tall as him and three or four meters wide. He stands motionless before the ship movers, who remain equally motionless and silent.

"That's so weird," Maxim says, watching the conversation.

Gabe returns to the team. "I have asked Botor and his team to position the *Ghost* near the entrance to the deep storage, in case we need to depart in a hurry." Behind him, the ship movers are spreading out underneath the *Ghost*. Two back up to the landing gear, their bodies shifting to wrap around the small warship's feet. A third moves under the forward section. A telescoping section rises from its body, magnetically latching onto the ship above.

The two droids at the landing gear groan as they move the ship upward a centimeter at a time. The forward droid is matching their progress to keep the ship level. The *Ghost* creaks as she rises, first a few centimeters, then a half meter off the ground. The three droids beep frenetically at each other before rotating in unison to point the Ankarran Raptor toward the spaceport ring wall and massive cargo and ship elevator to the lower levels of the complex and the long-term vessel storage.

"Neat," Wil whispers. Maxim shakes his head.

I HATE THE SUBURBS

During the ride from Dwihl Nora Spaceport out into the bedroom community of Gloin on the outskirts of Kalroa and near the smaller Dwihl Rel Spaceport, Zephyr is able to find them a home only a plorith from the port. A variable length rental, fully furnished with a sizable hover vehicle garage.

"Cool, space Airbnb," Wil says, looking over the home's pictures that his second-in-command shares with the team. "Book it."

The hover van makes good time, depositing them outside their home for the next few days. Sitting in a comfortable-looking chair on the front porch is Barbara Mress. She stands to great the team as they reach the door. "I thought it safer to meet you here." She nods to Zephyr. "Thank you for sending along your destination." The other woman smiles.

Mress continues, "After making my initial inquiries, security noticed some new faces loitering near the office."

"Danger?" Maxim asks.

The feline featured woman tilts her head, her tail swishing nervously behind her. "Nothing my people can't handle, at least for now. If you're successful, it won't matter."

"No pressure," Wil mumbles.

Bennie pushes open the door. Apparently, the designers of this community decided to keep things rustic with doors on hinges.

Maxim ushers everyone inside. "We should move this indoors." He taps Gabe's arm. "Can you do a sweep?"

The droid inclines his head, his optic sensors shifting to light blue.

As everyone but Wil settles into the sitting room, Gabe emerges from the hallway leading to the bedrooms. "I detect no listening devices or active networks beyond the home's built-in network and internex connection."

Bennie looks up from his wristcomm. He's sitting on the floor next to a display table, a wall panel open, exposing wires of various colors. "I've got control of the home network and am running all traffic through one of my custom firewalls." He places a small device no bigger than his wristcomm on the floor; wires are trailing out of it to splices connected to the wiring inside the wall alcove. Lights on the front of the device are flickering.

Wil opens the fridge to find it empty. "First order of business: groceries."

Maxim says, "Second is our timeline." Wil nods his agreement and moves to the lounge space.

Zephyr looks around. "Okay. We've got three potential targets, all landing here at Dwihl Rel. We're going to have to set up overwatch during each of the arrival windows, which begin in," she consults her wristcomm, "ten tocks. First thing tomorrow morning."

"Not much time," Mress observes. Nods all around. She produces a PADD from her stylish handbag—a handbag Wil looks at twice, realizing it probably cost as much as the *Ghost*. She places the device on her lap and begins opening files, sorting timetables and itineraries. "The first shuttle, the *Gitblim Fau*," she looks up, "a Zebulon Luxury Shuttles vessel, is first. It's the right model, but according to the public record, it's outfitted for mass transit. I'm thinking that it's out."

Maxim nods. "She's definitely using a private charter."

Zephyr nods her agreement. "We should put someone on the spaceport all the same, just in case."

Wil says, "One hundred percent." He looks at Barbara. "*Giblets Fair* comes in when?"

"Ten tocks."

He nods. "Cool. The next?"

She consults her PADD. "The *Ptoldan*. Comes in six tocks later. Private charter vessel. Right make and model, max passenger complement of ten."

"Solid candidate for sure," Bennie says. "Any idea who rented it, or a passenger list?"

Mress shakes her head. "Private booking." She looks at her PADD again. "Last up is the Judfuof Lines' *Cawdral*, similar in size and passenger space to the *Ptoldan*. Technically, a different space frame, but only because Judfuof bought the design. Like the *Ptoldan,* the manifest is marked private charter."

Wil stands. "Okay, we've got our targets and timetable. We need groceries and equipment."

"A little more intel wouldn't hurt," Maxim says.

"Maybe a squad or two of local security?" Bennie adds.

Mress shakes her head. "I'm afraid I'm all you've got. If the Yadro Collective is back, even if it's a ghost of its former self, it'll be deeply connected." She puts the PADD back in her handbag. "Outside Maltor, I can't trust that they don't have someone in Tralgot."

ALMOST THERE

"We're due to land in about twelve tocks," Margo says to the blurry silhouette on the screen mounted to the bulkhead in front of her seat.

"Good. Be careful. Her friends have been making inquiries."

Margo looks over her shoulder, then back. She taps a control under the display. A privacy field energizes behind her, cutting off from the rear compartment, and Cynthia. "Who? My team has surely killed her friends by now. They were more than a match for them, even in that broken down old clunker of a pocket warship. Add in the element of surprise, and they're dead."

"They must have placed a call or two before your team got to them. Barbara Mress of Tralgot started snooping around."

Margo runs a hand through her hair, her whiskers twitching as she does. "Will she be a problem?"

"That's still to be determined, but she seems to have exhausted her search. We're monitoring her. We're not quite ready to take out such a high-profile target. Yet."

Margo nods. "We will be, soon."

The silhouette dips its head. "Indeed."

Margo reaches forward, deactivating the privacy screen. "And the conclave?" She looks back at Cynthia, smirking.

"It will be ready."

"Justice will be served. Finally. I'll check in when we land."

"Acknowledged." The screen goes black.

From her seat in the rear, Cynthia says, "Lotta theater, that."

Margo swivels the chair around to face Cynthia. "I didn't see any reason you couldn't hear that. You'll face the justice of the Collective soon enough, and anything you know, you'll take to the grave."

"Just tell me why? Why bring the Yadro Collective back? Our own people fought against us to uncover and dismantle Yadro's roots." Cynthia spreads her hands. "Why bring back something so dark and evil?"

"Evil?" Margo scoffs. "The Yadro Collective gave me, and you, a purpose. It sheltered us, taught us."

"To be killers," Cynthia retorts.

"More than that."

"To whom? We were contract killers, assassins, and smugglers." Cynthia gets to her feet. "We killed whomever we were told: government officials, business people, whomever the highest bidder said to. There's nothing noble in that."

Margo smirks. "I see why you failed. Why you fled and disgraced yourself." Cynthia leaps at her. Margo barely ducks in time to avoid Cynthia's outstretched hands, but doesn't dodge the swift kick that follows the moment Cynthia touches the ground. She spins, launching a kick of her own that catches Cynthia in the midsection, forcing the air from her opponent's lungs.

Before Cynthia can recover, her hands snap together at the wrists. Margo wags a finger, tsk'ing. "Strike a nerve?" She points to the seat in the aisle opposite the one she had been in earlier. "Sit."

Cynthia bares her teeth. "I left Yadro because I valued my honor." She sits down.

Margo drops back into the seat she's been in. "We'll see what the Conclave thinks about that." She nods to the seat Cynthia vacated. "Sit."

Cynthia turns and returns to her seat with a harrumph. While

Margo busies herself with something, Cynthia thinks back to her time in the Yadro Collective.

The recruiter came to the orphanage one morning. The headmistress had the children line up in the play yard. Each child was scanned, given a physical exam, and then told to perform various tasks. Cynthia and four other children were selected, told that they were special and would be given a special education in a school for gifted children. The recruiter paid the headmistress for her silence and the van left the orphanage.

The training was strenuous. Two of the children from her original orphanage were injured early on and never seen again. The overseers said they'd been returned to the orphanage, but no one believed them. Cynthia and the other children trained every day. Even on holidays, they trained half the day.

For ten cycles, the children of Yadro Facility 43 trained. Each year, younglings were brought in as older students graduated. As the children neared graduation, they shadowed more experienced operatives until they could go out on their own.

Cynthia's first solo mission was when she was sixteen; a kill order had been issued for a socialite that had used her platform to speak out about certain parts of the government. Cynthia infiltrated a party at a high rise in Lirole. She flirted all night, working her way closer and closer to the young celebutante, until finally, in the early morning hours the next day, they were alone. Her target never knew what was coming and died happy.

EYES OPEN

"I've got the city's security feeds up," Bennie says, walking into the kitchen of the rental house. Maxim and Zephyr have gone shopping before heading to the spaceport to take the first watch.

Wil is sitting at the small dining table, a PADD propped up against a container of noodles. "Hold on, James." He looks up. "What?"

Bennie closes the food chiller, a food tube with a yogurtlike snack inside clutched in one tiny hand. "I said I finally got access to the city's security feeds. Took some of Gabe's infiltration code juju to break through. Pretty spotty coverage, but better than nothing."

Wil nods. "Cool, thanks. Now scram."

Bennie makes a rude gesture on his way out behind Wil.

James Hawthorne laughs on the small screen. "Hi, Bennie. Still a dick, huh?"

Wil turns his attention back to the PADD. "Don't engage him."

James laughs again. "Sorry. So, nothing new?"

"Nope. Babs gave us what she had and will help if we need more, but right now we're just waiting. We're pretty sure we beat her here, so now we just gotta get eyes on her."

"She'll be fine. You know that, right?" James' brown eyes twinkle in the harsh fluorescents in his office. "From everything you've told me, and having met her, it's gonna take a lot to take her out."

Wil sighs. "I know, but still. I can't help but think about all the worst case scenarios."

James smiles. "Perfectly natural. If it helps take your mind off things, the Mars colony had its first baby."

Wil's eyes go wide. "What? Really? Damn, those folks started the moment they landed?"

James leans back, affording Wil a view of the large window behind his friend and the newly reconstructed space command facility visible through it. "Technically, they got started aboard the *Calder* while we were en route."

Wil chuckles. "Nice. I still don't understand the point of a colony on Mars. You visited Epsilon Eridani. You're collecting drone data now, from what? A dozen nearby stars? I never looked at maps of that area, but surely there's a planet with an atmosphere you could colonize."

"Yeah, there are, and those plans are in the works, but with the increased scrutiny our system is getting now that the word is out that we're not protected, the Governing Council decided that having a few bases and early warning, and defense facilities throughout the system, wouldn't be a bad idea. Those pirates that buzzed us a year back, they weren't the last."

Wil frowns. "Shit. I knew it. Anything serious?"

James waves him off, then runs a hand over his hairless scalp. Once his dark black hair started to go gray, he shaved it all off and kept it off. "Not as yet. We've been making pretty good strides with the archive now that more countries are onboard with the global government." He beams. "We've provided power to third world countries. There isn't a person on Earth that lacks heat, cooling, lights. I never woulda thought I'd live to see a united Earth, but shit, man, it's looking promising."

"What about those Earth First creeps?"

"Still there, still loud and annoying, but their base has lost a lot of its strength."

"Good. I won't lie, I didn't know how this whole get-together-or-else thing was gonna work out."

"It was only the human race at stake. What could go wrong?"

Wil shrugs. "Right?" He smiles. From the other room, something makes a screeching, keening noise. Wil leaps to his feet, the chair clattering to the floor behind him. He looks at the PADD. "I better go."

"Take care and kick some ass." The screen goes black.

From outside the kitchen, Bennie shouts, "Wil, get out here!"

Rushing into the living room, he sees Bennie standing on the sofa, a large something standing on the short table in front of him, purple fur bristling, yellowed fangs bared. It opens its mouth and makes the same noise Wil heard a minute ago.

"The hell is that?" Wil shouts, drawing the creature's three pale blue eyes toward him. He pulls back into the kitchen. "Shit." He leans around the door frame to see Bennie flapping his arms to keep the angry creature at bay.

"You have a damn laser sword!" Wil shouts.

"Oh, yeah!" Bennie stops waving his arms and unclips his beam saber. The snap hiss of its activation is drowned out by the growling of the angry purple space raccoon thing.

"What is it?" Wil asks from the kitchen.

"I don't know!" Bennie hisses, waving his beam saber to keep the thing at bay. "It just walked in!"

"You left the door open?" Wil leans out and back in again.

"We're in the grolacking suburbs! How would I know wild animals just wander around?" He's about to say more when the purple-furred creature leaps. Bennie screams and swipes his beam saber in a wide arc.

Wil leans out of the kitchen just in time to see two halves of a purple space raccoon fall on a still screaming Bennie. He sighs. Ichor splashes from both halves as they land.

Gabe enters from the garage. "I am almost done setting up the monitoring equipment." He looks around. "What is going on?" Spotting the carnage on the floor, he holds up a hand. "Never mind." He returns to the garage.

CHAPTER SEVENTEEN

CONTACT

THE SHUTTLE JOLTS once as it sets down. Margo stands. "Welcome home." Cynthia scowls. Margo motions her up. "You have two choices. Play nice and walk off this shuttle and out to our ride." She raises the arm with her wristcomm on it. "Or, I stun you and rent a grav-gurney, and you wake up in a cell."

Cynthia spreads her hands. "I'll play nice."

"Good." She taps the intercom button. "Payment in full once my friend and I depart the shuttle."

"Very good," the pilot replies. The side hatch opens, dropping to make a ramp.

"Let's go," Margo says, motioning for Cynthia to exit the shuttle first.

Stepping out of the shuttle, Cynthia looks around. "This isn't Lirole."

Margo shoves her forward. "You're right." She gestures toward the pedestrian entry to the reception hall. "Go."

"So, the Collective is no longer enjoying the finer things in the capital?"

Margo scowls at the back of Cynthia's head. "For now. The Collective chose a less conspicuous place to restart."

The reception hall is moderately crowded; mostly Tygrans coming and going, with random other beings here and there. As Cynthia looks around the large hall, her gaze falls on a Brailack sitting in the room's corner, face buried in a PADD, paying no attention to the room. She coughs. No response.

"What's wrong with you?" Margo asks, shoving Cynthia toward the exit.

"I have to pee."

"Go when we get there."

"Can't wait. If not here, in the car. Your choice." Cynthia angles toward the restrooms. She raises her voice. "It'll just take a minute."

"Fine." Margo shoves her again, this time toward the public refreshers set in the corner of the building.

Bennie finally looks up as the two women draw near. His eyes go wide as he spots Cynthia. He lowers the PADD but stops when she shakes her head once, the movement barely noticeable. He glances past her to her captor. The PADD slides back up, mostly obscuring his face.

When the two Tygran women enter the restroom, he taps his earpiece, sticking out at an odd angle from his lobe-less ears. "She's here."

"What?" Wil says from the rental house.

"I said she's here, you krebnack," he hisses.

The two women emerge from the restroom, Margo complaining, "That was your one and only shot."

Cynthia glances at Bennie, then back to Margo, shrugging. "Shy bladder. Sue me."

Bennie watches them head for the exit. "They're leaving," he whispers.

"Well, follow them, you little twerp," Wil shouts, causing the Brailack to wince.

Bennie stands and makes for the door. Exiting the spaceport, he watches Margo and Cynthia step into a glossy hover limo. The latter looks back in time to spot Bennie and smile. Two other Tygrans, men, are standing on either side of the vehicle's door. Once Margo and Cynthia are inside, the two men join them.

The vehicle powers up its repulsorlifts and glides silently away, merging into traffic. Bennie snaps a scan of the vehicle ID with his wristcomm. "Sending data now."

"Received. Initiating tracking program," Gabe says over the comms.

"Okay. Get back here," Maxim says.

"On my way." Bennie looks up and down the street before heading off for the taxi stand.

Back at the rental house, Wil looks at the displays before Gabe. "So...?"

"I am working on it," the droid replies.

"But—"

Gabe raises a hand. "I am working on it."

The team is in the rental home's garage. Since arriving at the house, nondescript deliveries, courtesy of Barbara Mress, have been arriving nearly nonstop. The garage is now a moderately well set up command center.

Several large displays are arrayed before Gabe, seated at the single chair. His hands are splayed out over the keyboards, data tendrils snaking their way into the keyboard and computer core next to it. He turns his head. "Bennie was not wrong. The city's surveillance network is spotty at best. I am tracking the vehicle, but I am concerned we may lose the track."

Two of the displays come to life, a map of Kalroa spanning them with a pulsing red dot moving along the road.

"Don't lose 'em," Wil growls.

Zephyr puts a hand on Wil's shoulder. "He won't," she whispers.

"I have lost them," Gabe says, turning to look at his friends. He focuses on Wil. "I am sorry, Captain..." Seeing his friend's face, he amends, "Wil." On the large displays behind him, the red dot that represents the hover limo is fading from bright red to pink on the outskirts of an industrial sector. They've been watching as Gabe deftly switched from camera to camera to track the vehicle, hacking into systems quicker than the others could follow in order to make up for the deficiencies of the municipal security system.

Wil shouts a series of expletives as he storms out of the garage-turned-command center. Maxim turns to Zephyr. "See if Barbara has any thoughts." She nods, and he moves to follow Wil.

"I am disappointed that we lost tracking," Gabe says. "That section of the city seems to be a dead zone, as it were, for video monitoring."

Zephyr smiles. "It's not your fault." She pats his shoulder, then looks at her wristcomm, placing a call. A moment later, Barbara Mress is on the small screen. "We lost them in the industrial sector north of the city." She leans forward to look at the display. "Qilton district."

The Tygran executive nods slowly. "We own some facilities up there. I'll be over shortly." The screen goes dark.

In the living room, Wil is sitting on the couch, face in his hands. Maxim drops into place next to him. "We got this. You know that."

Wil looks up, snuffling. Maxim rubs his nose and makes a face. Wil wipes his nose, looks at his hand, and rubs it on the couch. Maxim leans back, wrinkling his nose and squinting.

Wil looks over at his friend. "Dude, what're we going to do? She was right there and now we've lost her again."

Maxim inhales. "She's not lost. We know where she is. They wouldn't have taken her out there just to make a left and head somewhere else." He puts a thick blue hand on his friend's shoulder. "We know, roughly, where she is. We'll get her back."

Wil nods, snuffling. He wipes his nose again and looks down at the couch.

Maxim coughs. "I'll get you a tissue. So gross." He goes to the kitchen.

The door to the garage opens and Zephyr walks in. "Barbara is on her way. She thinks she can help."

"Cool," Wil says. He snuffles loudly.

She squints. "You have a…" She wipes at her nose.

Wil's cheeks burn crimson as he wipes his nose again. Maxim returns and hands Wil a towel. "Thanks."

Gabe steps past Zephyr, making his way to the backyard.

Wil and the Palorians watch him go, then look at each other. Maxim shrugs.

WIL OPENS THE DOOR. "HEY, BABS." He looks down. "Oh, you're back."

"Captain…Wil." Now isn't the time for formality. The hurt on his face is palpable. She steps inside.

"What do you mean, 'Oh, you're back'? Of course, I'm back, you krebnack." Bennie punches Wil in the crotch as he steps past him.

Straightening up, closing the door, Wil says, "So, you have some thoughts?"

She looks over her shoulder. "I do. Is everyone else here?"

Maxim steps out of the hallway. "I'll get Gabe." He heads for the door leading to the backyard.

Zephyr joins them from the hallway and gestures to the garage door. The other woman raises an eyebrow. Zephyr says, "Command center." She pushes the door open. "Such as it is."

Mress spies the bloodstain on the floor in front of the couch. "Trouble?"

"Space raccoons," Wil says, gesturing for her to enter the garage. He looks back. "Bennie, come on!"

The Brailack hacker emerges from the kitchen with several bottles of grum clutched in his arms. "I'm coming!"

Maxim and Gabe enter, the latter offering to help Bennie with the drinks.

Once everyone is assembled and drinks have been distributed, Mress offers Gabe, sitting next to Bennie at the makeshift command station, a portable data storage unit. "This has the Tralgot inventory of buildings in that sector on it. Plus, some routing software that should make searching the municipal network for leasing data easier."

Bennie reaches up and snags the device. "Nice."

CLASS REUNIONS

"You only take me to the nicest places," Cynthia says, stepping out of the limo. She sniffs and looks around. They're parked in front of a dilapidated warehouse. The sign over the small personnel door reads Lamonto Shipping in worn blue painted on letters. "It smells like rotten zslaggo."

The limo rises back up off the ground, the repulsorlifts causing a puddle under it to ripple. The two men who accompanied them from the spaceport are in the limo as it departs.

"Just go," Margo growls. She reaches past Cynthia to rest a fingertip against a recessed scanner set next to the door. The sound of thick security bolts sliding away rings through the door.

The inside of the warehouse does not, in any way, match the exterior. The lobby is immaculate, all dark woods and brushed metals. In the corner next to the door is a large potted plant with bright pink and blue flowers.

Cynthia whistles. "Swanky."

A tan furred young man looks up from the PADD he's reading at the reception desk. His eyes flick from Margo to Cynthia and back. "Margo."

"Kento."

"The board isn't here yet. We're still waiting on a few operatives, as well." He raises his head, tilting to the side. "Most everyone is gathered in back." He raises an eyebrow. "That's her, huh?"

Margo nods. "The one and only."

"I thought she'd be taller." His gaze roves up and down, taking Cynthia in. One of his incisors sticks out just enough to curl his lip.

"She's a letdown on many levels."

Cynthia growls, "She's right here."

Margo shoves Cynthia toward a door to the left of the reception desk. "Go."

The door slides open to reveal a short hallway with doors along its length on both sides. At the opposite end of the hallway is the opening into the warehouse proper. The doors they pass are all closed. Cynthia looks at each, then says, "I've never been here. New facility?"

Margo grunts. "After your betrayal, we had to make some rather prompt changes. They knew where all the safe houses and recruitment centers were."

Cynthia sighs. "I still don't know what you're talking about, but the Collective wasn't exactly a well-kept secret back then. Every elected official and corporate executive in Lirole, probably the planet, knew about and used our services."

They exit the hallway into what looks like a combination barracks and training facility. Children ranging from eight- to eighteen-cycles old are scattered around the central space, training: the youngsters doing basic tumbling and scrambling, the older children sparring with blunted weapons.

Cynthia inhales. "What?"

"Surprised?"

"Yes." Cynthia looks over her shoulder. "How is this possible?"

"Like so many others, you clearly don't understand."

They walk along the perimeter of the training area, various groups pausing to look at the new arrival. Many point and whisper as Cynthia is directed to the rear of the building. The rear of the warehouse is housing for the more senior operators, with a notable addition. One of the smaller rooms has been modified to be a cell; the door has been removed and replaced with a force field barrier array. Inside the small room, everything but a cot has been removed.

Cynthia peers inside. "Homey."

Margo shoves her inside, and as the force field activates with a snap and hum, says, "Don't get too comfortable." She turns and stalks off.

Cynthia steps to the door frame, being careful to not come in contact with the energy barrier keeping her inside. The trainees have gone back to their various activities. She watches for a while, then goes to the cot to lie down. Looking at the ceiling and sighing, she says, "I hope you all are doing something about this," under her breath.

PART 5

CHAPTER EIGHTEEN

PLANNING

"This definitely reduces the amount of ground we need to cover," Maxim says, nodding as he looks at the large display. The satellite view of the industrial sector is a sea of colors. Just under half the warehouses are owned by Tralgot or one of its subsidiaries. He looks to the Tygran woman standing next to him. "You're certain your facilities are above suspicion? I mean no offense, but if this Gerbil Collective —"

"Yadro."

"Them. If they're back, could they have infiltrated your organization?"

Mress shakes her head. "No. I mean, technically, anything is possible, but it's highly unlikely. There haven't been any major turnovers within management for some time, and those currently in power at the executive level are all people I hand-picked and trust implicitly."

Zephyr inclines her head. "And the subsidiaries?"

The other woman shrugs. "I can't be as certain, but I am confident that it would be hard to hide. Especially recently."

Wil nods. "Okay, so that removes almost half the warehouses. That's good—great, really." He points to the display. "How do we check these out? I'm guessing going in and knocking on doors would just send them running."

Mress grins, baring her incisors. "They'd probably just kill you."

Bennie chimes in, "Speaking of...They still think we're dead. At least, I assume they do."

Maxim grunts his agreement. "No reason they shouldn't."

"We can use that," Zephyr says.

"How?" Wil wonders.

Gabe turns. "Did you bring your image inducers?"

Wil nods once. "Yeah, I grabbed 'em. Well, mine and Cynthia's." He looks at Maxim, smirking. "Someone else keeps theirs in their quarters...for some reason."

The big man's cheeks darken a bit. "Two is enough." He looks at Gabe. "I assume."

The droid dips his head. "Indeed." Turning to Mress, and pointing to a section of the display, he says, "I suspect municipal utility workers are fairly commonplace in such an area."

The Tygran woman nods. "He's right. Companies coming and going, buildings changing hands and purpose." She points to the section of the screen Gabe indicated. On it, a hover van and three Tygran men in reflective vests are working around a piece of equipment. "I'd be shocked if there's a day that goes by that doesn't see city workers from one department or another somewhere in that part of town."

Maxim says, "Okay. Wil and I can go in disguised as Tygrans, see if we can snoop out which warehouse is our target."

Wil says, "I just need a few minutes to reprogram the inducers." He coughs. "I think their memory is currently full."

Bennie clucks. "Of what?"

Wil turns. "Of none of your business."

"And you gave us dren." Maxim puts a hand around Zephyr's shoulder.

Wil blushes. "Anyway. We can go in a bit."

Mress raises a hand. "It would make sense to go in the morning."

She gestures to the screen to cut off Wil's objection. "It's midafternoon. Work crews won't be going out this late, and they certainly won't be working after hours."

Wil scowls. "We can't waste time. She's in there now. We don't know their timetable."

Mress nods. "I understand, Captain...Wil. But getting noticed before we're ready will do her no good. Whatever this conclave of theirs is, it surely has to be set up. They didn't know they had her until they grabbed her."

Bennie nods. "She's right. Whatever they're planning, they're gonna have to set it up."

"Fine," Wil agrees, shoulders slumping. "I'll be in our...my...room."

The others exchange a look as the door closes behind Wil. Bennie says, "Maybe we should get him a pet."

Everyone is silent for a heartbeat or three, then Maxim says, "What?"

"A pet. Maybe a...what're they called? Doogies? Dougs? Think it's Doug." The Brailack shrugs. "We can swing by Earth and get one."

"What're you even talking about?" Zephyr demands.

Bennie shrugs again. "You know, cheer him up."

Zephyr holds up both hands. "I can't even." She heads for the house.

Mress shakes her head and follows. Maxim says, "You're dark sometimes." He follows the women into the house.

Gabe turns. "Your ability to be insensitive continues to impress." He gets to his feet and leaves the garage.

Bennie, alone, now looks around. "What? I meant as a wedding present."

FOLLOW THE LEADER

"You look good with fur." Maxim grins.

Wil, despite his mood, holds out his hands, turning them over, examining the pale brown fur that covers them. "You know, never tried this look before."

"Don't want to know."

Wil shrugs. "Let's go."

Barbara Mress hadn't stayed the night but arranged for a municipal utility van to be outside the rental house.

"We'll monitor things from here," Zephyr says.

Bennie leans to the side. "Where are your tails?"

"What?" both men say in unison.

The team hacker frowns. "Uh, unless you both were involved in a horrible farming accident, you're missing tails."

"Oh, damnit," Wil hisses.

"Can't be helped," Maxim says.

Bennie shrugs. "Those sensors are like the ones from the museum. Stick 'em where you can to give us as much coverage as possible."

"Please do not take any unnecessary risks," Gabe adds.

Maxim moves around to the driver's side of the van. "We'll be safe."

The van rises and heads off.

Gabe says, "We are being watched."

Zephyr and Bennie turn to look, spotting an older Tygran woman across the street watering her lawn, attempting to look inconspicuously at the new neighbors. A puddle is forming in front of her unmoving hose.

"There a problem?" Bennie shouts, taking a step forward, arms upraised.

Zephyr palms his head, waving with her free hand as the trio moves back into the house.

The drive to the industrial sector doesn't take long. Maxim looks over. "You have the layout?"

Wil nods, looking down at his wristcomm. "Hang a left up here. We'll start there."

Maxim guides the van around the corner and parks it next to a van for a different utility. "Busy day," he says.

Wil hops out and grabs the shoulder bag full of sensor patches and other supplies, while Maxim grabs the portable scanner unit that was in the van.

"Do you know what utility we're pretending to be a part of?" Wil asks. He points up a wide street that runs between six warehouses, none of which are owned by or affiliated with Tralgot.

"I thought you did," Maxim admits. He holds up the device he grabbed from the van. "No idea what this does."

Wil steps to the side. "Well, don't aim it at me."

"You think it's a vaporizer?"

"I think I might want kids, and I don't know what shoots out of the business end of it." He makes a face. "I don't even know which end is the business end." Maxim's eyebrow ridges crinkle, and he shifts his device to his side.

"Uh huh," Wil says. "Let's do this." He heads up the street.

A pair of general-purpose droids pass them on the street. One waves. "We are working in building 4F. If you require access, please use the rear doors."

Maxim inclines his head. "Thank you. We will, if needed."

Once the droids are behind them, Wil says, "Can cross that one off the list."

Maxim nods his agreement.

The first two warehouses are dead ends. Each is locked up tight, and as far as either man can tell, currently unused. Wil places a sensor disk in several windows of each building.

"This is one is clear, too," Bennie reports over the shared channel.

"Okay, we're gonna head to the next cluster," Wil says.

"Anything look out of place?" Zephyr asks.

Wil looks at Maxim, who shrugs. Wil says, "Well, Tygran warehouse districts are far less sketchy than human ones, and Max probably shoulda set his inducer to make him a droid, but other than that...no."

Bennie turns to Zephyr. "Lunch?"

"Sure, I'll take whatever you're making." She looks at him from the corner of her eye.

Bennie chews his lip, then opts to say, "Okay. Be right back."

When the door closes behind Bennie, Gabe looks at Zephyr. "Well played."

In the kitchen, Bennie is busy making a pair of sandwiches when he looks up and out the window that looks into the rear yard space. He comes face to face with the Tygran woman from earlier that morning.

Bennie screams, stumbling backward to crash into the food refrigeration unit. He leaps up and runs to the yard. "Who're you? What're you doing back here?"

The woman draws herself up to her full height. "Protecting my neighbors."

"From what?" he demands. "How did you get back here?"

The woman scoffs. "Where did you come from? Do you work nearby? What happened to the Kleron family?"

Bennie's mouth hangs open. "Lady, we don't owe you dren. I'm gonna give you to the count of ten to get off this property."

"Well, I never—"

Bennie walks back into the garage holding two plates.

"Trouble?" Zephyr asks.

"Nosy neighbor," he replies.

Gabe turns. "That could pose a problem if she calls the authorities. We do not know the extent to which the Yadro Collective is embedded in the local security forces."

Zephyr nods. "Especially this close to their operations."

Bennie hands her a plate. "She's tied up on the back porch. Want me to go kill her?"

"No!" both Zephyr and Gabe reply.

Bennie takes a bite of his sandwich. "Just checking."

"Tied up on the porch?" Zephyr repeats.

Gabe stands and leaves the garage.

"Is that even something Knights of Plentallus do? Tie people up?" Zephyr asks.

He shrugs. "The manual is pretty thick, written on actual vellum and all. I just scanned it. I think tying up is okay."

She sighs.

Gabe returns. "Our...hostage...appears to be okay."

Zephyr glares at Bennie.

Two HOURS after arriving at the warehouse district, Maxim says, "Hey. Look at that." Wil slows down. "Keep moving," he whispers, putting a hand on Wil's elbow to keep his friend from stopping. Ahead of them, four warehouses away, a hover car is pulling to a stop. A very nice, very out of place, hover car.

Maxim consults his scanner and points toward the nearest building on their side of the street. Wil nods and heads between the two buildings.

Wil taps on his earpiece. "Think we mighta found 'em." He creeps back toward the street, placing a sensor sticker as high on the building as he can, aimed across the street at the building the hover car is parked in front of. He returns to Maxim, handing him a few of the tiny sensor devices. Maxim offers the scanner as if either of them knows what the device's display is telling them.

"Be careful," Zephyr says.

The two men ease around the back of the building, peering through every window they can to make sure they aren't hanging out around Bad Guy Building 2. Reaching the other side of the building after making a slow circuit along the back and down the opposite side, Maxim places a sensor sticker on the wall of the warehouse so that they'll have an eye on the approach to the building. They place a few stickers on the windows of the building they're hiding next to, just in case.

Coming around the other side of the warehouse to join Maxim, Wil peers around the edge. "Car's gone."

Maxim nods. "Coulda been the building owner or, well, anyone."

Wil nods his agreement. "Yeah." He takes a step out into the street but pushes back against Maxim as another car glides around the corner of the street up ahead. It glides to a stop in front of the same warehouse. Two Tygran women get out and move to the door. A moment later, the car glides off, passing Wil and Maxim. Maxim studies the screen of the scanner, pointing at a utility box mounted on the wall of the building above them.

"Private taxi," Wil says, pointing to the nondescript vehicle as it continues out of sight.

Maxim grunts. "Guess that is the place." Wil nods.

"See any cameras or security measures?" Wil asks.

Maxim peers over his friend's shoulder. "No, which is weird."

In their ears, Zephyr says, "We're looking at the records for the building now."

Bennie cuts in. "Looks like that building and the one behind it are owned by a shell company, which is owned by a shell company. That goes on for a while."

"Turtles all the way down," Wil mumbles.

Maxim looks at him, then says, "Nothing suspicious there."

Wil puts a hand on Maxim's shoulder. "Okay, let's plant some more sensors and get out of here." He stands up straighter and walks out into the street, back in character as a utility worker.

Maxim follows him into the street, waving the sensor device around with purpose. Still not sure what the device does, he makes beeping noises himself and clucks along, nodding at the device in—he hopes— an approving way.

"What're you doing?" Wil whispers. He makes a show of

checking a power management box mounted to a pole across from their target, slipping one of the sensor stickers on the cover.

"I still don't know what this thing does."

"So, you're making beeping noises?"

The big man shrugs. "Most things beep."

Wil sighs and motions for them to continue up the wide street between warehouses. Another vehicle glides past them. "They're not being very subtle, are they?" He leans down to inspect an internex junction, placing another sticker on it.

Maxim says, "Guess they figure with utility workers and other warehouse owners and workers coming and going, they can do as they like."

After watching the latest hover car depart, Wil and Maxim head across the street toward the warehouse next door to their target.

Over the comms, Zephyr says, "Looks like the buildings on either side of our target are currently being used by two different firms for long term inventory storage. No indication that they're in any way tied to this Yadro group."

Wil nods. "Okay, cool. We'll check out both, then head back."

CHAPTER NINETEEN

"So, it's true," a voice says from the door to Cynthia's makeshift cell. The energy barrier distorts the voice a bit.

Cynthia sits up. The voice, even with the distortion, is familiar. "Sarah?" She throws her legs off the bed, turning as she does to stand.

"I honestly wasn't sure if it'd be you or someone they pulled off the street," the other woman says, her light pale green eyes bright against the dark gray of her fur. "After all this time." She shakes her head.

Cynthia stops short of the force field. "Sarah, I didn't do whatever it is that they're saying I did."

The woman she called friend as a child scoffs. "That so."

Cynthia nods. "It is."

"They killed so many in the raids," Sarah says softly. "Did you know that? Joz, Kildor, Mo, all dead."

Cynthia inhales. "I knew they disbanded the Collective, but..."

"But? But what? Didn't know that by giving them the location of all of our safe houses, you'd be signing the death warrants for people you called friends? For people who called you friend?"

"Sarah, I didn't—"

The other woman holds up a hand. "Save it. Just tell me this. Do you sleep at night?"

Cynthia growls. "Listen to me. I did not betray the Collective. Someone is lying."

"You."

"No!" She slams her palms on either side of the narrow door. "I didn't do it."

Sarah turns, her tail rigid. Over her shoulder, she says, "We'll see, I guess."

Cynthia takes a deep breath, letting it out slowly. "Dren. What is going on here?" She asks out loud, not expecting an answer.

"They think you sold us out after you walked away," a voice says.

Cynthia jumps back from the door, her instincts taking over as she lands in a combat-ready posture. "Who's there?"

"Not surprised you don't remember my voice. You never seemed to hear it back then, either," a woman says, stepping out from around a corner beyond the doorway. Where Sarah was lithe muscle under black fur, this woman is wiry to the point of malnourishment, with mouse brown fur shot through with white. She reaches the door. "Would it help if I spoke to you from inside a locker?"

Cynthia gasps. "Bee...Beatrix?"

"Got it in one." The other woman inclines her head. "I'd say it's good to see you, Cynthia, but well..." She shrugs, holding her arms out to encompass their relative surroundings.

Cynthia nods. "Come to tell me how evil I am? How I'm responsible for the deaths of countless people I cared about?"

The woman on the opposite side of the energy barrier stares at Cynthia, unblinking. "No." She takes a deep breath. "I just had to see you for myself. Look you in the eye."

"And?"

"Did you know you and Joz made my life miserable? I contemplated ending it, more than once. Not like I could just up and leave."

"I didn't—"

The other woman holds up a hand. "I never expected to get this opportunity, so you'll listen." Cynthia nods. "I looked up to the two of you. You were so confident and self-assured. You never seemed to be afraid. But I was always afraid those first years. Afraid I wouldn't make the cut and would disappear one night. Afraid I wouldn't measure up to the example you third years set."

"Beatrix…" When the younger woman doesn't stop her, she says, "I'm sorry. I know that rings hollow now, but I am. I've had a long time to think about—and, to a degree—process the trauma inflicted on us. This place wasn't…isn't healthy. It's bad. Evil. We were kids and the only way we had to process that was to pass it on to those below us." She inhales. "I found people, people that care about me. It took a while. First, I found people that didn't care about me but felt like what I was used to. They used me just like the Collective."

"Good for you," Beatrix sneers.

"My point is that there are other things than the Collective. That's why I left. You can leave. They make you think you can't, but I'm proof that they're lying."

"And yet, here you are."

Cynthia's shoulders slump. "Because the board needs to make an example. They rule with fear, and showing that they can snatch someone off the street from light years away will keep the rest of you cowed."

The younger woman looks Cynthia up and down, then says, "The conclave starts in a few hours. I hope you can convince them." She turns and starts back down the corridor.

"Did I convince you?" Cynthia whispers.

Over her shoulder, Beatrix says, "I don't know."

THIS PLAN STINKS

Maxim and Wil walk in, having parked the hover van three houses down the street. Wil looks around, spying the Tygran woman on the back porch tied to a chair, a sock in her mouth. He looks at the others, now sitting around the main lounge area at the front of the house. "Why is there a woman tied up on our back porch?"

"Ask Bennie," Zephyr says, setting the PADD she's holding on the table before her.

"She was being nosy," Bennie says nonchalantly.

Wil looks at Maxim, then turns to Zephyr. "I mean, I kinda expect you to be the levelheaded one here. We're kidnapping people now?"

"Technically, she's not kidnapped," Zephyr replies. She waves a hand toward the team hacker and Knight of Plentallus. "Sir Knight acted on his own initiative."

"What? I caught her in the backyard snooping around. Want her blowing our cover?" Bennie grouses.

Maxim clears his throat. "Now, what do we do with her?" He holds up a hand when Bennie opens his mouth. "No killing."

"Why does everyone think I want to kill her?"

"You offered," Gabe replies.

Wil sighs. "Okay, whatever. We can drop an anonymous call when we're done." He points to the lounge. "Speaking of, we gotta go now." Maxim joins Zephyr on the sofa. Wil moves to push Bennie off the chair next to the sofa.

"Are you sure?" his first officer asks.

Wil nods. "Yeah, whatever they're up to has to be going down. We didn't see any more arrivals the last thirty minutes we were there."

Bennie nods. "He's probably right. Whatever the conclave is, I can't imagine they'd diddle Dudley."

Wil makes a face. "Dilly dally." He shudders. "Poor Dudley. Anyway, yeah. She might be dead by morning. We gotta go. Now."

Maxim adds, "If they're keeping as low a profile as Barbara suggests, whomever that was arriving today won't linger."

Everyone nods their agreement.

THE CENTRAL AREA of the warehouse has been converted from wide open training area to a courtroom design with bleachers ringing it. The thick mats and sparring weapons are gone, the latter pushed against the walls, the former replaced by bleachers and tiered seating for the board and the accused.

"This conclave is begun," a voice booms from speakers somewhere in the ceiling. Cynthia is seated at a small desk in front of a slightly raised witness stand. Above and to the side of the witness stand is the long bench occupied by the board of directors.

The board of the Yadro Collective has always been the five oldest operators, the assumption being that if an operator lives long enough to be on the board, they must have some knowledge, or at least skill. It helps that by surviving that long, one tends to pick up political favors, insider knowledge, and other under-the-table leverage.

None of the five faces looking down at her are familiar or friendly. Probably not a good thing, she decides.

"We accuse Cynthia Luar of betraying the Collective," the hidden speaker intones.

"I didn't," she says.

"The witness will speak when spoken to," the ceiling speakers boom.

A man Cynthia doesn't recognize steps forward. "Hello, Cynthia."

"Hi."

"I'm Dareb."

"Don't care."

He runs a hand over the top of his head, smoothing his hair back between his ears. "You understand the situation?"

"I understand they have made me the scapegoat in all this."

He wags a finger. "So, you plead not guilty?"

She stares at the man before her. "Yes. Of course. Because I am not guilty. Of course, this isn't a court, so..." She shrugs.

"That remains to be seen." He turns first to the board, then the gathered operators spanning several tiers of the assembled bleachers. "Does anyone stand with the accused?"

Cynthia holds up a hand. "I'm sorry, what?"

One of the board members, the man nearest her, leans down. "Do you not require an advocate from those gathered here?"

"I don't even understand how this sham of a trial is supposed to work. We didn't do these when I was last here."

Dareb turns back to her. "You are entitled to an advocate who can work with you on your defense."

"Do we get time to prepare?"

"A tock."

"So generous of you."

From the audience, someone says, "I will be her advocate."

Cynthia leans forward to peer into the darkened space and the sea of barely visible faces.

"Beatrix?"

The younger woman makes her way down the steps. When she reaches Dareb, he nods at her. "We'll reconvene in one tock."

Zephyr inhales. "Okay. Then we need to plan." She grabs the PADD she was using to read and calls up data from the computer system in the garage. She looks at Gabe. "Mind?"

The droid makes a metallic rattle. "No." He activates his holoprojector. The area between the sofa and chair, over the low table, fills with scans of their target, the warehouse Cynthia is likely being held in. "We know from the sensor disks you placed that there is only one ground floor entrance." The image shifts. "We also know from the satellite data Barbara was able to provide us that there's a rooftop access point."

Maxim nods. "Glad we brought our real party clothes." Zephyr nods.

Wil holds up a PADD of his own and says, "Here's what I'm thinking." He explains the plan with the aid of the PADD screen, which is covered in multicolored arrows going every which way.

"I don't get it," Bennie says.

Wil sighs and points to the screen. "This is you." He traces the lines around the screen. "Then you come, here."

"Are we the blue or the purple line?" Maxim asks.

Wil glares at him. "You're the red. Gabe and I are the blue."

"Aah," Maxim says. He looks at Zephyr, who shrugs.

Bennie looks around. "So...the plan is we rush the building? No offense, but maybe you should come up with a slide show. Help refine the idea?"

Wil glares. "No, dum-dum. Gabe and I will go in as local security. Someone noticed suspicious activity. We'll need to check things out." He points again to the two Palorians. "Up and Over." He points to the Brailack. "And Under. Once we know where she is, beast mode."

Gabe tilts his head. Bennie says, "I don't know what that means."

"Nor do I," Maxim says.

Wil makes a face. "You know, beast mode. We unleash our beasts."

"Keep your beast to yourself," Zephyr says.

Wil leans back. "No, no. Not...well, thank you, but...no, not that." He waves a hand. "Never mind. You get the gist."

"This whole plan is a gist," Bennie complains.

Wil flips him off. "Okay, get dressed. We roll out in thirty." Everyone stands.

"So, you believe me, after all?" Cynthia says as she drops into the metal chair, one of two, in the small room that is serving as an office for her and her advocate.

"No," the other woman says, taking a seat. "But I believe you're owed a fair trial."

"That's something, I guess."

The younger Tygran woman cocks her head to one side. "So, level with me."

"I did. I don't know how to say it more clearly. I did not betray the Collective."

"But you fled?" She pulls out a PADD and starts writing on the screen with a stylus, taking notes.

Cynthia nods.

"Why?"

"Because I'd just killed someone for something stupid. Not because they had a political view or were a business rival. Because they possessed something someone else wanted, and one of the board members owed someone a favor." She sighs. "I looked at myself in a mirror and didn't like what I saw."

"So, you walked away."

Cynthia nods. "And never looked back."

Beatrix consults her PADD. "You didn't place a call to Tyr planetary security?"

"Nope."

"Or to anyone indirectly linked to planetary security?"

Cynthia holds up a hand. "I'll save you some trouble. I made no calls. I tossed my gear, stole some clothes and left."

Beatrix nods. She raises the PADD, turning it so Cynthia can see the screen. On it is a series of call logs. The ID codes of the incoming calls are highlighted with a metadata window floating above them identifying the caller as Cynthia Luar.

"The wurrin? I didn't make those calls."

"I'm still not sold on this plan," Bennie says from the back of the van.

"Good thing your opinion doesn't matter," Wil replies. He guides the van around a corner, then slows the van to a stop. "You're the one that's always crowing about turning off your sense of smell."

"Doesn't mean I enjoy walking through dren," Bennie retorts.

Wil shrugs as the van slows to a stop. "Out you go." The hacker glares but hops out of the van. As the side door closes, Wil guides the van farther down the street. The street behind their target is quiet. Wil pulls to a stop in front of the warehouse behind their target. Looking into the back at Maxim and Zephyr, he says, "Your turn." The two Palorians nod, their matte black scout armor shimmering as the active camouflage engages. "Good luck," Wil says to the empty back of the van. The door slides closed.

Wil guides the van back around to the front of the warehouse. He turns to Gabe in the passenger seat. "Ready?"

"Yes."

Wil activates his image inducer. Gabe watches as his captain shimmers. The compact hard light generator wraps Wil in a holographic image. "How do I look?" He's using the same image that he and Maxim used earlier in the day, just with a different uniform.

"Like a middle aged Tygran man employed by the planetary security service."

Wil shrugs. "Okay, then." He inclines his head. "Your turn."

Gabe's optic sensors dim as several small hard light projectors engage. After seeing how well the image inducers worked and their utility, he scanned the small devices and created built-in units. Gabe is replaced with a model of droid commonly employed as a security officer, physically not that different from Gabe's body, but bulkier, painted blue with white stripes down the arms and legs.

Wil purses his lips. "Nice." He opens the door. "Let's go."

Maxim and Zephyr are crouched two warehouses away from the building they're planning to break into, next to an access ladder that leads to the roof. Each of them has a rifle attached to their back and a pulse pistol on each thigh. The specially designed weapons interact with the armor, mimicking its active camouflage properties.

"Up we go," Maxim says to the glowing outline of Zephyr on his heads-up display.

Bennie taps his ear piece. "I'm in and moving. It's gross down here."

"Copy," Gabe replies as he and Wil step up to the personnel door of the warehouse.

Wil takes a deep breath and presses the announcer button next to the door. He rocks on his heels, trying to look as nonchalant as possible.

After a minute, Gabe turns. "Perhaps they did not hear the announcement?"

Wil shrugs and pushes the button again, then to be safe, pushes it a third time. He turns to Gabe and smiles.

The door slides open. "Yes?"

"Hi," Wil says.

Gabe steps in. "We are responding to a call of suspicious activity."

"Seen any?" Wil asks, smiling.

"No." The door begins to slide closed.

Gabe's hand grabs hold of the edge, stopping the door in its tracks. "We are still required to investigate."

The man inside steps further into the door. "We're quite busy here."

Wil grins, forgetting that he is baring Tygran teeth. "Sorry, we have to investigate all calls."

The Tygran man sighs. "Very well." He steps aside. "Come in. Be quick."

Wil makes a show of looking around. "So, what do you all do here?" He moves toward the reception desk.

The young Tygran man moves to intercept him. "We're an exporter of dry goods."

"Like candy?" Wil asks. Gabe turns to look at him.

The other man stammers. "No. What? No." He looks Wil up and down. "Where's your tail?"

"What?"

"Your tail?"

Over the comms, Bennie says, "Told ya."

Wil frowns. "Farming accident." The receptionist makes a face. Wil continues. "Horrible accident when I was young. Ripped it right off. Shredded it. So much blood." The other man's facial fur flattens as his eyes bulge. Wil shrugs. "Anyway. Big warehouse. How many work here?"

The receptionist's eyes narrow.

CHAPTER TWENTY

SEWERS

BENNIE IS WORKING his way through the sewer. Muttering to himself, he stops and looks around. "I hate sewers," he says out loud. He's at a three-way junction, looking left and right. Checking his wristcomm, he turns right.

Something up ahead makes a noise, a sort of warble cackle sound. Bennie stops and looks up from his wristcomm screen. "The wurrin?" he wonders, looking around. He taps his earpiece. "Just in case you forgot, I hate you all." He resumes his course for the spot his map of the sewer says is under the sublevel of the bad guy warehouse.

Rounding another corner, he comes face to face with something covered in matted hair and trash and who knows what else. Screaming, he falls back into the murky water he's been wading through. The thing before him emits a mewling screech as it backs up. Baleful yellow eyes peer through the slimy hair. Whatever other features the creature might possess are lost in the matted blanket of hair.

Bennie scrambles to his feet, hand grasping for his beam saber. The furry shambling thing raises its arms, palms out, fingers splayed. It makes a clucking sound.

"What the wurrin are you?" Bennie shouts. "Go. Shoo!" He waves one hand, while the other is still trying to get a firm grip on his beam saber. Slimy water drips off of him and it, making a firm grip difficult.

The creature yips, advancing toward Bennie. Its arms are still up over its head, waving side to side. It opens an—until that moment—impossible to see mouth full of craggy teeth. It roars, spittle flying toward Bennie. A piece of half decomposed food container stuck to its head falls into the water.

Finally getting his beam saber unclipped, Bennie screams, drowning out the snap hiss that comes with the ignition of his beam saber. The bright purple beam of light startles the shaggy creature, sending it staggering backward, emitting a bewildering series of yips, gurgles, and cackles.

"That's what I thought!" Bennie cheers, jumping into the air. He lunges forward, driving the creature back. "Don't mess with a Knight of Plentallus, you slimy, hair covered...whatever you are!"

The creature stops, staring at Bennie. Another mass of hair and sludge rises from the water. The new creature mewls to the first, who answers. The second creature is followed by a third and a fourth. All of them are nearly identical outside the different types and amount of trash clinging to their shaggy hair.

Bennie's eyes go wide. "Well, that's not fair." He takes a step back, moving into a defensive posture, his beam saber humming and casting the entire dimly lit sewer tunnel in purple light.

Two of the creatures advance. "I'm warning you," Bennie says, sweeping his blade back and forth slowly.

The leader, Bennie assumes, lunges towards him. Its slime covered hands move from their weird rhythmic waving over its head to fully outstretched before it. A quick sidestep and swipe end in warbling screams as the creature waves matching stumps in the air, the ends still glowing a little.

The other three hairy slime things exchange noises, then surge toward Bennie, shoving their now handless friend aside.

"Dren!" Bennie shouts, trying to get his footing in the disgusting water, stepping on something round and smooth. He swipes wildly with his saber, nearly clipping one of the creatures. One of them, with what Bennie hopes are noodles tangled in the hair on its chest, lunges. He sidesteps the attack, raises his saber, and slashes diagonally across the creature's back. The creature falls face first into the water, sinking under the ripples.

Before he can turn, another of the wet mop creatures is on his back, pushing him down into the water. He manages to take a breath a split second before his head goes under. His beam saber splutters, flash boiling the sewer water for a second before the built-in safeties engage, turning the device off.

Despite their thin limbs, the creatures are stronger than Bennie expects. He fumbles around under the water, churning up trash and other detritus. Realizing he's in trouble, Bennie focuses on his training. Getting his feet under him, he heaves. While strong, the sewer monsters don't weigh much. Bennie breaks the surface of the water, flinging his opponent into the air. The hairy beast spins, clutching the stone of the tunnel roof.

He flips the switch on his beam saber hilt, taking aim and releasing two bolts of bright purple energy up into the thing. It falls, splashing into the water, sinking slowly, the smell of burnt hair and trash the only evidence of its existence.

He turns to the remaining creatures, the one with no hands and one that has a set of bones woven into the hair under its mouth. Both retreat backwards, slinking deeper and deeper until all that's left are the ripples of their passage.

He looks around. "I grolacking hate sewers," he says, reorienting himself and continuing on.

SOMETIMES BAD IDEAS WORK

MAXIM IS CROUCHED next to Zephyr on the roof of the warehouse behind their target. "I spot only the one sentry," he says.

She nods, then realizes he can't see her any better than she can see him. "Agreed. Wonder why?"

The warehouse they're on the roof of, despite sharing the same owners, has no security that they can find. No guard patrolling the roof like next door. Only an easily bypass-able sensor array. The roof opposite the small alley that runs between all the warehouses, on the other hand, has at least one guard and a more advanced sensor array.

"Thoughts?" Zephyr says. As she pans her head to look over the building, her heads-up display fills with highlights and callouts for potential risks. "Wonder why this building is so much less protected."

"Maybe this one is just storage, and they didn't want to arouse suspicions with two well-protected buildings?" Maxim offers. He uses his wristcomm to highlight a section of the roof that looks like a blind spot in the overlapping sensor fields. Someone set up a sofa and chair at the corner of the building, both of which have created a shielded corner of the roof.

"How do we get there without making any noise? These suits don't have repulsorlifts," Zephyr says, studying the section of rooftop

Maxim highlighted. The sentry is passing by the makeshift lounge and will soon be making her way toward the front of the building.

"Think you can do that hang sideways thing you did back on that station in Barsoom sector?" Maxim wonders.

He can't see it, but she bites her lip as she calculates the distance. "Maybe. Yeah. If you can give me a boost across." She turns to his faint green outline. "How does that help?"

He grins to himself. "Well, if you can stick like a dart, then get up and over, then lure the sentry to the blind spot, I can land on her."

"Land on her?"

"Bad plan?"

"We really have been hanging out with Wil too long." She stands. "Let's go. She'll be back this way soon, and I want to make sure I'm in position." She takes several steps away from the edge of the building. Knowing that no one is around to see them, they disable their stealth systems so that each can see the other, knowing how tricky the next minutes will be.

Zephyr takes off at a run. Maxim gets into a squat, fingers interlaced in front of him. Reaching Maxim, Zephyr leaps, landing with one foot in Maxim's hands. He thrusts up, first with his legs, then his arms, propelling her up and across the gap between buildings.

Before Zephyr is even halfway across, Maxim has reactivated his cloaking system. She sails across the gap, and the moment her hands come in contact with the lip of the building's roof, she triggers several functions in her scout armor. Her shoulder, elbow, and wrist joints lock in place, as do her gloves, leaving deep grooves in the metal of the building. Her active camouflage also re-engages. The sound of her impact is little more than the sound of a piece of metal striking another.

In her ear, Maxim says, "She's coming back around."

Zephyr quickly clambers up over the edge to crouch next to the makeshift lounge seating. The sentry walks over, looking around for the source of the noise she heard. Zephyr taps an armored finger on the metal roof. The woman looks over, squinting, hand moving to rest on the butt of her pulse pistol. She edges cautiously around the sofa toward the small coffee table in front of the couch.

Zephyr scoots toward the tattered and patched chair, tapping again to lure the curious sentry into position. No sooner does the armed Tygran woman step in front of the sofa than she crumples under the invisible weight of a Palorian man. Maxim's armor shimmers as it tries to adapt to the quickly shifting surroundings of couch and the now very unconscious woman under him.

Zephyr tuts. "That worked better than I thought it would." She leans down, pulling a length of high tensile strength grappling line from a pouch on her lower back to secure the arms and legs of the sentry. "Don't tell Wil." Maxim nods.

"About twenty. Usually," the receptionist says, eyeing Wil with open suspicion now.

Gabe is looking the room up and down. Via Wil's earpiece, he says, "This lobby is heavily shielded."

Wil nods, never looking away from their unwilling guide. "So, there are...what, a few offices back there?"

Before the other man can answer, Gabe says, "What type of margins do you get?"

Wil turns toward him, eyebrow arched.

"I'm sorry?" the Tygran man says.

Gabe turns to face the man. "Margins. What does an exporter of dry goods typically clear?"

"Oh, uh...I'd have to ask one of the executives. I just manage the front office."

Gabe inclines his head. "We will wait. I am contemplating my next career."

Wil's mouth is hanging open.

It takes the younger man a few heartbeats to regain his composure. "I'm sorry. What was the nature of the complaint you received?"

"Oh..." Wil looks up at Gabe.

"I think perhaps we're good here, no? I thank you for checking on us. Clearly everything is okay here." The younger man holds a hand out, gesturing back toward the front door.

When he gets close enough to usher Wil toward the door, his hand grazes the edge of what he thinks is the armored jacket that security forces often wear, and that Wil included in his image inducer programming. The younger man's hand pauses, then pushes into the light construct to brush against Wil's light combat armor.

"What the—?"

Gabe moves faster than Wil can process, grasping the front of the young Tygran man's shirt.

If the younger man were just a receptionist, that would have been sufficient to detain him. Confirming that he isn't, the limber man jumps, twisting around to land on Gabe's arm, his shirt tearing free. He lashes out with a series of kicks to Gabe's head, knocking it back. The hard light construct from his images inducers flickers, then fails.

"Gabe!" Wil shouts, reaching for the receptionist only to get an open-handed palm to his face, sending him reeling backward to knock a generic-looking print off the wall.

"Who are you?" the younger man demands. He performs another move, spinning around and behind Gabe's torso, then between his legs. As the droid moves to grab the man with his free hand, a pair of rapid kicks and punches blocks Gabe's move.

In a flash, the not-really-a-receptionist leaps over his desk, presses a button, then turns to Wil, leaping directly at him.

Gabe's eyes turn red as one of his forearms shifts into blaster mode. He fires only to blast a chunk out of the wall, the Tygran man having leapt clear to land on the droid intruder's back after twisting in midair to grasp Gabe's head in both hands, trying to twist it off.

"He's so fast!" Wil shouts, holding his pulse pistol, trying to draw a bead on his target.

"Yes," Gabe says, spinning his torso this way and that, failing to shake loose his attacker. "He is also very limber." He makes a mechanical grunting sound as the smaller man climbs off his shoulders, wrapping his legs around Gabe's torso, raining blows on the lightly armored midsection.

"Who are you two idiots?" the younger man says, dropping to the ground and tackling Wil, knocking the pistol from his hand.

The two struggle, rolling around on the ground until the younger man manages to get a grip on Wil's pistol. He sits up, while straddling the intruder, gun barrel inches from Wil's face. "Stop. I will kill you."

"I would advise against such a course of action," Gabe says, resting the barrel of his blaster against the back of the receptionist's head.

"I don't know who you two are, but you've made the biggest mistake of your lives," an unfamiliar voice says, the sound of charging pulse pistols punctuating the sentence.

Wil cranes his neck to look beyond the man pinning him, and Gabe standing next to them, to the new arrival, a middle aged woman flanked by two younger women, each holding a pulse pistol.

TIME'S UP

BACK ON THE WITNESS STAND, Cynthia looks around the gathered faces, finding that none have gotten any friendlier or even sympathetic.

Beatrix looks at the board of directors, all seated in a row above her and Cynthia. "The defense is ready."

Dareb steps forward. "Then I will call my witness." He turns a slow circle, taking in the board and those gathered in the bleachers. "The Collective calls Cady Keral."

Beatrix looks at Cynthia, who shrugs. Beatrix whispers, "She was in the orphanage with us. A few years older. You probably never met her." The other woman nods once, turning back to Dareb and a woman with pale blonde fur and a bobbed tail making her way to the witness stand, just below and to the side of the raised board of directors' platform.

"You're Cady Keral?" the prosecutor asks.

"I am."

"And you know the accused, Cynthia Luar?"

"I do. I was in the same orphanage as her, a cycle or two ahead of her. I was also her handler during her last year as part of the Collective."

Beatrix looks at Cynthia, who again shrugs. She whispers, "Maybe? I mean, it was always *control* I dealt with. No idea who was behind the comm system."

Dareb nods. "So, you were her primary point of contact that final year before she fled the Collective." Cady nods. "Did you notice anything...suspicious...about Cynthia's behavior over the course of that year?"

She nods. "Yes. Several times, I had to remind Cynthia of her mission parameters. She routinely tried to alter them."

"Alter them how?"

Cady tilts her head. "Mostly offering and asking for non-lethal options when the mission was a kill order."

Beatrix opens her mouth, but before she can object, a series of lights along the ceiling begins strobing red.

As one, the board gets to its feet, four well-armed operatives ushering them down the steps and toward a door to the rear of the large open space.

Cynthia looks from Beatrix to the smug faced Dareb, then around the room. No one seems to know what is going on. Dareb snaps his fingers. Several guards move in to escort Cynthia and Beatrix out. Cady moves back to the bleachers.

Upstairs, Maxim looks at Zephyr. "Was that us?" The lighting in the corridor has shifted from the warm white it was when they entered to a pulsing red.

She shakes her head. They're in the stairwell, almost down to the top level of whatever fills the back and upper levels of the warehouse. "No way. Probably Wil."

They continue on, stopping at an intersection as three Tygrans run past, each with a pistol in hand and various blades strapped to their torsos.

"He's good at stirring up the gringler nest, that's for sure," Maxim says.

Zephyr nods and heads for a door marked Private. Maxim follows.

It takes Bennie's lock picking app less than a microtock to override the door controls. Zephyr looks up at Maxim. "You can never mention it to him, but some of his slicing is impressive."

Maxim nods, saying, "Someone's office."

Zephyr moves to a desk. "Someone important."

BENNIE LOWERS THE SCANNER. No one is in the room beyond the duracrete wall before him. One of the dead shaggy sewer monsters has floated back up to the surface behind him. He looks over his shoulder and shakes his head. "Sewer monsters. I swear." He ignites his beam saber and plants his feet.

He jabs the tip of the blade into the rocky material. The duracrete sizzles, smoke wafting up and away from the blade. With measured slowness, he guides the blade down, stopping just above the waterline. No need to flood whatever sub-basement is on the other side.

Once he's cut a square big enough to step through, he pushes with all his strength. The duracrete square barely budges. "Dren," he hisses, putting his back against the stone. After a few heartbeats of little progress, he swears several more times and ignites his beam saber once more. Driving the blade into the square, he cuts it into smaller, irregularly shaped pieces that he violently kicks until they fall into the room beyond.

Leaning in, he looks around. As expected, a sub-basement. As not expected, it is full of computing cores—racks of them, all blinking status lights and whirring faint noises.

He clambers into the server room. "Jackpot," he whispers.

CHAPTER TWENTY-ONE

CONQUER AND DIVIDE

"SOMEONE LIKES EXPENSIVE DRINK," Zephyr says, holding a half empty bottle of Trollack pond whiskey.

Maxim makes a face. "I've never understood why that stuff is so expensive. It's pond water that they have babies in, distilled." He shakes his head. "Gross."

She puts the bottle back in the drawer she found it in. "It must be good. I hear it goes for upwards of ten thousand a bottle. More if the pond is renowned."

"Renowned." Maxim shakes his head again. Pulling open a file cabinet, he says, "This must be one of the bigwig's offices." He pulls out a folder. "Old school." Inside are dossiers. Dossiers of children: name, location, special skills observed by the screeners, cause of parents' deaths, and often the name of the agent that took care of them, and more.

He accesses the scanner function on his wristcomm. He opens several folders, scanning their contents before opening his chest armor slipping a few of the folders inside just in case. The blinking red light in the hallway goes out, the hallway returning to its original lighting.

"We should get going," Zephyr says.

Maxim slides the file cabinet closed. "Yeah."

They find six offices similar to the first one, all fine woods, expensive alcohols, and files. Lots of files. Each occupant of the office must be in charge of specific regions of the planet, hundreds of orphanages in each region.

"Who are you?" asks the oldest of the three women, clearly the leader. The other two women who entered with her hoist Wil up off the receptionist. She looks at the younger Tygran man. "Rather disappointing, Kento." She leans over his desk and presses a button.

The man dips his head. "Apologies, ma'am." He turns to Gabe. "They were disguised as local security."

"Disguised?" She eyes Wil, then Gabe, appraisingly. "They look pretty undisguised to me."

Wil wiggles his fingers. "Magic."

The woman in charge looks at the two intruders. "Restrain them."

With a faint metallic click, the woman nearest Wil places a device on his back, between his shoulder blades where he can't reach it.

"Sir, I..." Jarvis slurs. All suit functions cease.

The other woman places an override bolt on Gabe's torso. A light on the small device blinks. Gabe's eyes flicker, his shoulders slump.

The oldest woman smiles. "Bring them." She turns to Gabe. "I assume you will behave yourself?" Gabe inclines his head, his eyes dimmer than normal. "Good." She turns and heads toward the back of the warehouse.

Wil feels the barrels of two pulse pistols poke into the back of his armor. "Okay, okay," he says, hands up in the air. "Can I put my—" One of the pistols moves to the back of his head. "Or, you know, I'll just leave them up. It's good for the circulation." He falls in behind the woman in charge, Gabe behind him, flanked by the two guards.

The receptionist, Kento, retrieves a shirt from a cupboard behind his desk. He smooths his new shirt out and begins straightening up the lobby.

After passing through a series of doors and a short hallway lined with more doors, the group emerges into a massive auditorium. Bleachers form a half circle, seemingly set up recently on top of training space. Wil can see rolled up sparring mats against the walls as well as a few racks of blunt edged training weapons.

At the opposite end of the large space is a multi-tiered platform. The uppermost section has five ornate looking chairs, empty chairs. Just below that is a smaller boxed in seat, the witness stand, Wil guesses. Before the platform are two desks, each with two chairs. The bleachers are full of Tygrans of various ages.

"Did we miss the show?" Wil asks.

"Hush," says one of the women flanking him and Gabe.

Faces in the bleachers are turning toward the intruders.

Wil waves. "Hi." A jab in the back of his armor hard enough to push him forward silences him briefly. He turns. "So, this is a conclave?" This time the barrel of the pistol raises to his face. He turns back to see a group of Tygrans filing back in at front of the chamber.

After the five older Tygrans take their seats, several others follow. Including, "Cyn," Wil whispers. She's ushered in by a pair of guards. She sits down next to a younger woman.

Wil looks up at Gabe, who nods, the motion unnoticed by their captors. He looks around. "So, what now?"

"Can we cut his tongue out?" one guard asks.

The older woman shakes her head. "Not yet." She strides forward between the twin sets of bleachers. When she reaches the raised platform, she says, "These are the cause of the alert. They were snooping around the front office, then attacked Kento. The timing seems rather suspect." She looks over her shoulder at someone Wil can't see, sitting in the bleachers.

The Tygran in the middle of the group of five says, "Bring them forward."

CREEPIN'

Over the team's earpieces, Gabe says, "Cynthia is here. Alive. We are in the main warehouse space. One hundred and eight hostiles."

Maxim and Zephyr look at each other. They've cleared all the offices on their level and found two armories. Each armory is now sealed shut with a little chemical concoction Gabe helped cook up. The doors won't open without a cutting torch.

The big Palorian says, "Guess it's almost show time."

Zephyr checks the power level for her active camouflage. "None too soon. My camouflage system is down to about ten percent charge."

"Same."

They creep forward down the hall, stopping at an intersection. Maxim leans out, spotting a Tygran man in light combat armor walking right toward them. He clicks his local comms twice, then once. Behind him, Zephyr taps his shoulder.

They back up a meter and wait. The Tygran man comes around the corner and stops short of the two almost completely invisible Palorians. The man's eyes narrow and cast about the hallway. He sniffs several times, his fine whiskers twitching, his tail held still. As his hand drifts to the butt of the pulse pistol on his hip, he's tackled, eliciting a startled yelp.

As the sentry falls to the ground, he grabs a knife from the opposite leg as his pistol. Maxim feels the blade bite into his torso armor, hearing the buzz of the energy that lines the blade and is cutting into the armor every second. The impact causes the camouflage effect to ripple. He rains blows on the man's face as another knife thrust strikes exactly where the first did, this time puncturing his armor. From hip to armpit on this left side, the light bending function fails. Maxim grunts as the still energized blade slices into a rib. Maxim shifts his body to pull away from the lethal blade.

The Tygran twists under the weight of Maxim, getting his feet between him and the much larger Palorian. Pushing with all his might, he gets some separation from his heavy opponent, enough to bring his knife to bear between them.

Seeing the potential danger, Maxim shifts his weight, this time to fall to the side, slamming against the wall.

Zephyr, seeing her opportunity, pulls a knife of her own and dives for the Tygran man. So far, he hasn't called out, but she knows that won't last. Likely on his way to secure arms from one of the armories, he'll be expected back soon.

As if waiting for her to finish the thought, a voice down the hall calls out. "Panthro, hurry up. They just brought in a Multonae and a droid I've never seen the make of before. I bet they kill them with the traitor." When his friend doesn't immediately answer, the voice repeats, "Panthro?"

Looking down, Zephyr sees Panthro open his mouth to call out and drives her blade into the struggling man's side, finding a gap between two ribs. He grunts and gurgles, the light leaving his eyes.

Triggering the face shield on his armor to retract, Maxim whispers, "Get the other one." His hand is clutching his side, blue blood trickling between his fingers.

Zephyr checks her camouflage: two percent. She creeps around the corner toward Panthro's friend.

Maxim looks back down at Panthro, his eyes wide and sightless. He reaches down and runs a hand down the man's face, closing his eyes.

Standing, he looks around. No easy place to hide the body, and assuming things are going semi-according to plan, it won't matter in a few more microtocks. He triggers his armor's medical function, feeling the pinch of wound seal a moment before the painkillers course through his body.

Bennie hears Gabe's announcement and nods to himself. He's done what he can in the server room. A secure connection is uploading everything on every server to one of his remote caches for later sifting while a virus is working its way through the machines, burning out their storage modules. Several of the servers were already dark, their cores burnt out.

He turns a corner toward the desk and control unit in the center of the sub-basement and collides with a portly Tygran man. "Hey!" the larger man shouts, dropping a mug of chlormax to the ground.

Bennie falls backward with a shriek. The larger man stumbles back, as well, clearly not one of the fighting members of the Collective. Bennie rolls, getting to his feet, hand scrabbling for his beam saber.

The Tygran man gets his wits back and lunges for the small intruder, tackling him before the beam saber can ignite. The man slams Bennie to the ground, sending the saber hilt skittering across the floor.

"Get off me!" Bennie shouts, small fists slamming against his much larger opponent. He wiggles about ferociously until the man's grip loosens. Without waiting, Bennie lunges up, clamping his teeth on the man's shoulder.

Stumbling back, the technician yelps, "You bit me."

Bennie makes a noise, spitting. "Yeah, and now my mouth is full of hair."

"That's gross..." the man drawls, the last syllable stretching until he falls forward to the ground.

Bennie picks at his lip. "Hair in my mouth." He shakes his head and looks around for his beam saber while making *pfft* noises to dislodge the remaining hair stuck to his lips.

EVERYBODY WAS KUNG-FU FIGHTING

WIL AND GABE reach the front of the makeshift court. Wil looks over to Cynthia, who shakes her head fractionally. He grins. She frowns. He nods. She shakes her head again, more aggressively this time. The woman next to her looks from one of them to the other and back.

Wil looks up at the assembled board members, then turns to Dareb. "Hey, man."

The other man scowls.

From the raised platform, the senior board member asks, "Who are you?"

Wil raises a finger, then points to the woman next to the chairman. "You know what? You remind me of the babe."

The Tygran woman looks at the chairman, then back to Wil. "What...babe?"

Wil grins. "The babe with the power." He glances at Cynthia, who sighs, slowly shaking her head. He looks up at the board members, making a *go on* hand gesture.

"Uh, what power?" the woman demands.

"The power of voodoo." He drops to the ground.

Before anyone can react, Gabe's eyes brighten and turn ruby red as his hands fold and morph into his forearms as the blaster barrels emerge. He slaps the bolt from his torso, then raises both arms, forming a T.

Shouts erupt from the bleachers as Gabe opens fire. Instead of the normal red of super charged plasma, the energy bolts leaping from his arm cannons are blue. Stun blasts.

The crowd of assassins in the bleachers springs into action faster than Wil expects. Dozens of trained killers drop to the floor, sliding between rows in the bleachers. Others leap from the topmost seats to a low balcony that runs around the perimeter of the building. Still others surge forward, angling toward the raised platform and the stunned but already moving board of directors, attempting to provide cover.

Those Collective members who reached the ground have distributed the blunt edged training weapons from the lockers arrayed around the building's edge.

Gabe turns left and right, firing stun bolts faster than most people could track. In this case, his targets aren't just any people. The lithe, feline-featured assassins are leaping and twisting, avoiding the stun blasts while getting closer and closer. Several are throwing things in an attempt to distract the droid. Several blunted throwing stars strike his head and torso.

As Gabe's shoulder mounted cannon deploys, tracking targets, Wil darts toward Cynthia. She stands, flipping the table and pulling the woman next to her down behind it. Wil leaps over the table, landing next to the two women.

"Hi," he says over the sound of Gabe's rapid firing of stun bolts and the return fire from small, but decidedly not stun, weapons.

"Are you insane? You barged into a building full of trained killers," Cynthia says. She points to the balcony where members of the conclave are sprinting toward the rear of the building.

The other woman crouched behind the table says, "The armories are back there. That level. This will go really badly for you once everyone is armed."

Wil smiles. "Love you, too." He winks. "Our friends should have the armories taken care of. I hope." He leans around. "Would one of you mind?" He reaches over his shoulder to point at the inhibitor between his shoulder blades. His fingertips fall a few inches short of the small disc shaped device. Beatrix reaches up gingerly and plucks the device from his armor. "Thank you." The helmet and faceplate of his armor deploy, enclosing him.

"Hello, sir," the prissy intelligence in the armor says. "It is good to be back."

"Hey, Jarvis. Welcome back. It's Iron Man time." He stands, raising his arms, palms out. Plasma bolts lance out of both palms, slamming into two women who were advancing on the table, leaving scorched holes in their torsos.

"Wil!" Cynthia shouts.

He shrugs. "Sorry, this armor doesn't have a stun setting."

"I can lower the power if you'd like, sir. It won't be quite the same but should prove non-lethal," Jarvis offers.

"Oh. Sure, do that," Wil says, spinning to fire on a large man with two blunt edged training swords in his hands.

When the big Tygran man falls to the floor, Jarvis says, "He will be in pain later, but he is not dead."

"I'll sleep better tonight," Wil deadpans, turning to find another target and keep the enraged assassins from getting too close to Cynthia or her friend. He looks at the smaller of the two women. "I'm Wil, by the way. Her fiancé."

Beatrix looks at Wil, then Cynthia. "Congratulations?"

THIS IS...SOMETHING

"Boom, Kim Kardashian!" Bennie shouts, bursting into the room through a side door, a dead Yadro operator falling to the ground before him. "Gross!" He steps over the body.

Wil turns looking to the side door. "It's booyakasha."

Bennie waves the correction away, ducking under the swing of a wooden staff. Raising his beam saber, he cuts the staff in two and sends its wielder to the ground, cradling the stump where a hand had just been. "Did you know this place has sewer monsters?" He dodges a woman with a training sword in one hand and a very much not-training knife in the other, rolling under first one, then the second, strike.

Jumping to his feet, Bennie slashes down across his opponent's training sword, cutting it in half, leaving both halves burning. He smiles. "Run away." When she doesn't, he deflects her knife thrust and slices across her torso. Her body falls to the ground.

Across the room, Gabe reaches over his shoulder to rip a smaller woman from his back, hurling her at the raised platform that the board of directors vacated. "Perhaps now is not the best time to discuss the underground fauna," he says. His shoulder mounted blaster swivels, tracing fire across the room, blasting a section of the bleachers.

Bennie opens his mouth but shuts it as a line of energy blasts lances toward him, forcing him to leap out of the way. He swipes his beam saber to deflect the nearest bolt of super charged plasma. The blade snaps off as Bennie takes aim and fires a bolt of purple energy, causing two attackers that have secured pulse rifles to leap behind cover.

He runs over to dive behind the table. "Hi, Cynthia." He turns to Beatrix. "Well, hello there." He ducks as a piece of the table explodes.

Cynthia leans over, rolling her eyes. "Not now. We need weapons!"

Bennie shrugs. "Sorry, only carry this now." He leans up over the table and fires a purple bolt of energy that strikes a man in the leg, sending him spiraling to the ground. He drops a pistol. It clatters toward the table. Bennie darts out around the table, diving into a roll, snatching the pulse pistol as he passes. "Catch!" He tosses the pistol to the two women.

"WE'RE LATE!" Maxim says. They can hear the weapons' fire from the hallway.

"Then let's go!" Zephyr says, grinning.

They round the corner but stop short when Zephyr holds up a fist. She motions for Maxim to step back. Up ahead at the next junction, a procession of Collective operators surrounding five older Tygrans rushes past. Three lightly armed operators in front, three in the back. They're heading down the hallway to the offices and armories.

"They're gonna be mad when they get to those armories." Maxim grins.

Zephyr looks at Maxim, returning his grin. She taps her wrist-comm, activating the team channel. "Wil, we're going after a group we just saw heading…" She looks around. "Heading back toward the offices. Some guards and a couple of oldsters."

"The board of directors. Good call, we'll probably want them. I think we have things—oh shit! Sorry, I think we have things mostly under control here," Wil replies.

Reaching the junction, Maxim leans out, wincing. "Clear." They head down the corridor back toward the rear of the warehouse.

Knowing roughly where they're going, the two Palorians take it slowly to not alert their prey prematurely, since their camouflage systems are fresh out of power. Rounding a corner that will take them back to the offices they cleared when they got into the building, they spot the rear guard standing ready. The doors to the offices are open, and from at least a few of them, they hear urgent shouts. They watch for a minute or two until the other three armed operators appear from two of the rooms. One says, "Form up. We're moving."

The group heads for the end of the corridor, where one of the older Tygrans places a hand on a barely noticeable scanner panel on the wall. The wall—a door, actually—swings in on silent hinges.

"Always a secret passage," Maxim says. He grins at Zephyr. "Maybe we should install some at the office."

Zephyr smiles, and they head for the door the moment the last of the rear guard vanishes out of sight. They reach the door just in time for Zephyr to slide her hand in to block the latch. She turns to Maxim and wiggles her eyebrows, smiling.

CHAPTER TWENTY-TWO

Bennie has moved off toward the front of the large warehouse, doing his best to not kill his attackers, but with only a beam saber, there are going to be a lot of Tygran ninja assassins in the hospital later, with fewer than the standard number of limbs.

"Cynthia!" a familiar voice shouts.

Cynthia rises over the remains of the table to shoot and sees Margo. The other woman is standing in the middle of the melee, weapons' fire and scrambling Tygrans all around her.

Wil, standing off to the side fighting a woman with a training sword, turns to see Margo stalking toward Cynthia and the other woman...Beverly? He parries a strike from his opponent's sword, kicking her in the stomach. Before she can get back to her feet to attack Wil, he darts off toward Margo.

"Oh, no you don't!" he shouts, leaping into the air, plasma bolts leaping from his palms.

Margo stops dead in her tracks, spins, and leaps into the air to deliver a savage kick that stops Wil in midflight, sending him spiraling off in the opposite direction.

Wil crashes to the ground. "Get up, loser!" Bennie shouts,

ducking under the swing of a thick staff. He slashes, cutting the staff in two. His opponent grins, twirling the two halves. Bennie groans.

Wil stands. "Margo." He stalks towards her. "I have something for you."

She turns. "Oh?"

Reaching her, he lashes out with an armor powered kick. "An ass ki—" He's interrupted by a fist slamming into his face. He falls on his back, rolling to avoid a kick. He lashes out with a kick of his own, this time connecting, sending her sprawling to the ground.

"Sir, perhaps I should close the face shield if you are going to continue to get punched in the face," Jarvis offers.

"Shut up," Wil growls, wiping a gloved hand under his nose to clear the blood momentarily.

"Wil!" Cynthia shouts, ducking to avoid a bolt of plasma. She turns to return fire.

"I got this, babe!" Wil says, stomping toward Margo, his armored palms glowing.

Margo pinwheels her legs, spinning like a top as she gains her footing. She looks at Wil, sneering. She lunges in, sliding under his plasma blasts to drive punches into the softer parts of his armor. A split second before another fist slams into his nose, the faceplate drops into place.

"Thanks, Jarvis!" Wil shouts, falling back, trying his best to block the flurry of punches the lithe Tygran ninja assassin is dropping on him. Despite his armor, he's feeling more and more of the blows.

"Of course, sir. She is quite strong. The weaker parts of the armor may not last indefinitely under this attack," the AI warns.

From across the room, Bennie says, "Doing good, boss!" He jumps up and over a spinning kick. He aims his beam saber hilt and fires, burning a scorch mark across the torso of his opponent. The wound is, he thinks, in a non-lethal location.

"Shut up!" Wil says, turning sideways to use his forearms to block another powerful kick.

Beatrix, still crouching next to Cynthia, asks, "Should you help him?"

Cynthia twists, firing into the legs of two men rushing towards her, sending them to the ground writhing. "He's a grown man. He can ask for help."

"Well, this is not at all what I was expecting," Maxim whispers as they peer through the window of the small control room. Beyond the window is a ship about half the size of the *Ghost*, sleek like an atmospheric craft, except for the much-too-stubby nacelles that end in FTL engines.

"You think those platinum inlays do anything?" Zephyr says, pointing to the intricate scrollwork that winds around the ship's hull, forming an abstract image of a large scaled animal.

"Beyond advertising how expensive that ship is, doubt it."

The board of directors has moved aboard the ship, while the six guards are milling around the hidden launch bay floor. From a speaker somewhere in the building, a voice announces that preflight checks are nearly complete.

With the groan of metal that hasn't moved in tens of cycles, the roof splits down the middle and slides apart.

Maxim looks at his partner. "Haven't we done this before?"

She clucks. "Should be easier this time. No deadly space gas."

He turns. "Space gas? Like gas, in space?"

Zephyr frowns. "Don't tell Wil."

BOOM, BOOM

WIL STRIKES THE WALL, sliding down into a sitting position.

"Sir, this is not going well," Jarvis says.

Wil shakes his head to clear the stars that are floating in front of him. Even with his armor on, Margo is taking him apart one punch and kick at a time.

He looks at Cynthia and the other woman...Bethany? "A little help here."

Cynthia tilts her head. "That took way too long." She vaults over the remains of the table, leaving her borrowed pistol with Beatrix. "Margo," she growls.

The other woman spins. Wiping a trickle of blood from her lip where Wil got a lucky punch in, she says, "I was wondering if I'd have to kill him before you found your courage, traitor."

Cynthia rolls her head, stretching her shoulders. "I guess I'm going to have to beat the truth into you." She assumes a combat ready stance.

Margo charges, unleashing a flurry of kicks and punches. Cynthia blocks and parries as fast as her opponent can attack, barely taking a step back. Seeing an opening, Cynthia takes the initiative, driving her opponent back several steps.

A spin kick swoops in to be blocked by a raised leg, taking the impact on the side of the shin. A roundhouse punch whistles in to strike upraised forearms. Two quick jabs precede an uppercut.

Wil gets to his feet and fires a blast into a man Bennie is engaged in fighting. "Hey! Where's Gabe?" The Brailack looks over, then ducks under a chair being swung at him. He turns, swiping his beam saber blade through the chair. He shrugs.

Wil frowns. "Jarvis. Where's Gabe?"

"Gabe is in the lobby. Shall I contact him?"

Wil shakes his head, moving toward the hallway that leads back to the front of the building. "No, thanks."

Looking at the sleek escape craft, Zephyr says, "Ready."

"Ready," Maxim repeats.

Nodding to each other, they step out of the small control room, firing. Two of the Tygran guards fall immediately, but the remaining targets scatter.

"Gabe, Bennie, anyone—the bigwigs are trying to make a break for it. Any chance at overriding the bay doors, or their ship, or, I dunno, something?"

"Busy," Bennie says.

"I am afraid I am otherwise occupied," Gabe replies.

Maxim sighs, ducking behind a landing strut as return fire tracks them. Plasma bolts strike the strut, raining sparks. "Always up to us." He takes aim and fires both pistols at the engine nacelle over them. Zephyr takes aim with one pistol while using the other to lay down a minimal amount of suppressing fire, keeping the four guards busy.

The whine of repulsorlifts drowns out the energy weapons fire.

Zephyr darts to the other landing strut, firing as she moves. Maxim adds to her fire. Several bolts strike her side, sending her skidding the last meter, her armor smoking.

"Love?" Maxim says, leaning out to fire first on the Tygrans near the boarding ramp of the ship, then back at the engine nacelle that's sparking sporadically. Damaged, but not enough to keep it on the ground.

"I'm fine. We're about to lose our cover." She points to the ship.

The ship rises, the hydraulic pistons of the landing struts wheezing as the pressure on them eases.

The four guards dash for cover as the boarding ramp raises. Maxim, in a similar situation as the guards, darts away from his strut for cover.

Zephyr rushes toward the boarding ramp, diving and tossing her pistol up into the ship a moment before the ramp seals closed. She lands with a thud, firing her remaining pistol at the nearest guard.

The ship roars as it gains altitude. Zephyr rolls over and looks up. She gets back to her feet and sprints towards Maxim. "Cover!"

The escape ship clears the roof of the warehouse, both nacelles buzzing under the sound of the repulsorlifts. As it turns, angling away from the building, a section of it explodes. The boarding ramp, bent and smoking, slams to the ground next to Maxim.

The guards all look up as the ship lurches, belching flames from a large tear in the hull. Smoke is pouring from the wound as the vessel begins to twist. The starboard repulsorlift, the one Maxim has been firing on, is flickering wildly, trailing sparks. Another explosion rocks the ship, this one internal. The damaged nacelle splutters and dies.

The guards regain their composure and charge the two Palorians.

CLEANING UP

Wil reaches the lobby and looks around. He whistles seeing the six —he hopes—unconscious Tygrans, including his old pal Kento. The whistle turns to a croak when his gaze reaches the front door and a battered Gabe. "Damn! Gabe!" Wil shouts, rushing to his mechanical friend's side.

"Hello, Captain," the droid says. One eye is a smoking crater, the other is flickering. His left arm is gone at the elbow. There's a sizable hole in his side. Internal components are sparking, and something is leaking out. Wisps of smoke that smell like burnt electronics are drifting up from dozens of places inside the droid.

"You've seen better days." Wil kneels down, putting a hand on Gabe's shoulder.

"I have. This body, while highly adaptable and generations more advanced than any other droid frame in use in the GC, is...not suitable for...com-combat."

Wil smiles. "You have a high-powered rifle-thing that deploys from your back."

Gabe smiles his uncanny valley smile, pointing to the unconscious Tygrans. "The cannon did not impress them."

"Their loss."

Gabe nods. "I was endeavoring to execute the final phase of the plan."

Wil nods. "Success?"

Gabe nods once, sparks shooting from a damaged section of his neck. Wil looks up. Now that he's listening, he can hear sirens in the distance. Something somewhere explodes, drowning the sirens out briefly. He pulls a face. "That's probably not good."

"Agreed. Probably whatever Maxim and Zephyr are working on."

Wil reaches under his friend, using what's left of the augmented strength his armor provides to lift Gabe to his feet. "God, you're heavy."

"I am made of metal."

Wil smiles and shakes his head. "Let's go."

THE ESCAPE SHIP crashes back to the ground, crumpling the side wall of the fake warehouse. Maxim ducks a punch from one of the guards, parrying another series of blows before getting a chance to plant a kick into the man's chest, driving him back. He feels his wound reopen a moment before his armor informs him of a second dose of painkillers and wound seal being administered.

Over the sound of the metal crunching under the settling ship and the flames that have sprung up everywhere, the sound of sirens grows.

Maxim shouts, "Zee, cavalry inbound!"

She dodges a punch but misses the kick that follows and crashes to the ground. "Good timing! Go, Gabe!" The woman standing over her takes aim with her pistol but flinches as an explosion rocks the crashed ship and the remnants of the warehouse wall it's lying on. Zephyr kicks out as hard as she can into the knee of the woman, sending her to the ground. Zephyr scrambles to get the woman in a chokehold. Her scout armor protects her from the flailing blows until her opponent goes limp.

Maxim looks at his current opponents. "You should probably run. I'm guessing your government won't go easy on ya. We don't give a dren about you, but I bet you'd make excellent scapegoats."

The man and woman opposite him look at each other, then the flaming wreck a dozen meters away. They turn and break for the lowest part of the ruined warehouse wall. He smirks. Turning, he spots Zephyr getting to her feet, her opponent unconscious at her feet. "We should see if we can save one or two of those board member folks."

She nods and heads for the wrecked vessel. He falls in next to her. Wincing, he says, "So, this has been fun."

Seeing his face, she puts a hand on his arm, lifting it to look at his wristcomm. "Your vitals are not looking so good."

He grunts and climbs up to the ruined ship. "I'll manage."

She looks up at him, shaking her head. "Think it'll ever get old?"

He laughs, pulling himself into the wreckage. "When the pay stops being worth it."

Raising an eyebrow, Zephyr asks, "Who do you think is paying for this one?"

Maxim thinks it over. "Dren."

"Look what we found," Maxim says, pushing three wounded Tygrans through the door into the completely wrecked training-area-turned-courtroom. He shoves the trio toward what's left of a section of bleachers. "Go sit down." One turns to scowl. "Go on, scoot."

Bennie is sitting cross-legged on an unconscious Margo. "You two missed a pretty epic fight." He pokes Margo's head twice. "Cynthia kicked her ass up and down the room." He turns to Wil standing nearby, holding Cynthia close. "After Margo kicked Wil's ass up and down the room." He chuckles. "I got some video."

Barbara Mress walks over to the remaining three Yadro board of directors. "You disgust me." She turns to a pair of droids in security colors. "Keep your eyes on these three. Triple your forces around them at all times."

One droid inclines its head. "Of course. I have notified regional security, as well, to request additional resources." It helps the trio up and flanks them as they follow the other droid toward the front of the warehouse.

Barbara turns to Wil and Cynthia. "Well, this went...in a direction." She smiles. "Glad you all are okay." Putting a hand on Cynthia's arm, "Especially you. We were all worried."

Cynthia smiles through a split lip caked with dried blood. "I'd be lying if I said I wasn't worried. She," nodding to Margo's inert form, under Bennie, "told me you were all dead. That she blew up the *Ghost*."

Bennie nods. "She tried. She set some bounty hunters or mercenary types on us. Took a while to shake. They busted up the *Ghost* something fierce."

Wil pulls her close. "You know we're harder to kill than that." He beams.

She rests her head against Wil's chest for a moment. "True." She looks at Margo again, then the ruins of the platform erected for the trial. "I don't know what this was all about."

From his perch, Bennie says, "Oh, I do." He stands and walks over, his arm held up to present the screen of his wristcomm. "Once we were done, I looked through some of the data I collected from the servers in the basement. From what I can tell, one of the board member's spouses ratted out the group after being arrested for something else. He sold out the group, told his wife so she and a few others could lie low for a bit." He turns to Mress. "I'll forward it all to you when I get to the *Ghost*. Should be more than enough to shut these drennogs down for good." The Tygran woman inclines her head.

Cynthia shrugs. "Then why pin it on me? Why was it even a thing?"

Bennie makes a face. "No idea. I'm sure it's in there, but if I had to guess, someone asked questions, they started talking about being betrayed. You left the fold, and they pinned it on you out of convenience."

"People suck," Wil says.

A security officer approaches the group. "Excuse me. We've rounded up the wounded." He looks over at Margo. "Most of them." He points to the unconscious woman and two officers move to pick her up. Turning back to the group, he says, "Thank you. The Yadro Collective is a societal black mark we all thought was in the past."

Wil nods. "We'll make sure to mention that when we send the

invoice." The officer quirks an eyebrow, his tail twitching. Wil smiles and waves him off. "Don't sweat it."

Maxim taps his wristcomm, swiping to the officer, whose own device beeps. "I snapped scans from files upstairs. I don't know if they destroyed the real ones or not, but that should be enough to at least do some damage." He pats his armor. "Oh, and I grabbed a few physical files too." He releases the chest piece on his armor. The files he removes are covered in blood. "Oh, maybe these won't be as useful."

Wil's eyes go wide. "Dude."

The security man takes the bloodied files and steps back as Wil and Cynthia move in.

Maxim holds up his free hand. "I'm okay."

"Like hell you are," Wil says. He looks at Mress. "Gabe needs a mechanic. Max and Cyn need a doctor."

THE NEXT MORNING, the members of the team that didn't need to stay in the hospital are gathered around Cynthia and Maxim's beds. It took some arguing and begging, but the hospital staff agreed to put both of them in the same room. The hospital that Mress secured is a short drive from the rental house. With her help, the nosy woman Bennie tied up on the back porch was released, and no charges were pressed.

"Hey, losers," Bennie says, hopping up on to Cynthia's bed. A kick sends him back to the floor with a yelp. Hopping up onto Maxim's bed, he makes a rude gesture at Cynthia.

Zephyr, Wil, and Barbara Mress enter the room. Wil says, "You're looking good."

Cynthia smiles. "Nothing some medical grade painkillers couldn't handle."

Maxim grins. "Those are good meds."

Zephyr moves to stand next to the bed, next to Bennie. "Doc says you can leave in a bit. No serious damage to either of you."

The big Palorian man nods. "Told you I was fine."

Zephyr makes a face. "You lost of a lot of blood."

Wil sits next to Cynthia, planting a kiss on the top of her head.

One of her ears has a good-sized notch cut in it. Touching the tip with a finger, he asks, "Memento?"

Nodding, Cynthia reaches up to touch her ear. "Yeah."

"Looks good on ya. Very bad ass," Bennie says.

Wil joins Cynthia on her bed. "We stopped by the facility Babs set up for Gabe. He said he'll be ready to go by tonight. Looks like he's making some changes to his frame." He looks around the room. "I've been thinking. Maybe I've been trying to make this wedding thing more than it needs to be."

"What does that mean?" Cynthia asks, a worried expression crossing her face.

Zephyr glances at Maxim.

Wil holds up both hands. "Just that I don't think I want to waste any more time. I placed some calls this morning before we came over here."

Barbara Mress smiles. "For what it's worth, I like his idea."

"I still think we shoulda used the money from the Tygrans for something else," Bennie grouses. Maxim elbows him. "Ow. What?"

"Eat your cake," the big man says, nodding to the plate before the surly Brailack.

The crew of the *Ghost* is sitting at a round table in the hangar portion of the Rogue Enterprises building, under the port wing of the still-in-need-of-some-repairs *Ghost*. Near the large hangar doors, wide open to let the Fury sunset in, Wil and Cynthia are sitting at a separate table, whispering to each other. Behind them, several shuttles are parked in the open space outside the building.

Zephyr turns to Rhys Duch. "What did you think?"

Next to Duch, Grell, the squat purple apelike being, says, "Ah thaht it wahs pretty."

Zephyr smiles. "It was."

Duch sips his drink. "This was definitely an interesting ceremony." He looks over at the newly married couple. "All of his people go through this whole thing?"

"According to the data uplinks we've seen, most of them do it multiple times in their life," Maxim says. The Multonae man on the other side of Zephyr shakes his head.

"And the expense. This is the toned-down version, and it still cost a fortune," Bennie adds. He looks at Duch. "Where's Tah'tu?"

The Multonae crime boss shrugs. "Someone had to keep things running back home. He volunteered. I don't think he likes you guys."

"It's mutual," Bennie says. He raises his fluted glass and clinks his fork against it. Occupants of the dozen tables scattered around the hangar pick up the call. Wil looks up, smiling, and kisses Cynthia to cheers from the guests. Bennie grins. "That's fun. It's like they're puppets." He moves to strike his glass again but loses his fork to Maxim. "Hey!"

At a table nearby, Prathea, Xan, and Jor'Lu are bickering about something while hunched over a PADD. At the same table, a group of Tarsi are talking amongst themselves.

At the table next to that, watching the scientists argue, James Hawthorne and seven other humans are talking amongst themselves. The chief engineer of the *Wil Calder* leans in and says, "Holy shit, you guys." She motions toward the hangar space. "We're at a space wedding, surrounded by all kinda of aliens." She grabs her comm unit and activates the camera mode, snapping a few crowd shots. James laughs and looks to the front of the room, and his friend. When Wil looks over, James smiles and nods. Wil returns the gesture.

Standing, Wil and Cynthia work their way around the tables.

They reach the table with the gaggle of scientists and Tarsi. "Prathea, everyone. Thanks for coming," Cynthia says.

Wil smiles. "Bloomin' onion, Councilwoman Grythlorian." The Tarsi councilor and her Tarlack aide both incline their heads. The former says, "Thank you for inviting us to your joining ceremony."

Prathea looks up from the shared PADD. "Thank you for the invite." She looks at Wil. "Congratulations."

Xan strains to push Jor'Lu's chin up so that the Burzzad engineer is looking at the hosts. The Olop physicist says, "I thought you'd die alone, so, you know, congrats." She winks.

Wil smiles, pulling Cynthia close. "Thanks."

Cynthia grins. "Good to see you again."

Xan nods. "Glad you took my advice to not try to bed Bennie." The furry scientist grins, baring her teeth.

Wil's mouth forms an O as he looks at his wife. Cynthia chuckles. "Yes, good advice." She pushes Wil away from the table, toward the crew of the *Wil Calder*.

At the human table, Wil slaps his old friend on the back. "So..."

"Dude," Hawthorne replies.

"Right?" Wil beams. He looks at the others. "Thanks for coming. I know you don't know us and all, but..."

James' executive officer, a dark-haired Asian woman, smiles. "A chance to go this deep into GC territory without risking an attack from opportunistic pirates? The president of Earth Gov. practically begged us to come."

Wil grins. "I hope this means we see more humans out here soon."

"Gods help us all," Cynthia whispers.

Wil elbows her lightly. Looking around the table, he says, "Don't get yourselves into trouble."

At the Rogue Enterprises table, Gabe turns to Bennie. "How long do we expect this to last? I cannot begin upgrades to the *Ghost's* missile loading system until we clear some of these tables."

Maxim laughs. "That's probably going to have to wait until tomorrow afternoon sometime."

Gabe makes a rattling noise. "I see."

Bennie leans in. "How're you liking this version three design?"

Gabe holds out a hand, a matte blue-gray color like the rest of his chassis. "I feel that this body better encapsulates what I want my role to be."

"No shoulder cannon?" Zephyr asks.

"No shoulder cannon," Gabe confirms.

Maxim sighs. "That was a cool cannon."

"Indeed."

The reception lasts a few more hours. Slowly, groups begin to peel off either to their shuttles to head home, or to the upper floors and the makeshift guest rooms the team has set up.

Zephyr and Maxim are standing next to the control panel for the large hangar door. Reaching over to press the button to close the massive doors, Zephyr says, "I can't imagine a better path for our lives."

Maxim puts an arm around her waist, pulling her close. "I could do without Bennie, but..." He leans in for a kiss as the grinding of the door mechanism starts up.

"I heard that!" Bennie shouts from the table he's at, several plates of cake arrayed before him.

THE END

THE NEXT MORNING, everyone is at the kitchen table on the third floor. The last of the guests have departed for the spaceport.

Wil looks at everyone. "This was fun. Thanks."

Cynthia nods her agreement. "What he said."

Gabe, standing near the window that overlooks the street, says, "I am pleased that we could take time to do this." At a lower volume, he adds, "Even if it interfered with my maintenance schedule."

Bennie turns in his seat to look over at his mechanical friend. "Yeah, I still think it was outrageously expensive, but it was fun." His wristcomm beeps. He blushes a deep green.

Maxim smiles. "Xan?"

Bennie grins, baring his teeth. "She showed me how much she missed me last night."

"That's what that sound was," Zephyr says. "I thought a felga bird got stuck in one of the cooling units on the roof." She grins.

"Whatever." He scoops some more food onto his plate.

Gabe says, "Someone is approaching the building."

Wil looks up. "Someone forget something?"

Gabe shakes his head. "It is not one of the guests." He nods to a screen mounted in the living space next to the kitchen. On the screen, a small Olop is approaching the door.

"Who's that?" Wil asks.

Cynthia shakes her head. "She looks kinda familiar."

Bennie rubs his eyes. "Oh, grolack."

Maxim squints. "Hey! It's that little kid from our shuttle." He looks at the others. "The one that helped Mr. Knight retake our shuttle and save everyone. Blip? Wic?"

"Nic!" Zephyr snaps her fingers. "Was traveling with her grandmother."

"Oh, yeah," Wil says. His face turns serious as he turns to the team hacker. "You didn't..."

"What?" Bennie frowns.

"You know...she's a kid..."

"What? Oh! No! Gross, you krebnack. She's a little kid." Bennie is scowling at him.

Cynthia shrugs. "Sometimes with you we—"

"A little kid!" Bennie screams. He hops from the seat. "You guys suck."

On the screen, the young Olop is standing at the door waiting.

"Should I—" Gabe starts.

"I got it," Bennie grates. He moves to the stairwell, grumbling about his lack of friends.

The others wait until they see the door open on the camera footage. Wil turns to Gabe. "Audio?"

The sound of Bennie's voice immediately fills the room. "What do you want?"

The girl scowls but says, "Hi to you, too, Grandpa."

Wil chuckles. "I like her." Everyone nods.

"Hi. What do you want?" demands Bennie from off screen.

The girl rocks on her heels as she fumbles for what to say. Finally, she looks at Bennie. "I want to train with you. To be a Knight of Plentallus."

"Didn't see that coming," Cynthia says.

ENJOY CHAPTER 1 of 'Long Days, Short Knights' the first book in the next series of the Space Rogues adventures!

NEW ADVENTURES

CHAPTER 1

Wil dropped the crate and stretched to rub his back. "Okay, this is the last one. Not sure why I had to unload them all."

Lounging in a folding chair near the *Ghost*'s cargo boarding ramp, Maxim looked up. "Because Zephyr and I gave you our share of the Moklan Pleasure Station credits we got from that cruise ship gig." He grinned. When Wil and Cynthia moved their wedding up, they also changed their honeymoon plans.

Wil sighed but nodded along. "Right. Seemed like a good idea twenty-two crates ago. Well, the client will be here to collect these in a week or so." The other man nodded. Wil continued, "While we're gone, you mind ordering a new gravsled or three?" In their haste to leave Nom Clamma to save Cynthia, they had left their gravsleds behind in a hotel.

"Sure thing." Maxim stood and walked to the crates. "These are what, again?" He rapped his knuckles against the plasticoid material. Kneeling down to look at the label, he read, "Fungal growth medium?" He stood and backed away. "You gotta stop taking jobs without telling us."

Wil waved his hands. "Hey, I ran this by y'all. I distinctly remember you were reading something on a PADD and said," he lowered his voice as low as he could, "'I'm not going, so do whatever you like.'"

Maxim rubbed his chin. "That does sound sort of familiar." He smiled. "You excited?"

Wil turned to his friend, beaming. "I am. Two weeks on what's supposed to be one of the most luxurious locations in the GC, all expenses paid. Can't wait." He nodded toward the front office. "What do you two have planned?"

From the door connecting the small front office space to the hangar that the *Ghost* occupied, Zephyr said, "I plan to keep him plenty busy."

Wil leaned to look past the deeply blushing Maxim to grin at Cynthia and Zephyr as the door to the front office closed behind them. He whispered, "I know what you think she means, but I bet she means finally painting the exterior of the building." He winked as Maxim frowned.

Cynthia's tail was swishing languidly as she walked toward Wil and the *Ghost*, a duffel bag slung over her shoulder. "You aren't packed."

Maxim released a sigh. Wil looked up at him, grinning. He turned to his wife. "I know." He pointed to the twenty-two crates haphazardly stacked against the near wall. "I was busy." He lifted an arm and made a face. "I'll shower and pack." He grinned. "I don't expect to need many clothes."

Zephyr blushed, looking at Maxim.

From across the hangar, Bennie shouted, "No! I told you, thrust, then parry."

"I'm trying!" a higher-pitched voice replied. "You suck as a teacher!"

"You suck more as a student!"

Everyone turned to look at the stairs in the opposite corner of the building. Bennie and his apprentice, Nic, the Olop girl he and Maxim had met while on their way to meet the others aboard the *Galactic Empress*, were coming down the stairs. The juvenile Olop had tagged along with Bennie when his and Maxim's shuttle, en route to the docking hub and waiting *Galactic Empress*, was hijacked by pirates looking for vengeance against the *Ghost* crew members.

During the incident aboard the luxury star liner, Bennie had forbidden her from getting involved, asking a massive Xelurian scientist to keep an eye on the young woman and her grandmother.

After the team saved the cruise ship and its passengers from certain doom, the young girl had hung on Bennie's every word as he told the story to anyone who would buy him a drink.

Nic had arrived at the Rogue Enterprises offices a week ago, with a note from her grandmother giving her permission to train with Bennie at a "special school," whatever that was.

Bennie tried to send her away that first night and several times a day since then. She continued to refuse, insisting she was ready to be a Knight of Plentallus, like Bennie.

When not fighting, the two were sparring and training. Bennie was doing his best, despite only learning what it meant to be a Knight himself not that long ago.

"Hey!" Wil shouted. "Give it a rest, you two!"

"She started it!"

"He started it!"

Wil sighed. He turned back to his other teammates. "I'm going to shower and pack." Cynthia grinned and followed him toward the nearer staircase.

As Bennie and Nic reached the two Palorians, Maxim said, "What's the problem now?"

Nic's mouth opened, but a green three-fingered hand moved in front of it.

"She doesn't listen," Bennie complained. "She never listens."

Nic slapped Bennie's hand away. "He keeps changing what he wants from me."

Maxim inhaled. "Look. If you're gonna continue down this path, you gotta figure it out." He pointed at Bennie. "Have you checked in with Nexum? Maybe there's a training program for Knights? Or a guidebook, or something?" Pointing at Nic, he added, "You need to realize you're the student. Be open minded. He's learning to teach. You need to learn to learn."

Zephyr leaned to the side. "Well. That's deep."

Maxim grinned. "I can do deep."

GABE AND CYNTHIA were standing on the *Ghost*'s cargo ramp. Maxim, Zephyr, Bennie, and Nic were a few meters away.

"Have fun!" Zephyr shouted over the growing rumble of the small warship's engines spooling up. Wil was already aboard, finishing the pre-flight checklist.

The ramp rose, and Cynthia shouted, "Have a good staycation!" She turned and ushered Gabe up the ramp with her as it sealed shut.

Gabe was returning to Arcadia, the homeworld of the newly minted Mechnoid Nation. The society created by droids from across the GC had been granted personal autonomy and civil rights. Gabe had helped to create this new society and, for several cycles now, had been fending off pleas to run for public office. He was returning to Arcadia to participate in some government stuff that none of the others really understood. Despite turning down public office, Gabe still held a lot of sway among his people.

The *Ghost* rose off her landing gear, the hydraulic pistons sighing as the weight of the ship left them. With clanks and whirs, the two powerful legs folded up into the body of the ship, armored panels closing over them.

"He won't..." Maxim started to say.

The *Ghost* was rotating to face out through the huge hangar doors.

Zephyr looked around, then turned, pushing Bennie and Nic toward the door to the front office portion of the building. "He might."

Maxim followed the others as the *Ghost* tilted, dropping her nose slightly, allowing the ship to drift forward on her repulsorlifts.

Once the *Ghost* cleared the large hangar doors, her atmospheric engines lit off with a boom, pushing the ship up and away from the building.

From the safety of the conference room, Bennie looked up at the two Palorians. "I thought he'd do it."

"Do what?" Nic asked.

Bennie turned. "Kick in the atmo engines while inside the building."

"Wouldn't that be dangerous?"

"Very," Zephyr agreed.

Bennie cleared his throat. "So, anyway, we're gonna be taking off."

Nic looked at him, her mouth hanging open.

Maxim looked down at his friend. "Oh? Where are you going?"

Bennie rocked on his heels. "Nexum. I spoke to C7K2 last night. He said there are lots of materials on the apprentice training program at the Tower of Plentallus."

"There's an apprentice training program?" Zephyr asked.

Nic made a high-pitched squeal, clapping her hands.

Bennie looked at her, making a face. "Do you even know anything about Nexum?"

She shrugged. "I like road trips."

Maxim smiled. "I'm glad you got some direction. If there were materials, why didn't C7K2 send them along when you told him about training her?"

"Well, I never really told him. I mean, I assumed I could do it."

"With what? Those training holos he sent when you left the Tower last time?"

Bennie nodded. "Yeah, that's what I've been trying to use on her." He hitched a thumb toward Nic. "I guess he curated that stuff for self-guided learning from a certain point in the training. C7K2 has a whole other, more in-depth set of records for how a Knight should train his apprentice. Apparently, once a Knight got to a certain level, they always found a kid to tag along with them. Do grunt work stuff and all that."

"Grunt work?" Nic murmured.

Zephyr said, "Booking a shuttle?"

Bennie clucked. "No. Not since that last time. I've decided that public transport is for losers." He looked at Nic. "No offense." She made a rude gesture but said nothing. Bennie said, "I rented a private shuttle. It should be ready by the time we get to the spaceport."

Zephyr shrugged. "Can't say I blame ya on the public transport thing. Private shuttle, though. Pricey way to travel." She raised an eyebrow.

Bennie smirked. "I may have hacked the rental company's reservation computer."

Zephyr groaned. "I didn't hear that."

Bennie turned to Nic. "Why are you still standing there? Go pack."

The hangar doors rattled as they rolled closed, sealing off the space from the dry, dusty surface of Fury. The Palorian couple watched first Nic, then Bennie, head back upstairs to the residential floor.

Maxim turned to Zephyr. "We're actually going to be alone for... well...a while." He grinned.

"Let's celebrate when those two are safely on a shuttle leaving orbit." She winked.

THE SHUTTLE BENNIE hacked a rental for was spacious. It was about twice as long as the *Ghost*'s cargo hold, sleek and modern, unlike the aged Ankarran Raptor. Better still, it was almost entirely automated with a state-of-the-art sentient intelligence system for a pilot. Since Bennie didn't actually know how to fly a ship, that was welcome news.

The Brailack hacker and Knight of Plentallus tossed his duffel bag onto the bed in one of the three small single occupant berths near the front of the ship. He made sure his unwanted student took the berth furthest from him.

Bennie still wasn't sure about training Nic. For one thing, she annoyed the wurrin out of him. For another—if he was being honest with himself—the larger concern was that he didn't know if he was up to the task of training a potential future Knight. His own training was far from complete.

Her persistence had largely taken his second concern out of his hands. Since her arrival, he had tried time and again to send her home or really anywhere else that wasn't Fury. She refused, often vehemently, sometimes violently, to leave.

The speaker in the ceiling played a pleasant chime before saying, "We have been cleared for departure. Please secure for takeoff. We will lift off in five microtocks."

Bennie remembered how hard it had been for Wil to wrap his head around common Galactic Commonwealth units of time. Bennie never understood how twelve and sixty units made more sense to the human than simple base ten units. But, Bennie had learned over the years, from Wil and the humans he had met on Earth once, that humans were anything but rational.

Bennie walked out of the small berth to the seating area directly behind the cockpit. Nic was already there, seated and belted in. She was practically vibrating. "You've traveled before. Why are you so excited?" he asked.

"I've never been to Nexum."

"It's not that great, believe me." He dropped into a seat opposite hers. Fastening his belt, he added, "The locals are okay, the food is fine—"

"It's the home of the Knights of Plentallus!" she interrupted. "The Tower is a GC treasure!"

"It's okay." He nodded.

"How can you say that?" Bennie shrugged. She continued, "Built before the founding of the Commonwealth. Before, the, Commonwealth."

Bennie shrugged again. "Okay. So?"

"So? The Knights of Plentallus date back thousands of cycles. They roamed the stars dispensing justice and being good examples to others. Then they vanished." She leaned forward. "Don't you find that weird?"

Bennie looked up from his wristcomm. "Sorry, were you talking to me?"

Nic opened her mouth, but the ceiling interrupted her. "Prepare for takeoff."

It thrilled Bennie that the announcement distracted the young woman. He leaned back, letting the thrum of the atmospheric engines lull him into sleep. He had learned enough about the history of the order and its demise at the hands of the Tarsi in their creation of the Peacekeepers as galactic police force. He did not want to talk about it. He did not want to dash the dreams of his annoying young companion.

After cycles aboard the *Ghost*, Bennie was really liking letting a ship take care of flying while he focused on other things.

He had been tempted to dig into the pilot's core routines but decided against it since he wasn't sure a crash of the system wouldn't equal a crash of the shuttle.

He and Nic were sitting in the small cargo area at the rear of the craft. It wasn't what anyone would call spacious, mostly designed to hold the luggage of those traveling aboard the shuttle.

Given the relative size of both passengers and their lack of luggage, it made for an acceptable training space. Bennie was sitting cross-legged opposite his student.

"You have to keep a lot of variables in your head at one time: your physical surroundings, beings nearby, weather, vehicles, and more," he said.

Nic, her eyes closed, opened one eye. "Easy for you to say. You've got processor implants."

Bennie smiled, his eyes still closed. "It doesn't hurt. But I'm told that all the Knights could do it, and few, if any of them, were enhanced."

"How?" the young woman pressed. She was struggling to keep her focus on any one thing, let alone holding multiple things in her mind.

"Meditation. Practice. Rinse and repeat. Close your eyes."

"They are," she lied, closing her eye. "So, you just sit here?"

Bennie shifted uncomfortably. Sir Jarek Ruus had never really been super clear on that point. C7K2 hadn't either. "I mean, sorta. Open your senses. What do you hear? What do you smell? Is there a breeze? From which direction? That sort of thing. The more you can train your brain to pick these things out, the more it becomes second nature."

After a pause that almost forced Bennie to open his eyes, his young charge said, "I hear the engines, the air circulation system. I can smell the...I don't know what it is, but something is in the air, pungent."

"Sorry," Bennie whispered.

"Gross!" Nic's eyes bolted open as she scrambled to get some distance from her teacher.

Bennie chuckled, getting to his feet. "Okay, enough sitting on our asses." He looked up at the chronograph display above the hatch connecting the cargo area to the rest of the small ship. "We've got time for one more lesson before lunch."

"What's for lunch?" Nic rubbed her stomach.

Ignoring her, Bennie reached for a small tool that was fastened to the bulkhead. Placing it in a pocket on his canvas trousers, he said, "Okay. Come see if you can get it."

The Olop girl stared at him. "Uh, no thank you, Grandpa Creeper. I am not putting my hand in your pocket."

Bennie's mouth opened. "Wha—? No, that's not..." He removed the small tool and the light over-tunic he was wearing, placing the tool in the shirt's pocket and hanging the shirt on a luggage strap hanging nearby. "Okay, here. Try to remove the tool from my jacket without rustling the fabric."

"Picking pockets? That's the next lesson?"

"Yeah." He pointed to the jacket hanging between them. "Go for it."

"That's a thing Knights of Plentallus do? Pick pockets?" She moved to stand in front of the garment. Wiggling her fingers, she gingerly reached into the pocket. The jacket moved and, before she could react to that, a thin wooden dowel slapped across her arm.

Jumping back, rubbing the stricken arm with her other hand, Nic snapped. "What the wurrin is that? Where did you get a stick?"

Bennie was leaning on a thin wooden cane. "Never mind where I got it. Rustle the over-tunic, get a whack." He motioned to the hanging jacket. "Try again."

"Why are you teaching me how to steal?" she complained.

"How much do you think being a Knight of Plentallus pays?"

She shrugged. "I dunno. A lot, probably."

After collecting himself from laughing hard enough that his stomach hurt, he said, "Nothing. It pays nothing."

"What?"

He held up a finger. "That's not the point, though. I'm not teaching you this so you can rob people."

"Let's circle back to the pay thing." She scowled.

Bennie waved a hand. "That pocket won't pick itself. Try again." He tapped the end of his stick on the deck.

CHAPTER 2

Bennie and Nic spent the rest of the shuttle trip practicing. Sometimes it was mental exercises, sometimes physical. In between the training, they argued.

By the time the rented shuttle was entering orbit, the young Olop girl was moderately proficient lifting things from pockets. Bennie had explained that it wasn't so much about robbing someone as being able to liberate evidence or other vital findings. The role of a Knight was always ambiguous, and it paid to be flexible.

To his surprise, she'd taken to code slicing quickly. Still far from his skills, but no slouch.

Her swordplay needed a lot of work still.

The ceiling speakers chimed. "We have received landing clearance. Please secure all loose items and prepare for atmospheric entry."

Bennie took the training sword from Nic. "You'll get it. I wasn't that awesome with a sword at first, either. I mean, who uses swords?" He smiled.

"Right? Will mine be a blaster like yours?" She followed him into the seating area. "Speaking of, when do I get my laser sword?"

Snapping the harness around his waist, Bennie smirked. "Beam saber, and not any time soon." He held up a hand to stop her protest. "When the time is right, you can make your saber however you like."

The shuttle's pilot intelligence did a remarkable job traversing Nexum's atmosphere. It brought the vessel to a gentle rest on a small landing pad in the Tower's rear property where the public wasn't permitted.

After the conversion to public museum, most of the Tower had become a tourist trap, open sun up to sun down under the guidance of C7K2, the matte black caretaker droid. Bennie was never sure what the GC Council or Peacekeeper's thought about that. He honestly did not care.

Once the two passengers stepped off the boarding ramp, it rose as the pleasant computer voice said, "Thank you for using Aldon Shuttle Services, a subsidiary of the Draplin Combine." The shuttle was impossible to see with the naked eye by the time Bennie and Nic reached the rear entry to the Tower. C7K2 and DV-0 were waiting for them.

Bennie smiled. "Hi, guys. This is Nic." Before either droid or the Olop girl next to him could say anything, he added, "Show her around, get her situated. Bye." He waved as he headed straight for one of the lifts, his wristcomm beeping as he neared it, allowing him access. The lift doors closed behind him, leaving the stunned trio staring at the closed doors.

The two droids turn in unison to Nic.

C7K2 said, "Hello, I am C7K2, and this is DV-0. I am the caretaker of the Tower. DV-0 handles training when Sir Ben-Ari Vulvo is in the Tower."

"I'm Nic'ole Thot'la. You can call me Nic." She offered a small furry hand.

Each droid took the offered hand. C7K2 said, "We would be happy to show you around." He extended a hand toward the lift Bennie had just taken. "You may leave your bag here with Sir Ben-Ari Vulvo's. We will collect them later."

The heavy door slid shut, cutting off the landing area. Nic

followed the two droids through a twisting maze of rooms and floors, some open to the public where she had to fight through crowds, and others for official use only.

"What's this?" Nic asked upon entering a dimly lit room lined with holograms of worlds and beings, most of which she didn't recognize.

C7K2 said, "This is one of the Halls of Remembering. The Knights believed that it was important to not only celebrate their wins, but acknowledge their losses. Each of these displays is such a loss." The droid pointed to a blue and green world covered in clouds. The holographic planet was slowly rotating. "Vimdash Three. Destroyed by a plague."

Nic leaned closer to the holographic world. She turned to the droid. "Everyone died?"

"Three thousand cycles ago. Yes. The Knights of Plentallus were unable to help them."

"The whole planet?"

The droid inclined his head. "Several dozen Knights were there to help. Several of the best minds among the order did everything they could."

"Why doesn't the GC talk about this?" Nic asked, leaning in to gaze at the hologram.

"The Tarsi are not fans of history that predates the formation of the Commonwealth, particularly history that highlights the good the order did. All but the most prestigious schools have stopped teaching it entirely." He pointed to the ceiling. "The historical archives contained in the Tower are some of the most complete in all the Galactic Commonwealth."

While Nic was getting a tour, Bennie was in the beam saber lab, his saber hilt taken apart on the Brailack-height workbench and a cracked power cell casing off to the side, discarded. "That explains that," he whispered to himself, pulling a new power cell from a bin of similar units. After ensuring it was unblemished, he inserted it into the housing and connected a few leads. A PADD next to him, connected by wires to the main control unit of the beam saber, scrolled a diagnostic across its screen, finally settling on "Diagnostic Complete. No Warnings."

Bennie was disconnecting the PADD and reassembling his weapon when C7K2 entered. "Sir Knight."

"Hey, CK." Bennie didn't look up from his work. "Get my annoying new problem settled?"

"Yes. She is...remarkably curious. She has retired to guest quarters on level 18. Would you like me to provide her quarters on the residential floors?"

Bennie clipped his beam saber to the loop on his belt. "Not yet, not until I know what I'm doing with her. I tried meditating. On what I should do about her."

C7K2 stepped far enough into the room to allow the door to slide closed. "And?"

Bennie sighed. "And nothing. I sat there for an entire tock in the dark. I finally had to stop when I couldn't get a song I heard the other day at the office out of my head." He shrugged. "How did the others do it? Find answers in meditation, I mean."

"Many used drugs."

SEVERAL TOCKS LATER, after Bennie got his belongings settled in his room on the 38th floor of the Tower, he was knocking on the door that was assigned to Nic. "Open up. We're going to dinner."

"Hold on," came the muffled reply.

The guest quarters on level 18 of the Tower were nicer than most hotels and far nicer than the budget stateroom Nic and her grandmother had shared aboard the *Galactic Empress*.

The luxury cruise liner, the biggest pleasure ship ever built, had run a GC-wide contest, and her grandmother had won. The entire trip had gone sideways when some of the ship's investors hired mercenaries to destroy the ship in order to get their investment back through the insurance payout.

The door slid open. "Where are we going?" Nic was wearing an outfit similar to Bennie's earth tone tunic and trousers. Where his outfit was pale browns and off whites, hers was all darker browns and blacks.

"Dinner." Bennie waved toward the lift at the center of the Tower. With the exception of the floor that separated the Knights-only floors from the publicly accessible floors, a central pair of lifts ran up and down the center of the building.

"What? No comment on my outfit? CK gave it to me." She fell into step next to him, fidgeting with her belt as they headed for the lifts.

Bennie glanced over. "He shoulda asked me first."

Nic was silent the rest of the way out of the Tower. She knew she was capable of being a Knight of Plentallus. She didn't understand why Bennie was so against it.

The doors to the restaurant swung open. "Sir Knight!" The hostess beamed as Bennie and Nic entered the restaurant. "We have missed you!"

"Hello, Gertrude," Bennie said, walking up to the podium.

"Is there something wrong?" Nic asked, glancing from Bennie to the woman behind the host podium. "Your voice is all low and gravelly. You need a glass of water?"

Bennie waved a hand, shushing her.

The Trollack woman looked up from her podium. "We have your table, of course. Just you and your," she looked at Nic, "assistant?"

"Apprent—" Nic started to say.

"Thank you," Bennie interrupted.

The restaurant was as busy as usual. When Bennie had first discovered the place, he used the clout that the Tower offered to convince the owner to leave a table open for when a Knight was in the Tower, knowing full well he was the only Knight.

"This is so fancy. I thought you said we didn't get paid?" Nic said, looking around. Tables were scattered just far enough apart that their well-dressed occupants had privacy. Nexuu occupied most of the tables, but here and there, Nic saw other GC races.

She'd never seen Nexuu before. Their lidless blue eyes were entrancing.

"Who's we? You got a turd in your pocket? You're not an anything, yet," Bennie retorted.

She beamed. "'Yet.' Not 'never.'"

Bennie scowled. "Anyway. Part of being a Knight is that we rely on the kindness of those we serve."

She looked around at all the well-dressed Nexuu and other beings. "Who in here do we—

you—serve?" She cocked her head. "Is that why you do that thing with your voice?" She leaned in. "Does it hurt? Should I do that, too?" She cleared her throat. "How does this sound?" Her voice was thick and deep.

Bennie scowled and was about to answer when the server came to take their orders. Nic ordered a pasta dish with Nuflonog and a fizz-pop. Bennie said, "I'll have jerlack steak and qorrum fries."

The server left and Nic said, "You did it again! Your voice is all deep, like Maxim's." Her eyes went wide. "You've conned them into comping your meals here!"

Bennie shushed her and whispered, "Don't ruin it! Did you see the prices on the menu?"

The pair ate in relative silence until Nic asked, "So, what's the deal with all this?" She pulled at the sleeve of the outer tunic she was wearing. "Why is mine all browns and blacks?"

Bennie set his fork down. "I haven't read all the manuals yet, but I guess that's what they did way back when. Apprentices." He held up a hand. "I'm not saying you're an apprentice yet. They dressed that way to make it clear they were part of the order but not Knights. You might as well dress the part." He looked around. "Plus, it ensures they comp your meal, too."

Nic sighed. "Is it supposed to be scratchy?"

Bennie nodded. "Supposed to keep us humble or some dren. It helps if you run them through the clothes refresher a dozen times."

"Good night, Sir Knight," C7K2 said as Bennie and Nic entered the lift. He nodded to Nic. "And you, young miss."

Nic waved. "'Night, CK." The lift doors slid closed. "So, what now?" She looked up, a little, to Bennie.

He turned. "You go to bed. I do some work. That's what's next."

"Boring. I'm not even tired. I want to see more of the Tower."

Bennie said, "There's plenty of time for sightseeing." The doors slid apart on the level where the young Olop's quarters were located. Bennie shoved her out. "Bye."

She turned in time to scowl at the smiling Brailack as the doors closed.

As far as she knew, she was the only resident of the entire floor. Turning a slow circle, she headed off in the direction directly opposite her room. He didn't say she *had* to go to bed.

The public areas of the guest room floor were pretty sparsely decorated. Hallways branched out in four directions from the central lift column. Each hallway had four doors, two on each side. The first set of doors was smaller, leading to more triangular rooms, without windows—at least, real ones. C7K2 had mentioned that they had large display screens to simulate the view from the direction the room faced. The second pair of doors led to larger rooms with floor-to-ceiling windows. Her room was one such room. She was sure that if Bennie had been consulted, she'd be in one of the smaller rooms.

She stopped at a door. Each had a control panel set next to it. Hers had been keyed to her wristcomm. She waved the device near the reader on the off chance that all the doors on the guest floor had been keyed to her wristcomm or left blank. The panel beeped and flashed a red light. She should have known a droid wouldn't be lazy enough to just assign all the doors to one wristcomm, even if no one else was using them.

Well, that was okay. This wasn't the first locked door in Nic's life. She looked around to ensure she was alone and pulled the access panel from the wall. A few microtocks later, the door lock clicked, allowing the door to slide open. She wasn't useless, even if Bennie thought so.

The room was one of the interior ones, a wedge with a large—but not floor-to-ceiling—

display where the window would be if the room were on the exterior of the building. She looked at the view. "Not bad, really." She rested a hand on the display. Turning, she said, "There you are." Above the door to the small refresher was a grate covering what she assumed was the air duct—an air duct that connected to every other floor of the Tower, including the non-public floors. She grinned and moved a chair over to the wall so she could reach the grate. The chair wasn't enough. She hated how many things were designed around "talls." She spent a few microtocks dragging the dresser across the room, then hefting the chair up to precariously balance on top of the dresser. Olop were natural climbers, so the wobbly furniture tower wasn't an issue. She was prying the grate off the wall in no time.

The ducting was a tight fit, but doable. It took very little time to work her way to the center of the Tower where the horizontal ducts met the larger vertical ones.

"Okay, I'm on 18. Let's start at the first Knights-only floor, I guess." She braced her feet against the opposite side of the large vertical duct and climbed.

The 27th floor was one large open space, a gym of sorts. More weapons than she could even identify were racked along all four walls. The floor, and oddly, the ceiling were all padded. She peeked out into the space but didn't see any reason to leave the ducting for that room.

The 28th floor was interesting. The lift lobby was larger than on the lower floors, with several doors leading off of it and only one corridor leading to more doors. After walking around the floor to get the lay of it, Nic was back in the ducts thanks to a large planter that she was able to drag under the vent. The first room she peeked into on the next floor was some type of media room. "This looks fun."

The room was about twice the size of her guest room. Several overstuffed seats designed for different physical configurations faced a blank wall. There was an older model holoprojector mounted to the ceiling. Resting on the arm of one of the chairs was an equally dated PADD. Nic hopped into the seat and began browsing the options.

ON THE NIGHTSTAND, Bennie's wristcomm beeped. Then it beeped again. Then it said, "Sir Knight. Wake up!"

Bennie rolled over and pushed the talking device onto the floor.

"Sir Knight, we have an issue," the voice from the wristcomm said.

Bennie opened his eyes. "What?"

"Your not-an-apprentice is missing."

"CK?"

"Yes, who else would it be?"

Bennie sighed. "Where are you? I'll be right there."

"The command center."

Bennie frowned. "We have a command center?"

"Level 29."

CHAPTER 3

"Dren," Bennie whispered, stepping into the command center. "How did you not tell me about this place?" He looked around the room. It took up most of the entire 29th floor. Screens lined the wall, and the floor was covered in workstations, each with a few displays mounted on it. There was a raised platform in the center with what looked like a gaming table on it. He was pretty sure it was not a gaming table.

C7K2 and DV-0 turned. The former said, "It did not come up."

Bennie made a face. "So, where is she?"

DV-0, the training droid, said, "We are scanning floor by floor. As with most things in the Tower, the floor sensors are a bit dated. We have to scan each floor versus the entire building at once."

"Efficient," Bennie griped.

"There," C7K2 said, pointing at the flat display on the wall, a wireframe of the Tower on it. "Level 28, the archives."

"I thought the archives were up on 42?"

"We have many archives," the matte black droid said. "That room is dedicated to longer historical archives and stories."

Bennie rocked on his heels. "Okay, whatever. Let's go."

The door to the archive viewing room slid open with a *swoosh*.

Nic was curled up, watching something projected on the wall before her.

"What the wurrin? Are you trying to give me a reason to ship your ass back to your grandmother?" Bennie stormed in, two droids behind him.

She looked up, the fur around her eyes dark and wet. She pointed at the image being projected.

On the wall, rendered in grainy holographic particles, a Multonae Knight was leaping between a group of Trollack, cutting them down. The Knight landed in a crouch, spun, and stabbed his beam saber blade into what looked a lot like a juvenile Trollack. An unarmed juvenile Trollack.

Bennie's mouth hung open. He turned to the droids. "What the wurrin is this?"

Before the droids could answer, Nic said, "There's more." She tapped the PADD, then wiped her nose on her sleeve. The holo image shifted to a recording that looked a bit more recent than the previous one. A young Olop man was jumping and dodging through a crowd of Ruknak, his beam saber slashing through their rock-like skin like it was paper. It wasn't clear from the footage, but it looked like the Ruknak were fleeing the knight.

Bennie spun on the droids. "Explain. Now."

C7K2 stepped forward. "The history of the Knights of Plentallus is...complicated."

Bennie flapped his arms. "What do you mean, complicated?" He pointed to the flat image. "He's cutting people down! Isn't that Gelflux Prenta?" The holographic Olop Knight of Plentallus slashed his blade across a Ruknak, dropping it.

"Sir Gelflux Prenta, yes," C7K2 replied.

"Those people are running from him!" Bennie screamed. "How did I not know about this place? What else have you not told me?"

DV-0 inclined his head. "We thought it best to not overwhelm you early on."

Bennie stood there. Nic hopped out of the chair. She snuffled, wiping her nose again. "I'm going to bed." She pushed between the two droids.

Bennie stared after, then turned his attention back to the droids. "Was all of it a lie? Jarek Ruus? Was he just a drunk grifter? Did he kill people?"

"Sir Knight." C7K2 spread his arms. "All Knights kill people. It is the nature of things." He held up a hand to forestall Bennie's retort. "There is much history, not all what we would like it to be."

Bennie ran his hands over his head, moving to collapse into one of the chairs.

The caretaker droid said, "Would you have us believe your history is all altruism, Ben-Ari Vulvo? Wanted in five systems for computer crimes. Wanted in two others for felony assault, wa—"

"Those assault charges were bogus!" Bennie waved a hand.

"And the inciting revolution and vote tampering?"

"Well…"

C7K2 approached the chair and put a hand on the back, looking down at Bennie. "The Knights of Plentallus were not perfect. No being or organization is."

Bennie exhaled. "I get it." He looked up at the two droids. "No more secrets."

"Agreed," the two bots replied in unison.

He sighed, wriggling in the chair. "I guess I should bone up on the history of the order." He made a circular motion in the air. "Roll it."

C7K2 exchanged a look with DV-0, then said, "The remote is right next to you."

The two droids left, and Bennie settled in to watch some of the more uncomfortable stories of the Knights of Plentallus.

THE CAFETERIA in the Knights-only section of the Tower had been closed for cycles. After the last Knight left the Tower, C7K2 shut it down and reassigned resources. Bennie met Nic in the public cafe on the second floor of the wide circular base of the Tower.

"Morning," he said, putting a cup of chlormax down as she arrived. "I got your breakfast." He pushed one of the two plates before him over to a seat on the opposite side of the table.

"Thanks." She dropped into the seat, not making eye contact. She poked at the pastry absently. "I think I'll—"

Bennie held up a hand. "Wait. I know last night was crappy. I didn't know that stuff, either, and it's really screwed up. I get it if you want to leave, but I thought about it last night while I watched more of that stuff than I ever want to see again. I think you should stay." Her head snapped up. "I'm not saying you're an apprentice yet." He stuck his tongue out. "But I think it's possible, and I think it's my responsibility to make the Knights of Plentallus an organization that I'm proud of."

"So, like, more criminal?" She took a big bite of her pastry.

"'Like more criminal,'" Bennie mocked in a high-pitched voice. "No. Not that. I was going to say you show a lot of promise, but now... no." She opened her mouth, but he held up his hand again. "Come on, we're heading into town." He stood and headed for the open archway of the cafe.

Nic hopped out of her seat, snatching the remains of the pastry as she did, trotting after Bennie.

The Tower of Plentallus sat at one end of the mid-sized city of Aqu Var. While the local Nexuu loved having the Tower and the Knights around, their society operated like any other. Gleaming towers full of businesses of all sizes, doing all sorts of things... boutiques, restaurants, and more packed the city center.

"Where are we going?" Nic asked for the third time. They'd been walking, seemingly without destination for several tocks. Bennie would occasionally stop and talk to someone that flagged them down, accepted some snack or trinket when offered. They didn't seem to have a destination.

He turned to her. "Does it matter? You got someplace to be?"

"Back to Cranky Grandpa, I see."

"Don't make me leave you at an orphanage." Bennie turned down a side street. He looked around, mumbling. "Supposed to be right here somewhere."

"I was thinking I could visit the workshop where you assembled your beam saber when we get back to the Tower."

Bennie paused. "What? No. No beam saber for you."

"Oh, come on."

"No."

She sighed. "Fine. What're we looking for?"

Bennie pointed. "There."

Nic followed the gesture. "What? That weird symbol on the wall?"

He frowned. "Weird symbol...yeah. It marks places under the protection of the local syndicate."

"I thought you said you and Maxim shut that down last year."

Bennie nodded. "We did, but I heard some rumors that someone had moved into this place. Figured we should check."

"And what if they did?" a voice asked from behind them.

Bennie looked at Nic. "You weren't watching the alley opening?"

"Did you tell me to?"

"I told you to train your senses. Make it like second nature to hear everything, smell everything."

Nic made a face, planting a hand on her hip. "You didn't."

"Excuse us," the large, well-dressed Nexuu man said from the entrance to the alley. He was wearing a tailored charcoal gray suit that complemented his darker-than-average green skin.

Bennie held up a hand, palm out. "We went over this on the shuttle," he scolded.

She pointed at the man and his small contingent. "You didn't smell them. Or hear them."

Bennie scoffed, "I was distracted."

"Grab 'em," the man growled, motioning to his two flunkies.

Two red-skinned, four-armed men moved out around their boss, followed by a pair of Harrith men, all four blocking any route out of the alley. One of the bigger four-armed men cracked first one pair of knuckles, then the other.

"Oh," Bennie said. He pushed Nic back behind him with one hand, while the other unclipped his beam saber.

"What're you doing?" She slapped at his hand before producing a wicked-looking blade half as long as her forearm. The same one she had when Bennie met her. She darted around him, teeth bared, blade held at the ready.

THE NEAREST MULTI-LIMBED thug screamed in surprise a moment before a small furry terror, armed with sharp teeth and a knife, landed on his face.

Bennie, slightly more used to the savagery, didn't miss a beat. The screams of Nic's opponent drowned out the *snap-hiss* of his beam saber activating. He charged the two Harrith toughs, letting a battle cry escape his lips. Unlike their colleague, the two Harrith weren't as easily shocked. Both dropped to a knee, pulling pistols free of holsters under their arms. Both drew down on the charging Brailack.

"Dren!" Bennie shouted, changing course, swiping frantically to deflect those plasma rounds that came closest to him as he dodged behind a small trash bin.

Nic was aggressively biting and stabbing one man, who then grabbed the back of her tunic. "The wurrin is this?" He tossed her down the alley with one of his upper arms as one of his lower hands pulled a pistol from a holster on his thigh.

Bennie shut off his energy blade, twisting the selector as he took aim. A bolt of purple energy shot from the end of the hilt, striking one of the Harrith men in the chest, burning a hole through him, igniting his suit jacket. The body hit the ground, flames engulfing it.

"Gross!" one of the thugs shouted, stepping away from the conflagration that was rapidly filling the alley with the smell of burned flesh and fabric.

"Give up now and no one else...gets lit on fire!" Bennie shouted from behind his trash bin. The answer was several plasma bolts striking the thin metal, melting holes through it. Bennie leaped out from behind his diminishing cover, firing randomly.

While the remaining criminals were distracted by Bennie's fire, Nic emerged from the back of the alley, screaming. She darted past Bennie to leap onto the head of the nearest Harrith man. The lanky man screamed, his long thin arms pinwheeling. *What is it with her and heads?* Bennie wondered.

He used the confusion to ignite his beam saber and dive into the fray. Two quick swipes turned one of the four-armed goons into a two-armed goon. Over the screaming, Bennie shouted, "This only ends one way."

The leader of the group raised his wristcomm. "Get out here. We've got trouble!" He took a few steps back as Nic's opponent fell to the ground, his face a bloody mess and his flat nose conspicuously missing. She looked up, growling, blood soaking the fur of her face, her pink streak nearly invisible amid the gore covering her.

The door that Nic and Bennie had been looking at earlier opened, slamming against the alley wall. Three Trollack rushed out, each with a pistol.

"Okay, two ways," Bennie said over the hum of his beam saber.

Nic looked over her shoulder. "See, I should have a beam saber."

"You look like you're doing okay without," Bennie said.

"Ahem," the Nexuu man said.

Bennie sighed. Snapping off his beam saber, he laid the hilt on the ground. Looking at Nic, he shook his head. She scowled first at Bennie, then the leader of the group, before tossing her blood-soaked knife to the ground.

"Lock 'em up inside," the leader told the three new arrivals. Turning to the rest of his original group, he ordered, "Clean all this up. Get Holvaro to a medical facility."

Bennie handed his beam saber to one of the Trollack men. Nic followed suit, dropping her bloody knife into the man's webbed hand.

Bennie and Nic followed the three Trollack back inside the building, down a series of steps that gradually angled back under the alley and the building next to the one the door was set in. "So, who are you guys?" Bennie asked.

"Shut up!"

After a few more microtocks of walking, the nearest Trollack said, "Stop." He reached past them to open a door. "In."

The cell, such as it was, was closer to a root cellar. "Cozy," Bennie quipped, making a slow circle.

"Now what?" Nic asked.

Bennie made a patting motion in the air, then pointed to the door and the sound of the three Trollack walking away. Once the sound of their footsteps and banter couldn't be heard, he said, "Now we escape."

CHAPTER 4

"Oh, you got a lock pick up your butt?" Nic replied. She had dropped down onto a crate that, according to the label, was full of tubers.

Bennie frowned. "No, I don't have a lock pick." He turned to look at her, smirking. "I do have a plan, though."

"Well, I'm reassured."

Bennie made a rude gesture that she ignored.

"So..." she continued.

"We need to wait a bit. Let them get settled."

She sighed. "Oh. Great." She picked at a piece of loose adhesive tape. "So, how did you meet your friends?"

Bennie had turned back to the door and was now slowly looking at every detail in the room. "Huh? What friends?"

"What do you mean, 'What friends?' How many do you have? The ones you work with!" the girl snapped.

Bennie stopped investigating the room. He inhaled. "Well, I met Wil a cycle or two before the rest. He had made it to Fury after his crew was killed, and he wanted a clean registration for the *Ghost*. Well, it was the *Raptor* then."

He rubbed his chin. "I did the job and sent him on his way, never gave it another thought." He shook his head at the memory, smiling. "I wonder if I'd still have my shop...?"

"Then what?" Nic was leaning forward on the crate, her hands cradling her chin.

"Then nothing. A cycle or two later, these two pushy drennog PKs show up at my door, saying Wil sent them. I knew I shoulda just left them standing there."

"Not very noble."

Bennie clucked. "Anyhow. They needed new idents and wrist-comms to match. No sooner had I gotten them set up and was about to push them out the door, more PKs came knocking on my door. All downhill after that. My lab was burned, then actually exploded. That last part was my safety feature more than the PKs. We scrambled through sewers until we met up with Wil at the ship. I didn't have any place else to go and figured my identity was burned, too, so..." He shrugged.

"Wow."

Gathering himself up, he said, "Yeah. Well. Okay, let's get out of here." He nodded to her. "Pretend you're having cramps or something."

Her light brown fur rippled. "What? No. Why me?"

"You're the girl."

"I'll save clawing your eyes out for later. You want a distraction?" She hopped off the crate. "Hey, out there! I think my grandpa is dying!" She turned and winked at Bennie's scowl. "Hey! He's puking all over the place! Hey! It's probably old age or a hearts problem."

Bennie growled, then hearing the footsteps, he fell to the floor and began convulsing.

Nic whispered, "Can you throw up?"

He glared. "Not on command!"

"What's going on in there?" one of the Trollack gangsters demanded.

Nic shouted, "Your Harrith friends—I think they hurt him up in the alley. He needs a doctor!"

The door opened. "Back up!" the thug urged, pistol held at the ready, pointed at Nic.

He moved to kneel next to Bennie's still shuddering form. "What's wrong with you?" He put a webbed hand on Bennie's shoulder, shaking him.

"Oh, nothing," Bennie said before a tiny green fist jabbed straight up into one of the unsuspecting gangster's eyes. Before the man finished falling, he had a small, brown-furred attachment on his back, and it reached around to claw at his face and remaining undamaged eye. Bennie rolled away and got to his feet. "Don't eat him. Just knock him out!"

"I'm try—" Nic started to say but was hurled from her opponent out into the corridor.

The Trollack gangster got to his feet, his remaining eye roaming the space to find Bennie. He lunged the moment he spotted the Brailack.

"Ah!" Bennie shouted, barely dodging the tackle. He kicked at the other man, moving to get some space between them. Before he could turn, Nic was sailing through the air to land on their jailer's back, small fury fists raining blows on the back of his head.

When the Trollack staggered, near collapse, Bennie waved. "Wait, wait!" He grabbed the man's collar. "Where's our stuff?"

The Trollack man stammered, "Upstairs...Mr. Lugo's...office."

"Thanks." Bennie punched him as hard as he could, square in the face between both eyes.

Nic leaped from their jailer's back before he hit the floor. "Now what?"

"Like I said—we get out of here." He held up his hand, waving it and wiggling his fingers. "Search him."

Other than a base model wristcomm and a few hard currency credit chips, the Trollack had little on him. Bennie stomped on the wristcomm after deeming it worthless.

Creeping through the hallway, Nic asked, "What about Gabe? Was he with Maxim and Zephyr when they came to you?"

Bennie slowed, looking over his shoulder. "What? Oh, we stole him later."

"Stole him?"

They reached the stairs, the same ones they had come down earlier. Bennie made a shushing sound, then pointed away from the door they had come through. Nic nodded.

They crept through the hallway, checking the few doors they came across until they found one that looked right. And was locked.

BENNIE LOOKED AT THE DOOR, then Nic. "I can't pick locks without my wristcomm."

She sighed. "Not very useful without gadgets, are you?" She smirked and reached for the access panel. "Keep an eye out, Gramps."

"I really dislike you." He turned and crept back down the hallway. He had gone only a few steps before being summoned back with a hiss and the snapping of tiny fingers. "Okay, you're pretty good. Explains how you got around the Tower so easy."

Nic smiled and stepped aside.

"Hear anything in there?" Bennie asked.

She shook her head.

Bennie pushed open the door. The office was empty. Sitting on a desk that looked to be carved from a single piece of pale blue rock were their wristcomms, Nic's savage little knife, and Bennie's beam saber hilt.

"Huh. This wasn't so bad," Nic whispered from behind him.

Bennie scowled. "Are you trying to jinx us?" He motioned to the office. "See if there's anything we can grab to give the authorities." He moved around the desk, pushing the chair aside. After slipping his wristcomm back on and clipping his beam saber to his belt, he tossed Nic her wristcomm, noting that it was not a child's unit but a model only a few levels below what his had started at before he improved upon it. *Not shabby,* he thought to himself.

He made a note to himself to check out what mods she had installed on the device later.

The desk drawers were mostly empty except for the one with a prodigious amount of pornography and a half empty liquor bottle in it. Bennie thumbed through the reading material before noticing that Nic was looking at him. Dropping everything back into the drawer and sliding it closed, he said, "What've you got?"

She clucked. She was next to a half height file cabinet in the room's corner, which for an Olop, made it a full height unit. She held up a folder. "I think these are time tables and a chart of accounts."

"Chart of accounts?" He held out his hand for the folder.

She handed him the folder as she said, "I took banking for beginners in primary school. I know a chart of accounts when I see one."

He pulled a face and nodded. "Okay. Let's go before they get back."

"Too late," the heavyset Nexuu man—*Mr., what? Luigi, loogie? Lego? Lugo.* Bennie was pretty sure it was Lugo—said from the doorway.

Bennie turned to Nic. "Seriously? He snuck up on you twice?"

"Uh, you too."

"Not this again," Mr. Lugo groaned.

Bennie moved his hand to his hip as slowly as he could. "Any chance you're in the market for an assistant? I mean, you've seen what she can do. Fair warning: she's a pain in the ass."

Nic spun. "You wouldn't—" Her hands were flapping anxiously. "How dare you—"

Bennie raised his beam saber, activating it as he did. A magenta glow filled the small office. The move was fast enough that Lugo didn't react until the blade was pointed at him.

"Okay, look, man. This can go two ways. We fight our way out, or you let us walk out."

"And then?" the crime boss asked.

Nic edged over to stand next to Bennie, doing her best to look intimidating.

Bennie waved his free hand. "You find a new place to set up. We'll call this a wash."

The Nexuu squinted. "You don't act like I expected a Knight of the Tower to act."

"I'm a new breed." Bennie smirked.

The other man didn't seem impressed, but he remained silent as he thought it over. Finally, he huffed, "Very well." He raised his arm, speaking into his wristcomm. "Our guests are leaving. Don't bother them. Start packing things up, we're finding a new base." He turned to Bennie, eyebrow ridge raised.

Bennie smiled, his beam saber clicking off. He looked down at Nic. "Let's go."

Thankfully, she didn't say anything. She edged past the big Nexuu man, who made no move to stop her. Bennie followed, throwing out a salute as he passed.

They made their way back to the door in the alley. Pushing it open slowly revealed the alley was empty, all signs of their earlier scuffle scrubbed away.

Bennie looked around, impressed with the cleanup. "Let's head to the local security office. I think it's a few blocks this way." He pointed. "We can drop off this," he patted the folder he had tucked into his outer tunic vest, "on our way back to the Tower."

After dropping off the folder to the local security office and providing a full statement, Nic said, "So, you stole Gabe?"

Bennie rubbed his chin. "Oh. Well, yeah, sorta."

"Sorta stole?"

"Well, we definitely stole him, but it was more like liberating him. They crated him up to be sold or destroyed. We don't really know." He smiled. "Once we opened the crate to take a peek, I don't remember who turned Gabe on, probably Wil. Once we did, and he told us his story, we knew we couldn't hand him over to Xarrix."

"Xarrix?"

"Yeah, bad guy and all around drennog. He hired us to steal the crate Gabe was in. Wil did jobs for him off and on for a few cycles. We finally killed him a while back."

"What?"

Bennie waved a hand. The Tower was in view now, a few blocks away. "Another time." He walked a few more steps, watching her from the corner of his eye. "So, I'm thinking if we're going to make a go of this whole apprentice thing, both of us should take it more seriously." He stopped walking and waited for the excited squealing and dancing around ended before continuing. "Done?" She squealed one more time, bouncing on the tips of her toes, then nodded. "I don't think it's gonna be easy. There's a lot of weight and baggage on our shoulders here." She nodded, her head bobbing up and down. "Okay, then. Let's go get started." He resumed walking toward the Tower.

"Does that mean I get a—"

"No."

"But I'm your apprentice?"

"I didn't say that."

THANK YOU

THANK you so much for reading this latest Space Rogues adventure

If you enjoyed it I'd love it if you left a review. Seriously, reviews are a big deal. They help readers find authors. They help authors show how awesome they are.

REVIEWS ARE social proof and go a long way to encouraging other readers to take a chance on an unknown author.

WANT A NEW SCENE EVERY WEEK?

ACKNOWLEDGMENTS

I couldn't do this without an amazing group of people who sign up to beta and/or ARC read for me. The Beta readers in particular have to suffer through an early draft to help shape the story.

Below are some of these awesome people (If I missed your name, email me and you'll be in the next one :D)

- Chris Boyd
- Rick Lindsay
- Jim Stiles

Also, a big THANK YOU to my Patrons!

- Thomas Ortega

Thank you so much, all of you!

As they say, there's no harm in asking, so here we go.

If you can help connect me with someone who can get The Grand human Empire on a screen (Big or Little) I'll cut you in for 10% (Up to $10,000) of whatever advance is paid.

Send me an email and we can discuss.
rights@johnwilker.com

Want to stay up to date on the happenings in the Galactic Commonwealth?
Sign up for my newsletter at
johnwilker.com/newsletter
You can also join my Patreon page for all
sorts of awesome goodies!

Visit me online at
johnwilker.com

If you like supporting things you love by sporting merch, well you're in luck! I've launched a Space Rogues Shop. Take a look.

The Space Rogues Series. Wil Calder and a bunch of alien misfits somehow keep finding themselves in the thick of it. No one ever checks qualifications when it comes to saving the galaxy!

The Grand Human Empire Series. Jax, Naomi and the droids are just trying to get by. New droid parts ain't cheap after all.